GALACTIC
STEW

Other Anthologies Edited by:

Patricia Bray & Joshua Palmatier

After Hours: Tales from the Ur-bar
The Modern Fae's Guide to Surviving Humanity
Temporally Out of Order
Alien Artifacts
Were-
All Hail Our Robot Conquerors!
Second Round: A Return to the Ur-bar

S.C. Butler & Joshua Palmatier

Submerged
Guilds & Glaives
Apocalyptic

Laura Anne Gilman & Kat Richardson

The Death of All Things

Troy Carrol Bucher & Joshua Palmatier

The Razor's Edge

Patricia Bray & S.C. Butler

Portals

David B. Coe & Joshua Palmatier

Temporally Deactivated

Steven H Silver & Joshua Palmatier

Alternate Peace

Crystal Sarakas & Joshua Palmatier

My Battery Is Low and It Is Getting Dark

GALACTIC STEW

Edited by

David B. Coe
&
Joshua Palmatier

Zombies Need Brains LLC
www.zombiesneedbrains.com

Interior Design (ebook): ZNB Design
Interior Design (print): ZNB Design
Cover Design by ZNB Design
Cover Art "Galactic Stew" by Justin Adams

ZNB Book Collectors #17
All characters and events in this book are fictitious.
All resemblance to persons living or dead is coincidental.

Kickstarter Edition Printing, June 2020
First Printing, July 2020

Print ISBN-13: 978-1940709314

Ebook ISBN-13: 978-1940709321

Printed in the U.S.A.

COPYRIGHTS

Table of Contents

SIGNATURE PAGE

David B. Coe, editor:

_____

Joshua Palmatier, editor:

_____

Paige L. Christie:

_____

Diana A. Hart:

_____

A.L. Tompkins:

_____

Esther Friesner:

_____

Derrick Boden:

_____

Andy Duncan:

_____

Chaz Brenchley:

_____

Howard Andrew Jones:

_____

Mike Jack Stoumbos:

_____

R.S. Belcher:

_____

Mia Moss:

_____

Gini Koch:

_____

D.B. Jackson:

_____

Jason Palmatier:

_____

Gabriela Santiago:

_____

Justin Adams, artist:

_____

INTRODUCTION

David B. Coe

I'll admit it: I'm a Foodie.

I hate the term, but I love the sentiment. Food, for so many of us, is about more than sustenance. It is a means to express ourselves creatively, to share unique experiences with people we love, to explore other cultures. And yet, for those of us who also love speculative fiction, food often receives short shrift in the stories we read and write. Generic stews, c-rations, even *Lembas* bread—it all gets a bit grim after a while.

Hence this anthology. In these pages, food is not a prop or a vague addition to setting. Here, food is the star, the centerpiece of each remarkable story. Aliens and witches, conjurers and warriors, hell-beasts and intergalactic travelers and would-be heroes: you'll find them all and more in *Galactic Stew*. And whether their next meal is their last, or their last meal was their best, food lies at the heart of all they do and seek.

So dig in! We offer you a feast for the imagination, a cornucopia of tales, a mélange of narratives, a roux of...well, you get the idea.

Enjoy! Savor! And then start again! With this banquet, every dish is rich and delicious and, best of all, there are no calories.

BLUE

Paige L. Christie

Power pulsed through the café's floor as an empty logging truck roared across the bridge and reverberated energy through the swollen river below. May looked out the window in time to see the truck's air wake set the roadside sign swaying on its iron rings. 'BLUE,' read the weather-worn letters, and below that, 'EAT,' and tucked between those two words, "If you don't stop, we're both gonna starve." Kicked-up gravel bounced off the placard, chipping more paint.

A tingle awakened in May's skull as the vibrations roused the stools at the counter. She stepped around to reset the sigils etched into the metal seats beneath the cushions. Quiet days, like the last few, meant she spent extra time keeping the directing spells attentive only to those truly in need. It was as if without work to do they became bored and started pulling beyond their intended range. She walked the row of stools, spinning each.

"Order up, May," Colin called from the cook station.

Grabbing the bowl from the ready counter, she stared at the order. "*Seven* eggs, Thad?" she called to the man seated at the corner table.

He grunted without looking up, scribbling wildly in the notebook before him. That was the biggest response she had gotten out of him since she took over the place from cousin Sunny a year ago. Shaking her head, she started across the room, but the warning tingle snarled her thoughts again. Pausing, she plunked herself down on the last stool, lifted her knees, and gave the seat a spin. The spell swirled out, tingled up her back and arms, and danced through the space. Colin chuckled and Thadeus waved a hand by his ear as though he was shooing away a fly. The noise in her head subsided.

Another rumble came from behind the building and Blue shook again, this time from the power of a freight train pulling by on the tracks across the river. Minutes thickened with noise before it drifted into the distance. She waited, but despite the rise of power, the stools stayed quiet.

Fast water. Empty trucks. Long trains. May wove through the scattered tables and set the bowl of hard-boiled eggs on the table amidst Thadeus' piles of journals. A day with things in motion usually brought some excitement.

Behind her, the main door creaked open, banged closed. She turned to see a man crossing the room as though drawn by a wire. He made straight for the stool nearest the back door, the one with the most powerful pull.

Colin knew as well as she what that meant and he greeted the man with a coffee carafe in hand. The newcomer nodded. A man in need of coffee. His shoulders rolled forward under his black parka and he folded his arms in front of him to grasp his mug with both hands. She studied his hunched shape. Black coffee. A traveler, a long way from home. May tipped her head. Or maybe not? She watched a moment more, then crossed the room to join Colin.

The stranger glanced up, just a flicker of his eyes and no body movement.

Contained, this one. And he smelled a little of old sweat and sadness. That made sense. Blue called to blue, always.

May gave Colin a glance. He shrugged. She grabbed the coffeepot and filled a mug for herself, then turned, pot in one hand and mug in the other, to the stranger. His cup was almost empty. "Dark brew on a bright day?" An offer, not judgment.

He half-tipped, half-turned his head to look at her. Older than she had first assumed, but not old, with gray at his temples and in his beard at the corners of his mouth. His eyes were the same, neither young nor old. They met her gaze, held, then dropped away in dismissal.

Interesting. She twisted and set the coffee pot back on its warmer. "Dark brew can wait." This one was going to be a challenge. May plunked her mug down on the counter beside his elbow. "We've the best breakfast—well, the only breakfast—in fifty miles. And you look like the road's well-worn behind you. What'll it be? Thadeus has already eaten half the day's eggs, but we've a few left."

"No, thanks," he said, eyes on his mug. His fingers tightened around the porcelain. Just a fraction, but enough that the dark liquid in the mug gave a little shudder.

She frowned. Those traveling alone often stopped at Blue. Some were just on their way to find themselves in the mountains. Some were true loners, either supremely self-confident, like Thadeus, or paranoid as hell. This man was of a third type: one of the handful Blue called off the highway because of desperate need. The seat spells always did their work on those.

"Cheers to the hot and bitter." She picked up her coffee, raised it.

He didn't respond.

Well, this one was caught up. "You're not toasting. You're not eating. At least let me freshen that up." She pitched the words low, put a little twist on the word 'freshen,' backed it with a whisper of request drawn from the etchings on the clay of the mug in her grasp.

He pulled back, just his shoulders and head, and stared at her, eyes narrowing as he slid his cup toward her. She picked up the coffee carafe and poured his cup full, then put her fingers against the side of his mug and slid it back toward him. She kept contact with the mug until his hand wrapped around the handle.

The door slammed in his face and he stood in the too-bright sun and stared at the white-painted panels of wood. Every wrong possibility in his heart stood redeemed. He should have known better. He swallowed down tears.

Damn. A scene like that—it should have been raining, then the metaphor would have been complete. She met his gaze as the vision of his most recent interaction outside of Blue tripped through her mind.

* * *

He sat in the car for an hour, staring at the peeling Victorian, at the cement steps leading up the hill to the level space where the house was perched. He remembered racing up them on hot summer days and the hard work of shoveling feet of snow from the concrete treads, sweating in the cold, waving to the neighbors up and down the block as they did the same.

Today, the idea of climbing those steps seemed the most daunting task he could imagine. Until he imagined knocking on the door of that house. He lifted the paper cup from its slot in the center console and took a sip to ease his dry throat. The coffee was long since cold and he winced. She'd always made fine coffee, his aunt Jean. He could hope for some, if she let him into the house. If he swallowed pride, and fear, and got out of the car and went up those steps, he'd soon find out. He pressed his lips together, contemplating another swig of stale coffee, but the sour scent deterred him. Then he snorted through his nose and cussed a streak flavored by two decades spent in the city among people even angrier than himself.

Pointless, to have come this far, eleven hours up the coast, into the backwoods-world he had once called home. Pointless, to sit here, with sour coffee and the beginnings of his own sour stench. Shit-fire. He should have found a gas station bathroom and sponged off. At least changed his shirt.

Too late now. If he drove away under the pretense of cleaning up, he'd never come back. No denying it. When it came to home, he'd always been a coward.

Swallowing hard, he unclicked his seatbelt, pushed open the door, and climbed out into the hot brightness of the street. Sun beat back at him from the pavement, down on him from a sky the same blue as police strobes.

He shoved the car door closed and walked across the street. A half dozen strides brought him to the base of the steps. He counted his way up. Fifteen. The age he had been when he left. Fifteen. Half-again the time he'd been gone. But Aunt Jean was still here. Her old car was still parked around back and the terrible curtains he remembered from his youth still graced the front windows.

He paused at the top of the steps and stared at the house. Well over a hundred years old, its three-story height was topped by a steeply-pitched roof necessary to slough off snow in harsh New England winters.

It was easier to fondly recall stairs in need of shoveling than to remember the final weeks living in this place. The hard arguments filled the old house to the rafters and the heat behind the words should have melted all the snowfall that winter.

The usual excuses of youth and stupidity did not even apply to him. He knew exactly what he was doing, what he was saying. And Jean knew he knew. Had he been able to claim ignorance, she might have forgiven his choices, his actions. But Jean Arden had the longest memory of anyone he knew. Why the hell had he even come? He grunted to himself. He'd come because sleep was impossible now that an unfamiliar knot of regret lodged tight in his chest and in the back of his mind. Because he needed her to know what else he knew—how wrong he had always been. How stupid. How mean. How selfish.

He glanced back down the hill at the car. Cold coffee and talk radio. Plenty of that behind him. And ahead as well. He faced the house again. Better a small chance at forgiveness than none. And plenty of chance to be hopeless if she turned him away. He walked up the path, climbed the steps to the porch, and rapped his fist against the door before he allowed himself another moment to change his mind.

The wait was not more than half a minute, but it stretched, piercing in the hot sun. Then the brass knob turned and the door swung open.

Dark-eyed, sun-wrinkled, and with short hair gone a steel gray, Jean stood looking at him with a gaze as flat and unreadable as any poker player's. Seconds ticked past.

"You do it?" she asked.

He pressed his lips together and held her gaze, not daring to hope.

She gave a single sharp nod and closed the door.

His nose a foot from the white-painted panels, he locked his knees to keep from swaying as his stomach dropped and nausea pushed at the back of his throat. Pure old New England that response, that door hard-closed without even a slam to emphasize the anger behind the action. Once, she would have sold her soul to have him home and safe and thinking clearly. But there were some things her stoic soul would never forgive. He should have remembered that. Or perhaps he had simply chosen to ignore it. Maybe, someday, the remembrance that once he had at least come to ask for grace would give her some peace. Or at least give him some.

He bent his head and turned to make the long descent to the street, and the bitter brew awaiting him in the car.

* * *

Damn. May hadn't seen an encounter that cold since she took over the cafe. Once, when Sunny was in charge, a man had come in with the burden of war-deeds on his back and she spent four days of talk and fine fare to get him re-centered. But Sunny was gone and *this* fellow was May's problem. And his problem was, perhaps, he didn't know how to live with the guilt awoken inside him.

May didn't have Sunny's three decades of experience. And it was always the older diners who she had the hardest time connecting with. May worried about that, but Sunny put it simply: someone was always going to think May too old or too young for something. What they thought didn't make it true.

So, May nodded a little and pushed a menu toward the stranger and turned away to start a fresh pot of coffee. "If eggs aren't your jam, Colin's French Toast is a wonder. Real maple syrup from up the road. Boiled down last fall. Can't be beat."

From down the counter, Colin made a noise of agreement without looking up from the bacon popping and crisping on the grill.

Oh, bless that sizzle. Bacon. Colin had called it before she even rounded the counter. This one was going to require pulling out all the stops. *All things in motion today.* This man needed to *move on, not back.* The idea pressed into her bones. He was leaving something behind, and he had tried to go back to make that escape, but comfort wasn't to be found there. He couldn't run from himself. Not past, not present, this one's hope for redemption lay only in picking the right path forward.

Well, where better than Blue, the ultimate crossroads, for such things to be discovered, and for futures to be realigned? And things were moving today, in every direction imaginable.

The front door opened and Jenna and Jonas, the twins who lived in the old house at the top of the notch, came in, dressed for spring hiking in layers of wool and fleece. Jenna gave May and the man at the counter a measuring look and steered Jonas to a table on the far wall.

"Two Baked Blue Breakfasts, Colin," May said, and was rewarded when Jenna called, "Thanks, May!"

Something tingled up May's neck. She picked up the coffee pot and set it before Colin. He looked at her, then took it in hand and carried the pot toward the twins' table.

"Your name's May?" The stranger's voice rose from behind her.

She paused. Her name had broken his reserve where a kind grin and the offer of food could not. That was powerful. She'd have to take care. Turning to face him, she said, "Sure is." She did not ask for his. "Amaya, if you want the whole. But they call me nothing but May."

"I've an aunt named June." Sadness laced the words.

Like stones skipping over a pond, she replayed the vision of his interaction with the woman in the old Victorian house. *June, not*

Jean. Not far off, but still, not the kind of mistake she usually made. And *her* name the trigger. *Names would be his key.* To find and use it, she would need his. But he had to give it freely and if she had to ask, nothing else she did would work. And this man needed Blue as badly as anyone she'd ever met.

"Spring into Summer," she said. She moved so she was not quite across from him and leaned her elbows on the counter again, her fingertips tapping the side of her mug. *Tap. Tap tap.* The spells etched in the clay danced a little song of power into the space between them. "Season's changing. Seems appropriate."

He shrugged. "I suppose. Yesterday was warmer."

His accent arched, shifting through those few words, feeding her knowledge. He was local. Or had been once. But that was overlaid by tones from the large city seven hours to the south. Assumptions formed: he had gone far, done damage, lost much, lost himself, and returned to no purpose. And here he was, heading west not south, on a winding, narrow road that had led him to Blue. "But the sun's still bright. Sure I can't interest you in an early morning feast?"

He freed a hand from the mug, pulled the menu closer, and the crack in his closed posture let in another bleed of insight. *A dirty bar with windows overlooking a papermill, the scent of sulfur blasting the air each time the door opened to admit someone new. At least the glass in his hand was clean and the scotch single malt.*

The scent dispersed as he spoke. "That bacon smells fine. And some of those eggs you mentioned."

"I'll toss in a slab of home-baked sourdough and some hand-churned butter."

That gave a little lift to the edges of his lips. It wasn't quite a smile, but it was another crack in the facade. The power of place. The mug and the stools. The scent of friendly cooking in the air. All those chipped away at sad privacy. All those gave May an in.

"Traveling far?"

He shrugged again. That he had come some way was clear—the clothes he was wearing in her last glimpse were the same he had on now—but the nearest mill town was an hour away. And houses like the one in her first vision were found more over on the coast. A long drive from the city. Time spent drinking and thinking too much. Then a drive here through the night to reach Blue in time for breakfast. "How do you want your eggs?"

"Scrambled," he said. He hesitated and added as though the word was a struggle, "Please."

Of course scrambled. She glanced at Colin and confirmed he was already working on the new order. He jerked his head to the side counter and she pushed back and straightened. "Be right back," she told the stranger, and took the two specials to Jenna and Jonas.

When she returned to the counter, Colin had the eggs half-cooked and a plate set out for the bacon. She washed her hands quickly, then opened the bread-box, pulled out the sourdough, cut a big hunk, and put it into the toaster. Bending, she opened the refrigerator below the counter and peered in at her options. Small bottles for different milks—each marked with Sunny's arcane script and for specific purpose—filled the top shelf. Below were the butters. She sorted, frowning, until she spotted the stone container of Blessed Yak Butter. How Sunny arranged to have it delivered here regularly May had never asked. She just paid the bill when it arrived and accepted the potent stuff into her repertoire.

Stone box in hand, she straightened just as the bread tipped over the back edge of the conveyor screen and slid into the crumb tray. She opened the lid of the butterbox, knifed out a generous pat, and whispered an expanding spell over the butter before spreading it across the hot bread. It flared with red-gold light, then melted smoothly into the nooks and crevasses of the bread. Colin slid eggs and bacon onto the plate to join the toast.

Satisfied, she turned with a smile and set the plate before the stranger. "Hot and fresh."

"Thank you, May." He met her eyes for the first time.

"You're welcome." She waited.

"David," he said.

She grinned and nodded. There it was. "You're welcome, David." She turned away to let him eat as the final pieces of the story she needed opened in her mind.

* * *

He found the bar and left it without even knowing what town he had stopped in or how he had gotten there. Dawn was an hour away when he turned the key in his car and swung the wheel to pull onto the freshly paved two-lane blacktop leading out of town. Long behind him now was the coastal town of his youth. But the look in June's eyes lingered in his mind. He wanted another drink and more miles burned under his tires before the sun rose and he had to look himself in the mirror and once again face who he was.

He turned up the radio, non-sensical '80s hair rock, but it did nothing to drown out the hoots and shouts of the other inmates as they offered their raucous congratulations through the length of his last walk down the too-polished corridor of the cell block. Freedom at hand after seven years. Good behavior and no fights to speak of. A reputation like his made for easy time compared to many. Even if in his heart he was no longer the man who had earned that wrong kind of respect.

You do it?

He had. God save him, he *had*.

The blood on his hands was real, bought and paid for. And he never wished for anything in his life more than he wished to take back that night. The girl shouldn't have been home. It was Homecoming. He'd watched for days, seen her return home with a fine dress and new shoes. She should have been anywhere but there. The job should have taken one swing of the bat and equaled one shattered leg. It should not have ended with a half-checked swing that caught a seventeen-year-old in the head and put her on a ventilator for the rest of her life. She shouldn't have been there. But he hadn't scouted the house again. He had assumed. Assumption had missed the fact that she had been in bed with the flu for three days. Assumption had cost her the rest of her life. And him? Seven years of freedom and any peace in his soul.

But that result ended in the consequence he deserved. The trial, the sentence, the hard time done and the long walk to a freedom he no longer had any idea what to do with. And June knew just enough to throw it back in his face. His old boss would welcome him, but the blood on his hands was spattered through a tangle of brown hair and across a face too young. He couldn't go back, and now he knew he couldn't come home.

The road sloped and twisted before him, narrow in places, wider in others. Heading west, away from the coming sunrise, as though he could outrun the light and just live within the darkness he felt, he followed the double yellow lines as though they were his own personal Yellow Brick Road. But ahead lay no Emerald City. And Auntie Em didn't want him back at all. Damn the sun. Damn this back-woods state. And damn himself straight on to hell while he was at it.

Small towns rolled by, set close together on the map and on the road. The speed limit changed every few miles, dropping low with every piddly set of buildings that rose out of the darkness. He didn't bother to match the changes. As long as he could take the curves with the car upright, there was only one speed at this hour of the night.

At last, stars faded and the sky ahead of him lightened from dark blue to musty gray. In the rearview mirror, a swipe of red slashed the sky, blooming, until the sun burst over the horizon and swathed the land in the tempered angles of morning light.

A headache began behind his eyes. Lower, his stomach rumbled. He needed coffee if he was to continue much farther. In a long, flat valley between mountains, with a river on one side and nothing but trees on the other, he held little hope of finding more than a wide spot he might stop to relieve his bladder.

But he didn't stop. The road swept on and he followed it, passed an oncoming logging truck traveling much too fast for the narrow highway, even running empty, and even at this hour. Not long after, a freight train caught him, traveling on the far side of the river, pulling hard enough to pass him by, moving away.

God, when had he been passed by a train? He looked down at the speedometer. Thirty miles an hour. When had he dropped that low? Ahead on the right, a small building sat where the road turned hard and crossed a bridge over the river. Just before the bridge another road sloped off the mountainside to meet the one his was on. A sign outside the square building read "BLUE - EAT." An open sign burned in the window and two cars sat in the lot. Luck or madness to have a place open at this hour in the much-damned middle of nowhere. He braked and his hands tingled as he swung the wheel, pulling the car into the graveled lot.

* * *

May watched his final few bites as she wiped the far end of the counter. Typical that someone tossed onto the road with no destination would find his way here. But the despair backing this stranger—backing *David*—was heavier than any she had encountered in months. And the names. Powerful as they were, it wasn't often they were the *sole* thing to turn a lock. In this case, they were everything. Why?

"More coffee?" she asked. "Or can I get you something else? We've got pie, early though it might seem to some."

Across the room, Thadeus's hand shot straight into the air. He didn't even glance her way, just waggled his fingers above his head. "Fine, Thad, I'll bring you a slice." The hand descended and furious scribbling resumed.

Brown eyes in a face crinkled by puzzlement met hers when she looked back to David. "You know all your customers by name?"

Ahh. "Even yours now."

He sat up straighter, stared at her a few seconds, then nodded, surprise and uncertainty etching themselves over his face. She smiled at him. That was it. She *did* now know his name. His *real* name.

May tugged at the fragment of thought, the one linked to his deepest pain, the regret coiled tight inside him. Like a thread unraveling, it led back and back, pinging in places against the fibers surrounding it, sliding easily past others. Striking down that girl was far from the worst thing David had done, but it was the one that had struck *him* down. The one that had given him fame and notoriety. The one that would have reached June's front porch as a headline in the local paper. Mostly killing a child, accidentally or not, was not something easily forgiven. Certainly nothing ever forgotten. *Especially when the news that landed in the home-town rag was graced only by a photo and the false moniker he'd proudly sported through the years.*

Back and back and back. May followed twists and turns. The girl's name, Helen. His full name, David Arden. The two now forever associated and wrapped like a tangled skein. May tugged some more, loosening, until she freed enough slack to continue down the lines of memory back to where David and June last connected. *An icy day with the wind kicked high, snow crystals sharp and brittle under his steps as he stormed from the house for the last time.*

"None of your damn TV gangsters ever have to pay for the hurt they cause, David! Think twice. None of them is gonna give a damn about you when things break sideways. And they will!" June's fierce words fell unnoticed as stones into a pond as he tramped down the steps to the awaiting car. New York City and a life of adventure awaited, and what was a dumb country-woman's rant compared to that?

David and June and Helen and Blue. His false name had once enabled him to repudiate all the teachings of his youth, to remake himself into someone who could do the terrible things he had done. And yet, in the moment he had hurt that girl, he had been David, and that was what stung. What ripped and bashed him apart and earned him the punishment he so justly deserved.

That was who June had turned away—not the masked man capable of crime and destruction—but the unmasked one she had raised, all too capable of the same. And that was whose regret and pain May had to acknowledge, to understand, realign to new purpose, before she sent him on his way.

To allow David Arden back out onto the road in the state he was in, uncertain of his ability to move forward, to do better, was to invite much greater damage and destruction in the future—to himself and possibly to others again. She could not change what he had done. But she could do what Sunny had built Blue to do: draw out the worst darkness inside him and fill him with enough caring and compassion to make a better future possible for him and all those he met, down the road.

"You said pie?" he asked. Then he took the last bite of bread and butter. The spell of compassion laced into the butter tripped live as he swallowed and his face shifted again, eyes widening. The muscles around his jaw relaxed under the beard and he looked younger than he had by a good five years.

"Coconut cream." She had him. He was open under the spell of kindness. Unbarred by the first offer of caring made with the complete knowledge of *who he was* to have touched him in decades. He blinked several times. She smiled. "It's made with that same butter." And milk and cream from the farm the twins ran at the top of the notch. And pie crusts made with wheat harvested from Thadeus' fields. Pie, in Blue, was love, and whatever else it needed to be.

He nodded once, staring at her, and she grinned back as she opened the glass-fronted cooler and carved him and Thadeus each a slice. She plated both and set David's before him with a fresh fork, then carried Thadeus his piece.

When she returned, David's eyes were closed and the pie half-gone. Without a word, she refilled his coffee mug and leaned her hips against the back counter, waiting. She whispered soft words to the crockery as he ate and drank, the most powerful words she knew, the ones Sunny had told her were only to be used when need hung heavy in the air. They swirled around him, backed by the magic of purposeful food, and tension ran out of his body like tears. By the time he had finished, the most violent portion of the fear and despair inside him had drained into the stoneware, trapped by the glaze, housed in the clay with each touch of his lips to the cup, and each scrape of the fork over the plate. In its place was judgment-free compassion for himself...and for others. That most of all. Not so much was taken or replaced that he would feel less himself, but enough that he would feel like the self he was *had hope.*

He smiled as he finished, and she nodded and scooped the dishes from the counter. "Coffee to go?" she asked as she set them in the blue bus tub beneath the sink.

"Please, May." No ripple of awareness tingled her spine as he spoke her name. Her work with this one was done as well as she could do it.

She plucked a to-go cup from the stack by the dessert case and filled it, popped on the lid, and handed it to him.

On the counter he placed a crisp fifty-dollar bill and waved her off when she sprung open the register for change. "Keep it. This was the best meal I've had in years."

Of course it was. May nodded, measuring the change within him. Solid work. Enough to matter. "Thank you, David," she said. "Come back and see us when you pass this way again."

"I will." The door clicked shut behind him.

Colin cut a glance her way. "That took some doing."

"Worth it," May said as she hefted the blue bin.

"You'll have to tell me later why. Where are you going with that? Storage?"

"Cleanse kiln."

Colin gave a sharp whistle and even Thadeus' head came up.

"Hell's fire," Jenna said. "Need my help?"

May shook her head. "Thanks, Jen. This one wants to be free. It'll just take me a little spelled heat."

She paused in the doorway. The blue car with New York plates was just turning west on the highway. From the east came a tan van, slowing, slowing. Its blinker came on well before the driver could possibly have read the weathered sign. The river rushing. Big trucks passing. The season changing. Feet on trails. Things were in motion.

She held the door with her hip and called back inside. "Give me ten to get the spell moving. And start another pot of coffee. Looks like we're going to have a busy day."

MY BROTHER'S LEAVES

Diana A. Hart

I glowered at the steam rising from my brother's corpse, his mycelia-swaddled remains peeking out of a mound of fermenting tea. Acid from weeks of dodging creditors' com-pings gnawed at my gut. "Always leaving me messes to clean up, Hahn..." I said, words echoing off the bare walls.

Still, a lump formed in my throat. I swallowed and jerked the bamboo shutters wide. Chill, humid air poured through the tea factory, pushing back the scent of wood and old meat. Fyorre's twin moons cast a pale glow across the plasteel floor. In the wan light, fungal strands gleamed silver.

Li, the labor-master, clicked her tongue. The past ten weeks hung heavy in her wrinkles. "Should have left him in the gorge, Lady Mei. Let the mud-hounds pick him over." She tossed me a pole. "Waste of good Dream Pu-reh."

"I need Hahn's codes," I said.

"He'll have drained the accounts. Too many bets, too little Yen."

Which was precisely the problem. With each cycle another race or hound-fight finished somewhere on Fyorre and another bet-master pinged Hahn's com demanding payment on his loss, unaware that two and a half months ago Hahn had drunk too much plum wine and tumbled into the canyon.

Lips tight, I stirred the maocha—fully-aged tea leaves, rich and woodsy from weeks of fermentation—pausing only to jam a few dark strands of hair behind my ear. Once they figured out Hahn was dead, the vultures would swoop in, seizing his share of the fields to settle his debts.

My knuckles whitened around my pole. *Damn you, Hahn.* Half production was only enough to pay the workers or the terraforming tax, then there was the importation of memory-rich bodies...

Anger sped my pulse. Losing half meant losing all.

"Fool man," Li said, as though reading my thoughts, tapping the floor with every turn of the tea. Her nose wrinkled up like cracked driftwood. "Fool woman. Drink too much bloom..."

Cold slithered up my spine. "I know."

In order for Dreamer's Bloom to cause visions the fungus had to be alive when consumed. The occasional cup caused only minor infection, easily purged by the immune system, but heavy consumption caused long-term, even fatal, effects. Rocks settled in my gut. Still, what choice did I have?

My knees, sore from years of work that Hahn never deigned to do, groaned as I crouched over the earth-brown leaves. I put a pinch of maocha in my palm and rolled it about, inspecting the Bloom that had spread from my brother to the tea. If we were lucky, one of the leaves held a vision of Hahn's security codes. I just had to find it and seize Hahn's share before the debt collectors came.

* * *

I rubbed my temple, hunched over Father's wooden desk as another message squealed through the uplink. "Sonthi's tired of waiting, Hahn. You will make a payment of fifty thousand Yen or we will petition the Magistrate for liquidation of your assets. You have seven days to comply." Fresh bile burned my throat. I passed a hand over Hahn's slim data pad, ending playback.

Noonday sun spilled blue through the windows, lending a cold cast to the rugs and carved jade that lined the habitat. The jade Hahn hadn't sold, anyway. I buried my face in my hands, letting out a slow, tear-heavy breath, and cursed my brother again. In the years after Father's death, Hahn drowned himself in drink and dice, leaving me to manage the entire plantation and stare at the growing gaps in Father's collection. *At least nothing else will disappear now.* Provided I could save the fields. I laughed into my palms.

The doorway hissed open and Li hobbled into the room. An aroma of wet clay wafted in with her. I pulled my head up, blinking back moisture. Clutched in Li's gnarled grip was a lacquered tray, laden with towel, hot water, a gaiwan for brewing tea, and a bowl of my brother's leaves. She set the affair down with an audible click. As she spread the towel over the desk, Li fixed me with a stern brown gaze.

"One cup."

I sighed and pulled Hahn's data pad closer. Fresh message alerts blinked inside the glass. "Li—"

She grabbed me by the wrist. "One."

Anger flashed through me, hot and fast, but a tremor in her grip made me pause. Though her eyes were hard there was a wideness to them, like the deer in Father's hunting scrolls, proud and strong but afraid all the same. Guilt bowed my shoulders.

"One," I said.

Li bobbed her head, sunlight glittering sapphire in her hair, and left me to my Dreams.

I pulled up a transfer of property form on Hahn's data pad, then loaded my brother's leaves into the gaiwan, setting them steeping. My throat tightened. Steam plumed from the smooth, maroon pot, reminding me of those moonlit nights stirring moist tea around Hahn's body. I shook my head, poured Pu-erh broth into a cup, deep-amber tea chittering against the chipped clay. Deep, wet-bark scents crept into my nostrils, laced with hints of Hahn's old flesh.

"Be useful for once," I said, raising the cup to my lips.

Wood and sap and earth rolled across my tongue, the overall terroir sharp thanks to Fyorre's acrid soil, before the mushroom tones crept in, smothering my senses like a twining blanket of mold. I tasted bad meat. Tasted Hahn. Then mycelial haze drug me down, darkening my vision until the world was nothing but blurs of color and teetering, leaden limbs. My head thunked on the table. Pain reached me like the echoes of a distant bruise.

Hahn's mind flooded mine. I caught glimpses of his time in the gambling dens. The clatter of dice and roulette, cigar smoke, sweet lungfuls of opium, chips and Yen and notes of credit passing fast as water between his fingers. Then there were the women, all sweat and pleasure and waking to empty beds.

Under his indulgence was emptiness, a yawing, years-old abyss that ached in his bones. Somewhere far away, I whimpered. I knew that pain, too. Hahn's fingers flicked across his data pad, mine twitching in involuntary echo, as he ordered more wine to fill the chasm inside.

The mushroom taste started to fade. A curse mumbled half-formed from my lips. He'd used the pad, but not his security key. I'd have to—

"Hahn!" A small girl tugged his shirt, staring up at him with wide, dark eyes. The factory windows let in wind and light. The scent of half-fermented tea hung thick in the air. The girl held up a bamboo leaf. "Show me the goose again?"

Hahn smiled. I could feel the bulge of it in my cheeks. He cast a quick glance at Father as the man stirred ripening maocha. My breath caught. In this vision, Father's hair was a solid braid of black and no wrinkles yet creased his face. He also towered half a meter above Hahn. Seeing no signs of disapproval, Hahn set his stirring pole against the factory wall.

"All right, Mei, watch carefully." Hahn crouched on the floor and took the leaf from his sister. My heart beat faster, a distant, echoing drumbeat. Hahn turned, bits of tea staining the knees of his jumpsuit as he let Fyorre's sun spill through the bamboo shutters onto his hands. He pulled apart the fresh leaf and cupped it between his palms, raised it to his mouth and blew. The strip of leaf acted like the reed in an instrument, buzzing against his skin as he produced a loud squawk.

Dream Mei laughed. Hahn grinned. My head swam, memories mixing with that of my brother until I saw both our smiles, felt the sun's heat on both our skins, lips growing numb as we squeaked strips of leaf.

The Dream faded to nothing, replacing joy's warmth with the cold smoothness of Hahn's data pad under my fingers and damp towel beneath my head. My stomach bucked. I lifted my head, muscles shaking. Ropes of drool sagged between my mouth and the desk. The sun's glow had faded to a dusky cobalt, submerging the habitat in a deep-ocean twilight. Flecks of blood dotted the towel, stains dark maroon in the fading light.

I wept alone.

* * *

"We should sell these bingcha to White Station," Li said, and passed me another pressed Pu-erh cake. "Hawk's Flight and Fish in Summer are almost ripe, and the colonists pine for glimpses of home."

My Brother's Leaves

I chewed my lip, setting the seventh disk of tea into a bamboo tong before lashing the container shut. Each brush of coarse fibers summoned unbidden memories. In the diffuse light that filtered into the wide room, the visions blazed clearer than reality. Hahn cobbled together little bamboo animals for a gap-toothed Mei, who then danced about the rack-lined aging room with her tigers and kirin, singing softly to herself. I shook my head, clearing my vision but not my ears.

"Yes. White Station is good. We can pay off the Xiu Xian dens, at least."

Li shot me a knowing look. "How much have you been drinking?"

"A cup a day," I said, keeping my eyes firmly on the bingcha.

"Every day? Lady Mei, that's too much! You'll—"

"It's too little!" I snapped. My brow creased as I fought with the next tong. Five days and still no code. "I get two, maybe three visions, and then they stop." *Except for these,* I thought, as little Mei played hide-and-seek with her brother. A toppled rack in a botched hiding attempt reminded me why the north shutters didn't work quite right. My lips twitched, caught between smirk and frown.

One of the workers cleared their throat. "Lady Mei?" I looked up. A teenager in a mud-stained jumpsuit leaned in the doorway. "There's a man waiting for you in the habitat."

My pulse rose. I nodded to the boy, dismissing him, before waving for Li to follow. We hurried through the tea factory, past piles of freshly moistened leaves just starting the fermentation process, and out into open sun. I drew up short, blinking against the blue light. Wind stirred the rows of tea bushes like waves. Beyond the sea of green sat a land-skimmer, a sleek, solar-powered hovercraft with a shape that reminded me of a crane mid-flight.

Cold sweat slicked my palms. *Not good.* This model was solely a speed craft, and out here on the frontier the only people who could afford something like that were government and betting-lords. I brushed musty tea-dust from my jumpsuit and rushed to Father's office. Li kept a close step behind.

The door hissed open. A Thai man with a thin frame and high, sharp cheekbones held one of Father's jade carp, examining the delicately carved coin it held in its mouth.

My jaw clenched. "Can I help you?" I barely kept the venom from my tone.

The invader turned, flashing a too-wide smile, and set down Father's sculpture. Li's countenance pinched. I couldn't blame her. Just being near him made my hairs stand on end.

"Ah, Miss Mei! Good to meet you." He extended a hand, fingers like soft, warm grubs in mine. "I'm Sonthi, representing Twin Moons Entertainment. We've been trying to reach your brother, but he's not responding to com links."

I pulled my hand free and resisted the urge to wipe it on my jumpsuit. My heart thudded in my chest. "I'm afraid he stepped out for a few days."

"Any idea when he might return?"

"No. Hahn mostly keeps to himself."

Sonthi's brow drew tight. He leaned closer. "Miss Mei, I cannot stress enough my need to speak with your brother. My employer has already secured a meeting with the Magistrate next week, but we'd like to settle this without government involvement..."

He proceeded to rattle off some boilerplate speech no doubt intended to soothe my conscience if I decided to cough up Hahn's location. I didn't listen. My insides were a churning storm of ice and acid. *They have an appointment with the Magistrate...* I glanced at the gaiwan sitting on my desk, still full of this morning's leaves. I was out of time.

I flicked my gaze back to Sonthi. Cut off his speech. "You might try White Station."

Li and Sonthi both cocked their heads, the first in disbelief, the second with almost tiger-like interest. "Miss Mei?" Sonthi led.

I shrugged. "Hahn enjoyed it when we were little." In one of my visions, Hahn and I had run through the dockside markets while Father sold tea, chasing rats that had snuck planetside aboard ships and watching the latest freighters touch down, spilling out fresh colonists like a split bag of soybeans.

Sonthi's eyes narrowed almost imperceptibly. "Are you certain?"

"No," I said, breezing past him. I whiffed jasmine cologne. My insides shook but I did my best to keep my voice level. "That's why I said you might *try* White Station." Sonthi stayed put. My pulse thundered so loud part of me feared he'd hear it. I nodded to Li. "My labor-master can help you. She's known Hahn and me since we were children and might have a few ideas where to look."

Sonthi clasped his hands together. "Ah, excellent. Your cooperation is most appreciated, Miss Mei."

Behind Sonthi, Li's expression darkened. She pulled in a breath, ready to protest, but I placed a hand on the gaiwan. "It won't be long, I trust?" Li's glower turned to a gape, comprehension bleeding the color from her face.

"Not at all, Miss Mei." Sonthi gave a tiny bow. "You'll be without her two to three days, at the most."

I smiled. My stomach burned even worse.

By the time Sonthi's land-skimmer lifted off I was already brewing another cup of tea.

* * *

Dreams and reality blurred together as cup after cup of my brother's leaves passed across my tongue. My senses overflowed with sweet plum wine. The thick smoke of opium. Gamblers chattered in my ears and money disappeared as Hahn stumbled from bed to table to bed again. Through the mycelial haze of the tea I kept my hand on Hahn's data pad, the cool glass beneath my palm my only anchor to reality.

I over-steeped the next batch until each sip summoned a monsoon of memories. I gripped Hahn's data pad tighter, forced myself to look at it as the fungal-induced storm raged through my brain.

Come on, damn you. Tell me the codes.

Hahn's memories trended ever more toward use of his data pad. Summoning women. Ordering wine. Teaching little Mei how to play music and look up videos of cats.

I surfaced long enough to brew more tea, spittle dripping like red streamers from my chin. I paused, blinking numbly. *Red?* I looked down. Goosebumps spread across my skin. The towel was mottled with blood, sprouting wisps of mycelia around the edges. Dawn light turned the mess a deep, dark purple.

I hesitated, cup halfway to my lips. Fungal must hung heavy in the room. My mouth felt dry, like I was rubbing cotton on the roof of my mouth every time I swallowed. Tremors started in my hand. *Losing half means losing all.* I downed the cup.

Luck must have smiled, because I soon spotted Hahn changing his security key at Father's desk, fingers flying across his data pad. Mine danced in echo, tapping the same alphanumeric string into the pad. I grinned, muscles soft as lychee pulp, and tried to sit up.

Hahn looked up from his data pad, watching me through the window as I walked out to the fields. I pulled in a sharp breath. I was wearing a new jumpsuit and Fyorre's second moon hung behind the first, as though hiding from the latest colony ship that sparkled low on the horizon. My breast ached. This was ten weeks ago, the last night I'd seen my brother alive.

Shame settled on Hahn's shoulders, bowing them beneath their weight. *How can you keep going, Mei?* Working in the fields, keeping Father's dreams alive... Hahn swallowed. His sister's retreating back was so straight and strong, as though no hungry ghost roared inside her, demanding to be filled.

Tears rolled down my cheeks. I wanted to follow his memory. I owed it to Hahn, the one from so long ago, to be with him in the end, but every moment I stayed risked the tea fields. Hahn went back to his wine. I pushed him away, alone and broken, and pawed at his data pad with spittle-stained fingers. His security code went through with a tiny ping, finishing the transfer of property. I laughed and let my head fall to the desk.

All I tasted was mushrooms.

* * *

A dim, yellow glow shone through my eyelids and a rhythmic beeping droned in my ears. I groaned and tried to roll over. A sharp tug in my elbow drew me up short.

"Don't move, Lady Mei," Li said. Bony fingers gripped my shoulder. I smelled disinfectant and a hint of jasmine. Cracking an eye, my gaze swept over a smooth, teal-colored room. Vitals glowed on a nearby display and an IV of off-colored liquid sprouted from my arm. I heard Sonthi in the hall, voice muffled by the glass as he shouted into his com.

"Hospital?" I croaked. My throat felt like I'd been eating sand.

Li nodded. Her eyes watered. "Found you when we got back, hauled you back to White Station. You've been out a week."

A smirk teased my lips. If Sonthi was yelling, that meant one thing. "Magistrate's upholding the transfer?"

Li smiled, deepening her wrinkles. "So far, yes."

"Good. And my brother's leaves?"

Li clicked her tongue and glanced back at Sonthi. "Burned them. No tea, no proof Hahn's dead." My blood turned to ice. I sat, stunned, as Li pulled my blankets higher. "You're still a fool woman," she said. "Doctors say you'll live, but it'll take a full month of fungicide to clean the last of the bloom from your system. The visions should stop then."

Deep inside, a roaring emptiness stirred. Would I remember the visions once the bloom was gone? I'd forgotten who Hahn was once already, the bond we'd shared before Father's death, and without it my love for him had rotted to nothing. Guilty weight bowed my head. *Losing half means losing all.* I sank deeper into the blankets.

"Li," I muttered, "can you get me some water?"

She murmured an assent, sparing a pat for my shoulder, and hobbled out of the room. Sonthi kept growling into his com, insisting I could find Hahn once I recovered. The door hissed shut behind Li.

Tears blurred my vision. I swiped a hand across my face, wiping away the moisture, but the ache in my chest didn't stop. Under it all, little Mei laughed. My jaw tightened.

A quick yank pulled out my IV. Fungicide dripped onto the floor. I leaned back into the pillows and closed my eyes.

A phantom wind played through Hahn's hair, carrying the scent of tea bushes and the promise of rain. Ahead in the fields, little Mei held Father's hand as he walked the grounds, checking the bushes for signs of pests. She saw Hahn and waved. "Hurry up, slowpoke!"

Still in my bed, I ran for them as fast as Hahn's legs would carry me.

SNOW AND APPLES

A.L. Tompkins

The coughing began just after first snow. By midwinter, there was a terrible, wet rattle in Marushka's chest that no herb or tincture could ease. She'd waved him off, said, "Don't fuss, Vanya." But she grew weaker day by day, fading with the sun.

Ivan was sitting at her bedside, one wrinkled, blunt-fingered hand wrapped around hers, when the end came. Her final choked gasp haunted his sleep for weeks, filling his nights with dreams of drowning.

He didn't sleep much anymore.

It took three days to chip a grave out of the frozen earth. He adorned her cairn with boughs from a spindly evergreen and the carved wooden birds she'd adored, because the toughest flowers wouldn't be breaking through the soil for weeks yet.

As the days crawled closer to spring, he found himself eating alone, tending to their home alone, and going to bed alone, for the first time in nearly five decades. No Marushka to laugh at how flat his bread always came out. No one humming as he sat before the hearth stone, twisting fiber into rope. No one to tuck her icy toes against his leg at night while he pretended to grumble about the cold.

Each day was heavier than the one before it, until something inside him snapped, like a branch weighed down with too much snow.

Tears were useless, and regrets were for the living, but there was one last thing he could do for his Masha.

He threw the last of the cheese and some tough rounds of bread into a satchel, only because he had to. Everything tasted like ashes to him, dry as dust on his tongue.

Breath pluming in the air, Ivan squinted up at the night. The first glimmers of green and azure flickered in twisting ribbons, streaking the dark. The Spirit Tide was building. When the colors of the spirit paths filled the sky, he'd have his chance to make an offering. Marushka deserved whatever comfort he could win her on her final journey. A cake or a bit of drink wouldn't do. She'd given him a lifetime of love and friendship. Only the best would be enough. For Masha, he'd find a ghost apple.

And if he had to cross the Forest Prince to do it, so be it.

He paused to rest his hand on her snow-dusted cairn. One last caress before he turned his back on their home and set off over the flattened brown grass of the steppe.

Ivan walked. He ate when he thought he should be hungry, drank when he was thirsty, and kept putting one foot in front of the other while his legs ached and the wind bit at his skin.

He'd been frozen inside since midwinter. He could take a little more.

Eventually the grass thinned, and the plain rolled up against the edge of the woods. Ivan looked up at the gray and black bark of the towering larch, at the sticky green needles of pine and spruce, and ran his tongue over his teeth in distaste.

Marushka never seemed to hold the forest any ill-will, but she hadn't complained when he'd insisted on building their home on the sprawling steppe where the only trees were sparse and slender things huddled by the river. Ivan was the one who clung to his grudge and made sure to keep his axe close at hand.

He knew he'd need all his wits once he crossed the forest's border, so Ivan dragged some evergreen boughs away from the tree line and picked up any fallen wood he could reach that looked dry enough to burn. He still had a long way to go, but if he didn't rest soon, he knew his body would decide for him.

The branches caught quickly, spilling heat and warmth into the night. Spruce boughs made a soft enough bed, but he felt the aching of his bones more deeply than usual.

In the flickering light of his meagre fire the trees seemed to shrink, drawing away from the flames, and Ivan felt a small flare of satisfaction.

If his concern was for himself, he'd march into the woods, blazing torch held high, and let the Leshiin, the Forest Prince, deal with his disrespect as he would. He wasn't there for himself, though. This was the last thing he could do for Masha, the last comfort he could grant her, and he would not fail.

The branches clicked together as the wind picked up, needles rustling with a low hiss. Ivan stared up at the shadow of the forest and felt the years fall away. He'd challenged the woods once before for Masha's sake, when he'd been a callow youth whose only thought had been to rescue his love from the creature that had stolen her from her home. He'd made curious friends, rescued a legend, and escaped with Marushka mostly through luck.

It seemed a lifetime ago.

His laugh was a raspy huff of air. *Because it* was *a lifetime ago, old man.*

The fire guttered wildly and Ivan huddled down into the fur of his coat to avoid the bite of early spring. He reached for his bag and fished out a hunk of dry cheese rind. Food could keep away the cold, for a time, so he forced himself to chew even though it made his jaw ache.

"It's been a long time, Ivan, son of Illyana."

Ivan flinched at the unexpected voice and ignored the protest of his back to twist around and face the speaker.

Golden eyes watched him from the shadow of the woods, unblinking. He'd started to reach for the axe laid by his side when he finally made out the pointed upright ears and russet fur.

The fox vixen slipped into the light of his fire and took a seat with her tail tucked over her black paws. Her nose twitched at the cheese still clutched in his hand, muzzle streaked with far more white than he remembered. "I hope you brought enough to share."

For the first time in more days than he could bear to count, Ivan felt happiness flare up, like a well-banked fire being coaxed back to life. He'd known Wise Beasts lived longer than normal animals, but he hadn't dared to hope he'd find her again.

He'd barely opened his mouth to welcome her when a high, sweet voice from above mumbled sleepily, "If I have to be awake without the sun, there had better be bread."

Ivan squinted into the dark until he caught the reflection of the fire in one shining black eye. Even in broad daylight, he would have struggled to see more. The nightingale's soft brown and cream feathers vanished in the forest, but he'd know that piping voice anywhere.

"Bread for you and cheese for you. All I have, you're welcome to my friends." He slid the rind to the vixen and broke open one of the small loaves to hold in his hand for the nightingale. "You've already done more for me than I can ever repay."

The vixen flicked her ears, dismissively. "I've always loved a good trick."

She didn't turn down the cheese, though.

The nightingale fluttered down to land on his palm. She was so light that other than the dry rasp of her little claws, he might not have noticed.

"I'm sorry to have been away so long—" he began, when the nightingale interrupted him with a flick of her wings.

"We understood, Ivan Illyanavitch." She tilted her head to look up at him with one eye. "The woods are old, and strong, and they hold onto grudges with every root and branch."

The vixen licked her muzzle, her tongue shockingly red against the white fur. "What brings you back here?"

Ivan kept his eyes on the fire as wood popped and sap sizzled. "I came for an apple."

He felt them exchange a look before the vixen spoke up, gently. "Apples don't grow in spring."

"This one does."

Nightingale fluffed up her feathers, tucking one foot up against her breast before she spoke again. "Why an apple?"

He hesitated, pulse thick in his throat. "Where do Wise Beasts go when they leave this life?"

"Well," the vixen began, cautiously. "There are options, of a sort. We can choose to dwell beyond the mists, in one of the kingdoms of the Beast Princes. Or we can go around again." Her voice lightened, taking on the cheeky tone he remembered fondly. "Maybe next time, *I'll* be the nightingale."

Somehow, despite not possessing a nose, the nightingale gave a surprisingly good imitation of a snort and for the first time since winter closed in, Ivan smiled.

He turned his gaze to the sky, the velvety blackness lightened to indigo by the brilliant array of colors snaking across the heavens.

"When humans die..." His throat closed and he had to clear it and try again. "We travel to the Thrice-Nine kingdom. It's a long journey. We have to pass through many lands in the mists. But when the Spirit Tide comes, and the spirit paths touch the mortal world," he lifted his chin to the ribbons of light twisting in the sky; green and blue and palest violet, "we can make offerings to those who have gone before us, to help speed their journey."

"What kind of offerings?" the nightingale asked with a sort of artless innocence, her head cocked to one side.

"Mostly food." His neck ached from being arched for so long, so he let his head tilt forward again. "Kavass, or little cakes dabbed with enough fresh blood to be of interest to the dead. But the best offering is a ghost apple."

The vixen's ears perked. "A ghost apple?"

"They grow in the deepest part of the forest, away from the sun. When I was a boy, I found some in these very woods. My brother dared me to eat one."

The nightingale hopped forward, eager. "How did it taste?"

His lips twitched at the memory. "Terrible. It was mealy, and grainy, and somehow both sour and bland at the same time."

Tail flicking in disappointment, the vixen wrinkled her muzzle. "An odd sort of offering, then."

Ivan shrugged. "My mother always said these apples weren't for the living. They saved their sweetness for the dead. One last taste of the world they've left behind."

Silence fell, other than the crackle of flames. The rasp of fur against grass and the gentle weight in his hand was the only way he knew they hadn't slipped away back into the dark.

The wood brightened, shadows stretching thin until they broke. Ivan frowned, squinting up at the sky. It was nowhere close to dawn, yet. The nights were cruelly long this time of year.

Gentle warmth fell around his shoulders, like a comfortable coat, and Ivan turned to face the trees.

The Firebird perched in the skeletal branches of a nearby larch, the magnificent cascade of her tail feathers dripping embers onto the ashy soil.

She was exactly as he remembered her, all scarlet and gold, blazing orange and palest white. She settled her wings, flames rippling across her feathers like embers. Almost too brilliant to look at directly, her form blurred like a heat vision in the heart of a fire, caught between magnificent crested bird and a dark-eyed, solemn woman.

For her, he smiled, his throat nearly too tight for words. "I hadn't thought we'd meet again."

The smile she had for him was frosted with sorrow. "I am sorry for the loss you've suffered, Ivan Illyanavitch."

Winter closed back in, snuffing the warmth camaraderie had kindled. Still, he couldn't bring himself to look away. "Humans don't last so long, dear lady."

She leapt down from her tree, strong wings flared wide, and knelt beside him, her gown of iridescent feathers trailing in the dirt. "You will always have my friendship, Vanya."

The vixen and the nightingale nodded solemnly.

"All I can do for my Masha is speed her journey." His voice was a dry, hoarse thing, strangled by too much unsaid. "Will you help me?"

The Firebird pushed snow-white hair back from Ivan's forehead. He closed his eyes and felt the brush of feathers on his skin.

"Sleep. I will watch over you until dawn."

It was more than he would have dared ask and Ivan settled down as well as he could on his bed of soft boughs. With the warmth of the Firebird so near, he didn't even bother to bury the ashes of his fire beneath his bed, trusting her to not let him freeze. His limbs grew heavy, pain fading before the blackness of sleep. There were no dreams to plague him, only peaceful dark under the protective eyes of the Firebird.

* * *

Ivan woke to aching legs, the scent of evergreen thick in his nose, and a little red fox curled up tight against his chest. The fire had gone out at some point, burnt down to ashes, but for once, he wasn't cold.

The sun was well over the horizon and the Firebird was gone. He offered a quick thought of gratitude to her. A restful night was a gift beyond measure, especially so close to the tree line. If he'd had any fruit on hand, he'd have offered it up to her in thanks. Of course, it was the Firebird's love of fruit that had gotten her into trouble in the past.

The looming woods didn't look any friendlier in the light of day.

It took some effort, but Ivan managed to haul himself upright. The vixen gave a small growl of protest, tucking her tail tighter over her face.

The nightingale flitted from his bag to a stubbornly upright stalk of grass, her little feet clinging while she ruffled up her feathers and sang, "Good morning," in her silver voice.

With a resigned grumble, the vixen relented. She rose into a stretch, black paws extended before her. "I hope you realize that you're insufferable."

The nightingale gave a twitter of laughter, but still prudently flew up to perch on Ivan's shoulder, out of reach of the vixen's teeth.

He was grateful for their company. Even their bickering helped feed the warmth the Firebird had kindled in his chest. It had been an absent sort of kindness that made him pause to free a little vixen's tail from a bit of deadfall—and to scoop a featherless chick back into its frantic mother's nest—when he'd gone to free Marushka from the Leshiin. Their fear had moved him. He'd wondered if his Masha was afraid, had hoped someone would help her. Then he'd mostly hoped his aid wouldn't get him bitten or pecked. He'd had no way of knowing then that they'd return his kindness ten-fold.

He felt it in his bones when they crossed the forest's threshold. As they picked their way through the shallows, stepping over the tender green shoots of emerging ramps and ferns, the hair at the back of his neck prickled in warning. The hiss of evergreen needles brushing against each other sounded like whispers.

The nightingale emerged from the hood of his coat, winging up into the bare branches of a larch tree, while the vixen slunk into the dead, dry underbrush. Ivan took a deep breath, let it out in a sigh that plumed in the air, and let himself ache, just for a moment. He wanted Marushka beside him so much it hurt, wanted her hand in his, as they'd faced the rest of the world over a lifetime.

At least he wasn't alone.

He wasn't sure how long he'd walked when the Nightingale gave a trill of warning up ahead. The trees grew thicker the deeper he wandered, blotting out the weak spring sun. He'd been moving as fast as he dared, but it was slow going. He couldn't risk a fall. Creatures that couldn't walk didn't last long in the woods.

At the call, Ivan slowed further. He used the handle of his axe to part the skirt of a spruce tree and peered ahead, trying to catch a glimpse of what the nightingale had seen.

Dappled light broke through the bare canopy here, the branches twisting together high above like the roof of a palace. The sunlight glittered off the surface of the pond nestled in the clearing, and off the milk-pale skin of the young woman bathing in its icy waters.

Her back to him, golden hair trailing down to drag across the pond's surface, she lifted a cupped hand to smooth water over her extended arm.

Ivan scowled, heavy gray brows drawing down. He didn't have time to go around, to double back and pick a safer way. So he bulled his way through the trees with a huff of breath, limping as fast as his tired legs would carry him.

The young woman turned at the first sound of dry wood crunching under his feet. Her face was all clean lines and full lips. Her eyes the same icy blue of the water that lapped around her hips, and when she smiled at him, her teeth were white and perfect as pearls.

She reached out to him, beckoning. "Swim with me." Her voice was lower than he thought it would be, more of a throaty purr than the high and clear tone to match her appearance.

Past all thought of caution and diplomacy, Ivan made a rude, nasal sound as he limped past. The shocked expression on the Rusalka's face was almost worth the danger.

"That didn't work forty years ago. It's not going to work now."

Normally Rusalka had no need to chase down prey, so Ivan was sure it was surprise that made her pause long enough for him to slip back into the trees.

The vixen gave a short bark of laughter. "That was bold," she said, one golden eye shining up at him from beneath a pine tree.

Ivan shrugged, but couldn't quite relax the white-knuckled grip he had on his axe. "I don't have time to be drowned. It's almost Spirit Tide."

The deeper they travelled, the thicker and darker the trees became. Evergreen trees parted to make way for broadleaf, bare branches pushing out tender buds. Mist lapped around trunks and pooled in hollows, making the lichen-covered ground slick and treacherous. Ivan had to slow, move more carefully, and he chafed at the delay.

He eventually had to pause, to lean against a moss-covered trunk and drink some water. His skin was clammy with sweat and his breath was heavy in his chest.

But there, up ahead through the twisted branches, he saw a glimpse of white.

The vixen's startled yip was his only warning before what he'd thought was a spruce tree shook itself and stood.

Needled boughs fell around the hulking figure's shoulders like a cloak as he stretched to his full height, antlers brushing the canopy. His skin was like bark, tough and gray, his beard a tangle of leaves and moss. Eyes glowed blue-green like foxfire in the dim light. The Leshiin slammed one massive foot to the earth before Ivan and the trees trembled, leaning away.

"I don't know if you're exceedingly brave, or just a fool to come back here." The Leshiin spoke in a voice of creaking branches and rustling leaves. "Did you think you could sneak by? I felt your presence the moment you passed over the first root. How dare you set foot in my kingdom after you stole from me?"

For once, the ice inside his chest was useful. Ivan knew he should be afraid. He'd only escaped with Masha before with help from his friends and a fool's luck. But he was tired, and he was old, and it seemed fear was beyond him. But pride wasn't, so he straightened his shoulders, despite wanting to sit to take the weight off his bad leg, and met the Leshiin's gaze squarely.

"Stealing implies ownership. I took nothing that belonged to you. Marushka has only ever belonged to herself."

The Leshiin tossed his head, antlers crashing against the canopy of branches. "All within the woods belong to me."

"She was only in the woods because you snatched her from the edge of the village." The handle of his axe felt heavier in Ivan's hand. He tightened his grip. "To harvest fruit and tend mushrooms you were too lazy to see to."

His dry tone seemed to enrage the Forest Prince, who raked furrows into the earth with claws of twisted wood. "She should have been honored to serve me!"

"Because you're so impressive?" Ivan snorted. "A half-dead forest with barely any birds or beasts to it, but you think you're something to be admired because you've claimed it as your own?"

Spruce needles bristled over the Leshiin's shoulders like the hackles on a dog about to bite.

Ivan pressed on, heedless. "You say this is your kingdom, but I walked these woods for years as a boy. I wager I know it better than you do."

The Leshiin paused and Ivan ruthlessly suppressed a smile.

"You'd wager, would you? And what would you wager?"

And that was the bait taken. It seemed the Leshiin was as prone to games of chance as the tales claimed. The Forest Princes were notorious for betting with each other over all manner of things, using the animals and birds of their woods as chits. A forest devoid of beasts was said to have an unlucky Leshiin.

"If I lose, you'll have what you tried to have of Marushka; a servant."

The Leshiin eyed him. "There's not much life left in you."

Ivan didn't dispute it, only shrugged. "You'd get what's left of it."

The Forest Prince considered. "Very well. And if you should somehow win?"

"I want an apple."

His sharp crack of laughter sounded like branches breaking. "Not much of a bargain, but as you wish." The Leshiin narrowed his fox-fire eyes. "So then, mortal man, if you know my woods so well, how many deer are grazing in the clearing to the north of us?"

The gloating tone was grating, as if he were convinced he'd won already, but Ivan ignored it. Instead, he pursed his lips and tilted his head as though he were considering.

In truth, he was listening.

From her vantage in the boughs of a nearby spruce, the nightingale sang four short, silvery notes nearly lost to the wind.

"Four," Ivan said.

The Leshiin froze. Wood popped as he clenched his fists. "Luck. How many squirrels nest in that larch?"

Ivan watched from the corner of his eye as a flash of russet fur disappeared behind a moss-shrouded trunk. The vixen gave one sharp yip, followed by two softer.

"Three. A mother and two kits."

The Leshiin swelled with fury. His hooves tore great clods of dirt free from the ground.

Ivan squinted against the growing light, but kept his gaze firmly on the Leshiin. "Now I'll ask you a question. What is in the birch tree behind you?"

"Nothing," spat the Leshiin. "It is a half-dead, useless bit of wood. Why? Do you feel some measure of kinship with it?"

Ivan clicked his tongue. "It seems I do know these woods better than you. The correct answer," he smiled so hard his cheeks ached, "is a Firebird."

The Leshiin went very still. His great head turned ponderously to face the birch behind him.

The Firebird perched lightly on a branch turned gray and sooty. Sparks cascaded from her wings, while her tail draped down the birch's trunk. Its papery bark already turning black and peeling.

"I do not fear you," the Forest Prince said, drawing up to his full, impressive height. "I defeated you once. I can do so again."

The Firebird looked down her wickedly curved beak at the Leshiin. "The Rusalka helped you trap me. But you've no water spirit to aid you this time."

She flared her wings wide and they burned with every color of flame. The orange-red of the hearth. The scarlet and gold of a wildfire. The blazing white light of the stars piercing the heavens.

The Leshiin turned and, with a sound like an enormous tree being felled, dove into his woods and disappeared.

Satisfaction in every line, the Firebird carefully preened one of her flight feathers back into place. "Go and fetch your prize, Ivan Illyanavitch."

He huffed a breath of laughter and limped forward to push his way through the trees. "Thank you, dear lady."

"Oh, no," she said, voice full of amusement. "It was my pleasure."

The wild orchard was small, only three trees clustered together in a little glen so thickly canopied it felt like perpetual night. The apples were stark white against the dark wood of the branch, so ethereal-looking he half expected them to melt away from his hand like frost. Some had already fallen to the ground to spoil. They bruised purple and red beneath the skin, more like flesh than fruit.

A careful twist of his wrist netted him his prize. It was too light for its size, cool in his palm, and so soft it felt half rotten already.

The vixen gave a little yelp of disgust. Ivan smiled. "I did warn you."

"You did," she admitted, and shook her head until her ears flapped, backing away from the ghost apple she'd sampled on the ground. "Ugh."

The trip out of the forest was far easier and faster than the journey in had been. The Leshiin had been playing games, Ivan suspected. Fortunately, the Forest Prince was too busy dodging the Firebird's vengeful talons for petty tricks, because when Ivan broke free of the tree line, the sky was full of light.

The spirit roads danced through the night sky in vivid jewel tones. Sapphire twined with emerald, and both were wrapped up with deepest amethyst. The light twisted and folded back on itself, spilling ribbons of color in all directions. The Spirit Tide was in full force.

Ivan sat heavily on the ground and set his axe to one side to free a hand to root through his bag. He didn't have dancers and his breathing was too labored to sing. There was no table groaning with tough spring vegetables, lamb, or new cheese. No offering cakes and no kavass.

But he did have a nightingale, a clever vixen, a ghost pale apple, and the friendship of a Firebird.

Ivan laid his offering on a little square of cloth he'd brought from their home and set both on a flat stone lying near him in the grass. The cold seeped into his legs from the ground, but it had settled into his bones so long ago he barely noticed.

"For you, Masha. One last bit of sweetness." His head dropped forward, eyes burning in the light. "Safe journey, my love."

He didn't know how long he sat there, head bowed, eyes closed, with his companions a silent honor guard. Eventually, the nudge of the vixen's nose against his arm made him look up.

His heart gave a painful thump.

There she was, his Masha, standing in the light of the spirit roads. Not the gray-haired woman she'd been, and not the slip of a girl he'd met so long ago. This was his wife as she lived in his memory, her back strong, but her face lined and her hair frosted with a dusting of silver.

Ivan's mouth moved wordlessly. He wanted to jump to his feet, to hold her. But he wasn't sure his legs could bear him and he could see the horizon of the steppes behind her, as though her body were made of fog and moonlight.

He tried to smile for her, to be strong. But he was cold, and he was tired, and there were an old man's tears on his face.

Ivan managed to force a single word past the lump of everything he desperately wanted to say. "Marushka."

She smiled at him then, a slow, sweet expression that warmed her face like the sun finally breaking through clouds. It wasn't until she leaned down toward him that he noticed his offering was gone.

"*Vanya,*" the wind sighed around them.

Even though she was barely more than a breath of air, more mist than woman, he felt it when she brushed her lips over his. Warm breath, familiar skin, and the bright taste of honey and apples on his tongue. He kept his eyes closed, trying to catch the moment, to keep it with him, and he didn't open them even when he felt her hand, insubstantial, effervescent, slip into his.

The world hushed and, even though his eyes were closed, he still saw vivid colors on the back of his eyelids. He was with his love, their friends beside them, and the wide brilliant path of the spirit roads opened before him.

SENSE AND SENSITIVITY

Esther Friesner

"All right, calm down, I've got this, it's nothing serious." Midge Devlin took a deep breath before uttering the last in her litany of lies: "It's only an allergy."

Her skin crawled as the words left her mouth. She knew there was no such thing as "only" where food allergies were concerned, having lost her beloved, shellfish-sensitive Aunt Vera to a portion of vegan risotto inadvertently served with the same spoon used to dish out jambalaya at a buffet.

Midge loathed sacrificing truth on the altar of interplanetary relations, but you couldn't guess her true feelings by looking at her. She was a top field operative, highly trained at keeping a poker face even when the game at hand was Lie Your Ass Off. Saving a life was important, but nowhere near as vital as saving the situation.

She hauled the slumped alien upright in his chair, produced the proper pill from the kit in her evening bag, and sent it flying down his warty throat, chased by a quick slosh of water. There was no harm in such a cavalier manner of administering the remedy. The aliens' capacious gullets were proof against having anything "go down the wrong way."

More's the pity, Midge thought grimly. *I wouldn't mind having a mob of them gag to death if it convinced the rest to go the hell home.* She grimaced. *Fat chance.*

Earth's unwanted guests were the embodiment of an epic self-interest that would leave the most lobbyist-leeching senator agape. Every Malkyoh was an island, entirely devoid of fellow-feeling. They could watch one of their number perish in the most ghastly manner and not raise a (nonexistent) eyebrow.

On the other hand, they relished the chance to *avenge* any deaths, injuries, or insults their shipmates suffered. This was not because they cared about their comrades, but because they liked nothing better than the prospect of making others suffer too.

The pill did its work. The alien's octagonal eyes irised open, he wiped a dribble of water from the corner of his mouth, and resumed chatting with the woman seated to his right, as if nothing had happened. Nothing *had* happened, if one went by the reactions of his fellow Malkyohs. Their colleague's collapse and subsequent reanimation had not put them off their feed for an instant. They continued to dismember and devour the plump, roasted quail *Veronique* on their plates and, in some instances, on the plates of any Terrans within reach.

The Terrans made no move to prevent their dinners from being pillaged. The Malkyohs were their planet's guests and, as such, their most churlish behavior must be indulged. This policy was two percent diplomacy and ninety-eight percent awareness that they had tech capable of turning a man or a metropolis into clouds of dissociated molecules. (Yes, they *had* demonstrated this capability, which was too bad for Poughkeepsie, but what *can* one do?)

Midge took a deep breath, poised to initiate the next stage of damage control. Phase One of the Malkyoh's allergic reaction was over once she saved him, but Phase Two was coming and it wasn't going to affect the alien alone. She cleared her throat, ready to sound the warning.

She did not get the chance; things happened too fast. The British ambassador's wife, hostess of the exclusive soiree, discreetly directed one of the wait staff to bring the recovered Malkyoh a fresh plate. It was brought at once, whereat the alien greeted this gracious gesture with a not-so-gracious:

"How dare you! Are you stupid or murderous? That blasted chunk of Earth-flesh almost killed me!" He shot-gunned the piping-hot quail full into the waiter's face. The poor man screamed and fled.

"Yes, run," the Malkyoh said with satisfaction. "I hope you scar, you thoughtless wretch. If our superlative scientists hadn't found a way to make your miserable excuses for medicine work faster, I would have missed dessert. I ought to—ought—ougggghhhh—ah—ah—ahhhhhh-CHOO!"

And there it was: Phase Two.

Midge's agency had learned early on that Phase Two always manifested within a short time after Phase One. It never failed to do so and it was never a good experience for any humans in the vicinity. When a Malkyoh sneezed, they didn't do so by halves, nor solely by noses. (They had two of those.) Glowing pea-sized amber droplets burst from every uncovered orifice of the alien's body, including some of the larger pores, spattering everyone at the table luckless enough to be seated in the splash zone.

Midge went into immediate, elevated emergency mode. The figurative dam had burst before she could patch the leak. Now all she could do was grab an equally figurative mop and get to swabbing.

She spared only an instant to thank heaven that her skin was coated with a thin layer of the petroleum jelly-based salve that was a mandatory precaution for all field agents. Her epidermis brought to mind *plethodon glutinosus* (Our Friend, the Northern Slimy Salamander) and carried a faint whiff of *eau de* NASCAR pit stop, but safety measures were seldom chic. It was her version of Kevlar and she wore it with gratitude; slick, stinky gratitude. She knew the awful consequences of a snot-spritz from an allergy-afflicted Malkyoh.

"Forks DOWN! Don't eat another bite!" She raced to the dining room doorway and made a dramatic gesture that bellowed, *Begone!* "If you have been hit, leave immediately. You'll see several uniformed representatives in the foyer wearing *this* insignia." Like a clown producing a rainbow river of handkerchiefs from his mouth, she reached into her evening bag once again and unfurled a microfiber banner emblazoned with the emblem of the recently formed Department of Extraterrestrial Respect and Protocol. "Follow their instructions *to the letter*! Do it *now*!"

Nine panic-stricken guests bolted from their seats. At least two of them abandoned places nowhere near where the amber droplets had fallen, but there was no preaching reason to a stampede. Chairs toppled. Shrieks and fearful gasps resounded. Cries of "GetitoffgetitoffgetitoffgetitOFF!" were cut short only when the pocket doors of the dining room rolled shut upon their exit.

The Malkyohs continued eating. Loudly. They found the Terrans' distress hilarious and laughed about it with their mouths full, adding to the mess on the table.

The remaining humans exchanged worried glances. Their darting eyes and trembling lips made it plain that they were having an inner debate on the subject of *Did I Lose My Chance to Get the Hell Out of Here, Having Missed the Rush, Without Torpedoing My Country's Relations With Great Britain and Also Without Insulting These Almighty Sociopaths From Beyond the Stars?*

It was not a *short* subject. Merely taking the time to pose that question left the unhappy guests with no option except staying put or faking their own deaths.

As the wife of a career diplomat, their hostess remained the picture of aplomb. She favored the table with a benevolent smile and made tiny circles in midair with her fork, a gesture intended to urge them back to behaving as if nothing untoward had happened. Perhaps she had inadvertently chosen the wrong fork, for it lacked the mojo to restore the festive tone of the pre-sneeze dinner. Her guests seemed to have forgotten their mad scramble to cajole, wheedle, and favor-swap in order to add the cachet of having dined with *actual aliens* to the family Christmas letter. They eyed the flotsam and jetsam of the abandoned places at the table uneasily. Most of these were directly across the feasting board from the Malkyoh who had sneezed to such devastating effect. Another was the seat to his right.

Strangely enough, the seat to the Malkyoh's left was still occupied. Midge stared across the intervening table in wonder at the gangly youth seated there. He was liberally sprinkled with alien snortage, but he wiped it from his face as casually as if it were raindrops.

"There we go," he said cheerfully, tossing away his sodden handkerchief. "All sorted. Not so bad. This'll be something to tell the lads back home, eh?"

"Young man—" Midge began. She groped for the guest's name. Her mission prep had included memorizing the list of attendees and their particulars. Her mind popped up a file labeled Calvin Lowell, nineteen, British, and already a multiple Olympic gold medalist in track and field. His fame, charm, and good looks made him a prize every D.C. hostess craved to have at her table. He had his choice of invitations and no doubt he'd accepted this one because—well, because *dinner with aliens!*

"Mr. Lowell, come with me," Midge said sternly, striding back from the doorway. "You need to be treated. We might still have time to—*what are you doing and stop it at once!*"

She lunged for him, but of course it was too late. The width of an embassy's formal dining table was between them. Her gallant body-surfing through a sea of dinner plates and alien snot was all in vain: the young athlete was an energetic eater and managed to get two mouthfuls of quail chewed and swallowed before the agent of DERP could reach him.

The results were everything Midge feared: Calvin Lowell's eyes bulged with horror. He dropped his fork and laid both hands on his chest, gasping for air. The color fled from his face. He was choking, but it was not the sort of suffocation caused by a foreign object blocking his trachea. It was the human version of the same reaction—what the alien had suffered before Midge worked her life-saving magic, the onset of a radically severe attack of anaphylaxis.

Ah, the wonders of exobiology! Malkyoh food allergies were *catching.*

Midge yelled for backup even as she belatedly pivoted on one hip and swung herself off the table on Lowell's side. Once again, she reached for her evening bag, that repository of so many tools of the DERP trade. The shout for team support had scarcely left her lips before she realized she'd dropped the bag when she'd made her futile dive to prevent this very thing from happening. Even as she began loosening the stricken athlete's clothes, a trio of her subordinates was with her, their own auto-injectors in hand. She grabbed one of the devices and administered the dose of epinephrine. Two more of her team raced in, bearing a stretcher and oxygen. The unfortunate athlete was trundled out posthaste, while the remaining human diners began babbling excuses to their hosts, childless couples insisting they had to get home before the babysitter's curfew, all of them calling for their coats and cars and dashing away.

The ambassador and his wife viewed the remains of their dinner party, now entirely ceded to the Malkyohs and Midge. Even though he was an accomplished British diplomat, there wasn't an upper lip stiff enough to help His Excellency weather such a debacle. He buried his head in his hands and groaned. His wife wept openly.

Midge attempted to comfort them, lest the Malkyohs look up from their feed, notice their hosts' behavior, and take it as an affront. She spoke soothingly *sotto voce* of similar incidents she had witnessed when entertaining the Malkyohs abruptly changed from the social coup of the year to the disaster of the century.

"I'm sure Mr. Lowell will be better before you know it," she said. "DERP is a new agency, but I assure you, we've already logged a *lot* of experience. We'll get him back on his feet as quickly as possible. As long as he avoids any further contact with the allergen, his acquired sensitivity will be—"

She stopped, uncomfortably aware that heaping pleasantries onto this particular garbage fire had led her to say more than she ought. She prayed that the ambassador and his wife had not noticed.

This was not to be. A diplomat who failed to pick up on every nuance of a conversation was not worth his salt. The ambassador's chin jerked up. His eyes met Midge's in a glare as keen and pointed as a lancet.

"'Acquired sensitivity?'" he repeated coldly. "Do you mean to imply that our young Mr. Lowell—the pride and hope of Britain's showing in the next Olympiad—was not suffering from a merely *transitory* reaction to contact with *that*?" He thrust an accusatory finger at the pattern of glimmering amber globules presently staining the tablecloth.

Midge sighed. "There's nothing transitory about Mr. Lowell's condition. I wish it were otherwise. Had he left the room as soon as he was struck by that sneeze, our highly trained team could have decontam—"

A scowl from the nearest Malkyoh made her bite off the rest of the word. The aliens had made it clear that they did not care to have any aspect or function of their bodies spoken of except with adulation and praise. Early in their visit, when for some inexplicable reason they'd touched down in upstate New York, polite requests from the Vassar College administration that they cease using the campus for toxic potty breaks had resulted in the aforementioned Poughkeepsie Incident.

(No one really knew if the Malkyohs took *actual* umbrage over such things or if they simply viewed them as an excuse-slash-justification for perpetrating mayhem under the mask of victimhood. It was the most human thing about them.)

"That is, he could have been *helped*," Midge said quickly. It wasn't an elegant save, but it was sufficient. The Malkyoh went back to gorging. "Our researchers have developed protocols for handling such situations. I'd be happy to elaborate, but I don't wish to divert your attention from your guests of honor." She indicated the aliens. The aliens indicated that they wanted more food by throwing their empty plates at the waitstaff.

While his wife bid the servers fetch dessert, her voice feeble and tremulous with nerves, the ambassador gave Midge a hard stare. "Calvin Lowell *was* one of our guests of honor," he said coldly. "He was Britain's pride."

"But that hasn't changed!" Midge exclaimed. "Lots of athletes have allergies and go on to add to their achievements. My department will see to it that he receives all the instruction he needs to prevent him from experiencing the second-level consequences of—"

"*Second*-level?" The ambassador bristled. "Is he in danger of a *worse* reaction?"

"Only if he's re-exposed."

"And then what?" Thunderclouds were gathering on the ambassador's brow. "Is his life in peril?"

"No, not really, but—" Midge raised her hands. "Your Excellency, this isn't the most...suitable time or place to go into details. If you'll visit DERP HQ tomorrow, I'll provide you with a full explanation." She smiled so hard she twinkled.

The ambassador pursed his lips. "Thank you, but that will not be necessary."

His wife dabbed away tears with one corner of her napkin and resurrected a feeble smile. "We would hate to take up your department's time needlessly. If the situation is indeed as you describe it, Mr. Lowell is actually quite lucky: the odds of him encountering quail *Veronique* in his daily life are rather low, wouldn't you say?" She forced a laugh.

Midge joined in, not because she felt this was a laughing matter, but to defuse a terrible situation. She remained at the dinner table until the Malkyohs finished their meal and left. They did not say *Thank you.*

They never did.

* * *

Lester Murdoch, leader of DERP, considered the glass of bourbon on his desk with the same world-weary gaze an ancient philosopher might give to the contemplation of a skull. He raised his drink to the American flag hanging on his office wall and proclaimed, "To the end of this proud nation as we knew it. We're harboring a plague. Our efforts at containment and control of the Malkyohs fail and fail again.

Poor Lowell's case is the latest, but it won't be the last." He set his emptied glass back on the desk heavily. "And my wife really wanted to see England. Damn."

Seated in a deep leather armchair across from her superior, Midge swirled her own drink and drained it, hoping it might mellow her mood. Alas, the magic of that beautiful bourbon fell short. She remained as snappish as when Lester first informed her that every DERP operative, from lowest to most highly-ranked, was now *persona non grata* in Britain.

"If you called me in here to throw me under the double-decker bus for what happened, I'll go quietly," she said.

"What? No! It's not your fault." Lester poured himself a second round. "You followed procedure to the letter. How could you have known that it wasn't the quail itself that caused that Malkyoh's reaction but the wine in the recipe?"

"I thought the wine cooked off."

"Not enough, apparently; not for the Malkyoh and not for Lowell." He shook his head. "You know, ordinarily it might be an advantage for an athlete to have an alcohol allergy; one less thing to worry about when in training. But in this case—"

"I know. I saw the video. It went viral." Midge shuddered. Lowell's second exposure to the allergen he didn't *know* was an allergen took place in one of Washington's temples of *haute cuisine*, a place famed for its exclusivity and refinement. None of that prevented the more iron-stomached of Lowell's dining companions from whipping out their smartphones to capture what happened when he innocently took a sip of a captivating Cabernet Sauvignon. Every Terran who'd caught a Malkyoh's allergy plus a secondary exposure reacted differently, but this case was a beaut.

"It wasn't just the tentacles," Midge said sadly. "I've seen the tentacle effect more than once, especially in the cases that sprang up before we knew what was happening. But these—! Purple ones with red stripes and yellow suckers, and so many—! And oh my God, they didn't just burst out of his sleeves; they erupted everywhere—back and chest, neck and arms, and even out of his—his—" She smothered her gag reflex.

"Ah, yes," said Lester, who had finished his second drink and was well into a third. "His legs were just about the only parts unaffected. He might still be able to carry on as a runner, except he can barely see past the fringe of cilia over his eyes and his new circumference takes up two and a half track lanes."

"Well then, if this isn't a disciplinary meeting, why have you called me here?"

"Troniu is stopping by." Lester licked his lips nervously. Despite the bourbon, they had gone dry at the mention of the aliens' leader. "He wants to see you."

"Me? Why?"

"Maybe he wants to reward you for saving his crewmate."

They shared a brief, cynical laugh.

Ever the realist, Midge said: "Maybe he wants me dead without the bother of hunting me down."

"Why would he want to kill you? That doesn't make sense."

"Why do the Malkyohs do *anything*?" Midge countered. "Anything that even comes close to making sense, that is."

A burbling, somewhat squishy sound came from the doorway. "Making sense?" said the Malkyoh leader as he barged into Lester's office.

Midge blanched. The alien had overheard her. Now the life-or-death question was...how would he react?

She was in luck: the Malkyoh brushed her disparaging words aside much as a battle-hardened mother would dismiss a furious toddler's "I hate you, I hate you, *I hate you!*"

"Ah, you Terrans and your thought-toys. Common sense! Logic! Reason! Amusing. Tell me: In a universe that is more random than regimented, what is the use of your attempts at sense-making?"

"Ex—Exalted Leader Troniu, welcome!" Lester hurried forward to receive the alien. He licked the palm of his hand, slid it down the length of the Malkyoh's upper nose, and licked it again. The aliens insisted this was the proper way for one superior to greet another, but Midge believed they'd just dreamed it up for giggles.

She offered her chair to Troniu. "A pleasure to see you, Exalted Leader," she said with a straight face. "To what do we owe the honor?"

The Malkyoh settled snugly into the leather-covered nest, upper limbs overhanging the arms of the chair like blubber doilies. "I have a grievance," he said. "*You* will make it go away."

Midge's stomach twisted. It was the first time she'd heard of the Malkyohs lodging a complaint. Usually they settled such things themselves, with extreme prejudice, malice aforethought, and *vaya con Dios*, Vassar.

"It's my privilege to serve you. What seems to be the trouble?" She braced for the worst.

"Dinner."

"Dinner?" It sounded so simple, so innocent and harmless! She might have been relieved, if only she didn't know better when it came to the Malkyohs.

"No one is asking us to dine with them. It has been twenty-one days since our last invitation."

"Twenty-one..." Midge did a quick calculation. "The affair at the British embassy?"

"That. You were our Earth-liaison agent there, so it is your fault that we have received no more invitations since then. You have done something wrong."

Midge's job (and survival instincts) precluded her from arguing that point, but her thoughts on the subject were free and enraged:

No, you grub-guzzling toad, this is all on you. Anyone with a working internet connection has seen Calvin Lowell's horrible transformation. That video was bubonic plague *viral! Points to Lowell for being a survivor, no thanks to you. Once he realized his athletic career was over, he made himself a new one, posting so many follow-up, tell-all vids that our takedown efforts were a joke. Now everyone knows what your allergies can do to humans—it's not just a rumor any more!— and "Calamari" Calvin made sure they also know you don't give a rat's ass about it! No one will risk having you at their table! So guess who's really to blame for—*

"Fix it." Troniu's pronouncement snapped Midge out of her inner rant.

She donned the mask of meekness. "Of course, of course. I apologize profusely. I will look into this." *Boil in your own noxious snot while you wait.*

"As you should. Attending your feasts pleases us. Have a new invitation by tomorrow."

"Er, it might take more time than that, Exalted Leader Troniu," Lester said. "The problem is—*might* be—that everyone with the means to entertain you in the style you deserve has already done so and fear that a second offering would fall short." (It wasn't a lie if it was the subjunctive.)

Nice one, Lester, Midge thought. *Too bad we can't just suggest they find fresh fields to poop over, leave the U.S.A., go harass some other country.*

She knew this was a futile dream. When the alien ship first landed on American soil, the rest of the world seethed with envy. If the star-travelers ever shared their advanced technology, surely the nation hosting them would get first dibs! Other countries tried to entice the Malkyohs away, only to have the United States issue stern *Back off!* warnings. But when the downside of entertaining the aliens became clear—along with the fact that they showed no signs of sharing the smallest scrap of knowledge as to their gizmos, doodads, and death rays—America had a change of heart. It was time for a government-approved suggestion that the egocentric E.T.s broaden their horizons and move on to some other nation.

Or planet.

Or galaxy.

The hint was dropped as gently as possible by Rasputin Mitchelson, afterwards known as the senator who drew the short straw. He broached the subject ever-so-tactfully, while escorting Troniu himself through the Lincoln Memorial.

Troniu heard him out, then made it clear that while he was happy to have abandoned what was left of Poughkeepsie for the attractions of Foggy Bottom, he'd done enough Earth tourism. He wasn't going to waste his ship's fuel—whatever that was—on globe-trotting. And since some might interpret a hint to visit other lands as a badly disguised *You're no longer welcome here,* Troniu made a cautionary closing argument that necessitated a thorough scrubbing of the Memorial's floor and a by-election in Kentucky.

Midge sighed. That was a mistake as it refocused Troniu's attention on her.

"Is what your superior says true?" the alien demanded, giving her a dose of orange stink-eye. She dared to nod. "Unacceptable! If there are no more humans able to regale us properly, it is because you are lazy, disrespectful, and unwilling to make the effort to meet our modest needs. We will avenge this insult!" He stood, ready to leave in a homicidal huff.

"Exalted Leader Troniu, no, please, you misunderst—That is, I failed to explain properly." Lester spoke at a terror-driven pace, desperate to outrace the Malkyoh's threat of reprisal. "I should have said that everyone with the *individual* means to entertain you has done so, but if they *all* wanted to get together to offer you a true banquet, an extraordinary feast worthy of your magnificence, it would take some time to organize."

The alien considered this for so long that Midge feared he'd tipped wise to Lester's *if*. But then: "A banquet?" He sank back into the armchair, mollified. "Tell me more."

Midge knew that Lester was great at coming up with Big Picture solutions but useless when it came down to providing details. She took over at once: "It will be a superb retrospective feast, a buffet featuring all the Earth delicacies you've already tasted. We'll have to host it in a venue large enough for all your people to attend at once, so none will feel left out. Naturally it will take us a while to find a site large enough for that. Perhaps within. . . two weeks?" *Time enough for us to do the arm-twisting we'll need to persuade any Terrans to set foot in that minefield*, she thought.

"Two weeks? Too long."

"Oh, I agree, Exalted Leader Troniu, I do agree!" Midge took the wheel of her preferred vehicle for dealing with the Malkyohs—an imaginary dump truck filled with butter and manure—and dropped the full load on the alien. "That's why I humbly implore you to lend us a little of your vast genius. We know that your advanced intellect will find an instant solution that our miserable, ineffective minds might never—"

"Silence!" the alien leader barked. "I am well acquainted with your stupidity. Be grateful that I have had one of my overwhelmingly brilliant inspirations. You will use the assembly space inside our ship itself! It is already large enough to accommodate all of us and as many humans as we wish. We wish many, for each shall contribute to the feast with a bounty of delicacies!"

"Ah, an intergalactic pot-luck." Lester brightened at how well things were going. "Excellent idea, Exalted Leader Troniu!"

"I know."

"And don't worry," Midge said. "DERP will see to it that every dish brought aboard your ship will be something you've already eaten. They'll all be clearly labeled with a list of allergens, to protect those of your colleagues who have, um, sensitivity to some of our foods."

Troniu made a disdainful noise. "That would be all of us. In the course of our stay thus far, each of my crew—my magnificent self included—has encountered at least one item of Earth cuisine to which we proved allergic. Some of our more overachieving colleagues have manifested sensitivities to multiple foodstuffs. You should know this!"

"Uh, indeed, but it sounds so much more authoritative coming from you, great one," Midge said. "So, all the more reason to label—"

"Why bother?"

"Well, to make certain everyone can enjoy the feast without fear of another reac—"

Midge's words were interrupted by a loud hiss as the alien leader's lateral vents abruptly discharged cloudy green streams of a pungent, revolting smell. It was the first instance any Terran had experienced of the alien version of *pull my finger*, but the two DERP staffers were insensible to the honor of being pioneers of science. Lester was just plain insensible, having crumpled into unconsciousness under the assault of that extraterrestrial stink bomb. Midge did not dare to check if he needed aid. The Malkyoh leader might interpret her action as criticism of his sublime self and she knew how well *that* would go over. She was above all deeply committed to maintaining her molecular integrity.

She turned to the alien, clenching her hands to keep from pinching her nose. "Exalted Leader Troniu, are you—?" she began shakily. "Are you feeling well?"

"Quite well. My health is, as always, the best health. I have come here directly from an excellent lunch. The cottage cheese was delectable. I had five helpings."

Midge's encyclopedic mind raised a red flag. "But—but you're *allergic* to cottage cheese," she said. "I *know* you are; I was the agent in place when you had your first incident."

"Bah. Our metabolism makes yours look like a steaming heap of *akn'donavi*. Once I survived my first encounter and then discharged the bulk of the bio-contaminants, *this* is all that now happens when I eat those tasty curds." He concentrated and another wave of verdant fetor burst from his body; a willful one this time. He smiled benevolently over his own eructation.

Oh my God, there's a Phase Three? *Gah!* Midge kept her thoughts to herself as she fought to stay on her feet and restrained the urge to upchuck her bourbon. "That's—that's wonderful, but—" She remembered the hapless waiter who'd gotten first degree burns from a hot quail to the face. "—I don't understand why, at the British embassy dinner, your crewmate was quite adamant that a second allergen exposure would be fatal."

"Oh, that was Arbit." Troniu said dismissively. "Bit of a hypochondriac. Ignore him. He was fine once he sneezed things out of his system."

"Ah." Midge's head swam from the second assault of fumes. She heard herself babbling about how special she felt, being among the first humans to ~~endure~~ experience this new aspect of the Malkyohs' glorious physiology.

Troniu preened. "If you would like to see it again, I will require more cottage cheese. It will take a brief while for the reaction to arise, but even the smallest amount of an allergen is sufficient for us to repeat—"

"*No!*" Midge immediately flipped that one-word death sentence into a *faux* indignant: "It would look too much as if *you* were performing a trick under *my* orders. Unthinkable!"

"True, true. Very well, let us instead turn to the matter of our banquet: We will require *new* dishes as well as past favorites."

Midge mentally raced through all the disasters that might occur at a spread including previously untried foods. *What if we serve them the one thing that gives a whole herd of them Phase One reactions?* "Wouldn't it be better to limit the menu to—?"

"No. If there is not at least one new dish at this feast, our outrage will be immeasurable, except in terms of residual radiation. Your pathetic planet's sole redeeming feature is its variety of tasty fare. Every meal is a revelation. In some small way, it makes up for the inconvenience of our exiiiiillllle—" For an instant, the alien leader looked very much like a human who had just given an honest answer to *Do these jeans make me look fat?* "—llllllong, glorious, totally voluntary voyage of interstellar exploration." He stood abruptly. "It is decided. I have provided you with the perfect venue. I give you five days to arrange our feast. Fail at your peril. Have a nice day."

The instant Troniu left, Midge opened all the windows. She then knelt to revive Lester, but she did so in a distracted manner. Her thoughts were elsewhere. They circled a single word, like sharks sussing out a bevy of body-surfers with nosebleeds. Lester awoke to her emphatic demands for a support team, a banquet budget, and permission to pay an immediate call on one Kendra Winslow, third top-ranked official with the intelligence-gathering organization that made the DIA, NSA, and CIA SAC resemble junior high girls passing *But does he* like *like me?* notes in class.

"What for?" he asked.

"Girl talk."

* * *

In an office that looked more like a cozy parlor, a cabal of two traded information over tea and petit fours.

"He actually *said* 'exile?'" Kendra Winslow smirked as well as she was able. "Troniu's getting sloppy."

"Sloppy or super-confident that we can't touch him," Midge said. She helped herself to another pastry. "So, it's true? They didn't come here on an exploratory vessel?"

"Nope. It's the good ship *Don't Let the Doorknob Hit You in the Ass*. My department's been doing deep intel on them since they hit Earth. Every Malkyoh aboard that vessel was kicked to the curb and booted to the stars by the folks back home, wherever *that* might be. They're not fans of enacting the death penalty, but if they heard that someone else obliterated Troniu and his gang, they'd celebrate." Her rubbery lips drooped even more than usual. "So would I."

Midge understood. The two women were friends as well as colleagues and she knew how much Kendra Winslow loathed the countless iterations of *Oh, you poor thing!* she'd had to endure from family, friends, and co-workers just because a Malkyoh's Phase Two reaction had left her face looking like a blobfish. To make matters worse, her transformed appearance also made her irresistible to many of the aliens, including their Exalted Leader. This was bitterly ironic, as it was he who had Phase Twoed all over her at a luncheon that took place before DERP mastered emergency treatment protocols for besnotted humans.

"I'd be willing to put up with those bullying bastards if there were the slightest chance that Earth could profit from their presence," Kendra went on. "No such luck. We haven't circulated our latest findings yet, but it's not good news: the Malkyohs *won't* share the scientific wonders of their ship because they *can't*."

"You're kidding."

"You heard me. They have no more knowledge of how any of it works than my cat. And Milady Bubbles is a very smart kitty!"

"But—but they flew across the galaxy! The zapped a senator! They slag-heaped Vassar!"

"And you drive a car, but do you know how to build an engine? You can flip on a light switch, but can you wire your home for electricity?"

"I see." Midge nodded. "That's excellent news."

"It is?" It was Kendra's turn to be taken aback.

"It means there's nothing to lose when our departments join forces and execute my plan. Together we can—we *will*—end this reign of gluttony-based terror." She leaned in and looked Kendra straight in her tiny, watermelon-seed eyes. "We're going to obliterate the Malkyohs."

Kendra pulled away sharply. "We can't do that!"

"Why not? They're exiles, not refugees; not by any standard. Hell, they're invaders in everything but name! They're the embodiment of entitlement! Of narcissism!"

"Yes, but kill one and the others kill you. Plus your entire city, if they feel like it."

"Not if we don't give them the chance." Midge's determination showed in her face, despite a smudge of petit four icing at one corner of her mouth. "Hear me out, back me up, and I guarantee my plan will get rid of all of them, *all at once*."

"Guarantee?"

Midge raised her hands. "All right, there *is* a margin of error. The plan hinges on a theory, but it's packed with enough plausible deniability to save us from annihilation if it doesn't prove true."

She told Kendra what she had in mind. As Midge spoke, the other woman's body language conveyed a mounting sense of interest, fascination, and excitement that her blobfish face could not hope to convey.

"Midge, that's brilliant," she said, when the DERP agent finished. "We'll do it. If we send out some science operatives to run a few covert field tests beforehand, we might even be able to significantly reduce that margin of error you mentioned. There's just one thing—"

"Yes," Midge said sadly. "For one person, this will be a suicide mission." She straightened her shoulders. "That will be me."

"Not unless you want to see your margin of error turn into a chasm. There's no credible way you can assume the role necessary to pull off this coup. The Malkyohs *know* you're a DERP agent. Use that to make it all run smoothly. Play to your strengths." Kendra clasped Midge's hand. "And let me play to mine."

* * *

From her place on the stage, Midge Devlin gazed out across the hordes who had gathered to celebrate International Kendra Winslow Day in Washington D.C. The event took place outdoors, as there was no roofed venue large enough to contain the representatives of every nation bent on honoring the woman who had given her life so that humanity might cease to live in fear of being sneezed on by aliens. Similar festivities were taking place world-wide. In the seating section reserved for those who, like Kendra, had suffered at the hands—or rather, the nostrils-and-other-orifices—of a Phase Two incident, "Calamari" Calvin Lowell wept openly.

It was the fifth anniversary of Kendra's heroic sacrifice, a day to be made special by the dedication of a monument befitting her memory. Midge smiled wistfully as she readied herself to accept the privilege of unveiling the commemorative statue. As the acknowledged brains behind the plot that saved the Earth, she'd had to fight off insistent admirers who wanted to include her likeness in this massive, stony tribute. It took years of rejecting the offer, always with the same words: *Compared to her, I did nothing. An idea is only as useful as the hands that give it the spark of life. What I did was, at most, choreography.*

She recalled the day of the banquet clearly. While all the Malkyohs sat drooling in anticipation at the tables set up inside their ship, she stood poised in the vast, hastily-erected nearby building needed to stage all the food for the feast. Before her were assembled the two groups of humans who would—fingers crossed!—make her theory a liberating reality. They awaited her words.

The first team consisted of the unwilling hosts of the banquet: all those who had entertained the aliens on occasions where one or more of the Malkyohs had fallen afoul of an Earth-allergen. Her instructions to them were simple: *Do whatever* they *tell you and you'll survive.* She indicated the second team.

They looked like waiters. So they were, in a way, but they were also the best operatives Kendra's agency could provide, backed by a substantial troop of DERP's finest. To them Midge merely said *Good luck* before she led the trembling members of the first team in to dinner.

She watched the march of "waiters" as they carried the food into the alien ship's assembly-space-turned-dining-room. She hoped they'd done a thorough job of using all the serving utensils to cross-contaminate every single dish so that there would be no possible way any Malkyoh might escape encountering his particular allergenic *bête noire.* (She'd named this mission *Operation Frequent Aunt Vera* for a reason.) She watched the Malkyohs swarm the buffet, gobbling and guzzling. She prayed that none of them would encounter a fresh allergen, forcing her to deal with new Phase One and Two reactions on this night of all nights. She was in the midst of a postscript prayer that sufficient numbers of the aliens would soon be touched by the spirit of Phase Three when the first report thundered forth.

Wave upon reeking wave, the wind from beyond the stars broke upon Terran ears. And noses! The humans gasped at their first breath of the Malkyohs' tertiary allergic reaction. Their distress was visible, almost palpable, which amused the aliens no end. Many of them took this as a cue to initiate their ability to release malodorous clouds *ad lib.*, even before their systems made this inevitable. They were so caught up in the glee of seeing Terrans topple that they failed to notice the waiters were not troubled by the change in atmosphere. The high-tech filters stuck up their noses worked like a charm. With *sang froid* any British butler might covet, some began conveying the unconscious from the ship while others coolly suggested that those humans still ambulatory might wish to come outside for a breath of air.

Now.

Midge stepped in quickly to cover the mass exodus by remarking to her dinner partner, Troniu himself, that this was such a pity because she had planned something extra special for dessert.

"You've never tasted this before, so you're in for a brand-new treat, just as you requested. It's not just delicious, it's an *event*. One of our best chefs is on hand to create it right before your eyes. Ah! And here she comes now."

Midge made a sweeping gesture to the doorway as Kendra, resplendent in a gleaming white chef's coat and towering toque, came in wheeling a tableside cart laden with a massive silver basin. Some of Hollywood's best makeup artists had labored over her for hours, using every trick they knew to make a blobfish into a beauty that none of the Malkyohs who knew her would recognize. The illusion was too delicate to last long. Sadly, it didn't have to.

She stopped in the center of the ring of tables and began to describe the dessert she was about to confect. She spoke in such eloquent detail that she soon had every Malkyoh on the ship quivering with greed. Some shook so hard that they discharged further contributions to the thick, emerald miasma now filling the room, but she seemed impervious to either the stench or the limited visibility.

Kendra was just elaborating on the succulent grand finale of her offering when Midge murmured, "I do hope those people come back quickly or they'll miss this. Exalted Leader Troniu, would you mind if I went to fetch—?"

"Fetch them and die," the Malkyoh leader said with a smile. "No dessert for those inferior creatures. More for us!"

Midge steeled herself for the final gamble, prepared to stake her life on what she knew of the Malkyohs. "You're right as always, Exalted Leader Troniu, and so gracious to permit me to remain and share—"

"I said no such thing!" the alien snapped. "Since you are so concerned about those weaklings, go look after them."

"But—" (Some objection had to be made, for the sake of plausibility.)

"*Go!*"

She walked out of the assembly area quickly, playing the part of the underling Terran eager to obey. Troniu never knew just how eager she was to get away, or how glad she was that she'd bet her life on his selfishness and won. She began to run as soon as she was out of the Malkyohs' sight, but tears for Kendra blurred her eyes and made her stumble as she fled the ship. Scrambling to her feet, she sprinted on, beseeching the gods of chance to let her put enough distance between herself and the ship before—

Her luck held just as Kendra's ran out and took the Malkyohs with it.

Now here she was, standing to acknowledge yet another effusive introduction, crossing the platform to take up the cord that would release the draperies concealing the monument, pulling it to reveal a new American icon as meaningful as the colossus of New York's harbor on which it had been based.

The people cheered. The artist had done well, giving them an inspiring image of their hero at the moment she'd saved the world. But while Lady Liberty carried an inscribed tablet, Kendra's left arm cradled a basin of cherries jubilee, the dish that was her cover story for unleashing the deadly weapon held aloft in her other hand.

It wasn't as large as Liberty's torch, but when Midge hit the hidden switch and that match flared to life, the crowd's roar was almost as loud as the blast that had destroyed the alien menace, hoisted into annihilation by their own methane-loaded Phase Three petard.

Life isn't fair, Midge thought. *But sometimes bad guys do get their just desserts.*

THE SILENCE THAT CONSUMES US

Derrick Boden

Dreams of Eri's unsmiling lips bleed into the afterimages of battle, the fire and the fall, the howling silence. I wake to alien constellations waging war across a sapphire sky.

I'm alive. Somehow. My breathing, hot and labored, is proof of that much.

The remains of my ejection shell dig into my back. Cracks spiderweb my visor. The wraiths of battle rage in my ears. My hands still shake from the impact with—

The squid.

Panic gnaws at my gut. I sit up.

Try again. Heavy gees sap my strength. Blood worms from my ear. Warnings carnival-light my visor.

Come on, girl. Breathe.

I'm sucking in atmosphere, have been since the crash. Like licking a rusty pipe, only worse. Terraforming of this vacant rock has been on the shelf for twenty years thanks to a dispute between Tango Mining and Central Population. Even if they do come to terms—unlikely seeing as how the two aren't talking—it'll be another seventy plus before the moon's fully oxygenated. I'm still alive, though, so fuck it. I wrestle my helmet off, let it clang to the ground.

Negligible probability of a hostile encounter, my ass. Command is as chock-full of neocon predators as Tau-B12 ever was and I'll bet my left kidney someone caught wind of my particular brand of social deviance. Shipped me out here to disappear quietly. Give someone a glimpse of your insides and they'll eat you alive.

Bygones. Right now, I gotta find that damn squid before it finds me.

The northern lunar surface is a wasteland of pumice and shale without even the sparse patches of purple lichen that have started to crop up near the equator. Obsidian teeth jut from the landscape, polished mirror-smooth by a million years of pounding wind. It's daytime, but the sky is twilight-dark. The planet's edge creeps like a ghost's head above the horizon, shimmering auroras for eyes. Smoke trails from wreckage at the lip of a crater: my ship, and the squid's. Pale Protectorate panels twist around the crimson fuselage of the alien probe, lovers wrapped in an awkward embrace. The probe's ends are popped like a stale calorie pack.

My lip curls. Got the bastard.

Shadows writhe within the probe. I reach for my pistol and my hand comes back empty, sticky with blood. My suit is torn down the side from tits to toes and I'm gouged at the hip. The blood has clotted black in the moon's off-balanced atmosphere. No sidearm, no utili-pack. No beacon. I stumble behind an upthrust of rock. When I peer around the corner, the shadows are still.

I blink hard. The air must be making me loopy. Nothing could've survived that crash.

A gust of wind howls across the crater, like cheap pneumatics blasting the mine shafts back on Tau-B12. It's been three years and twelve days since I tasted Eri's tears. Since the Skinners strung up Raul for not conforming to their breeding standards. Since Eri pleaded for the hundredth time—*say something*—and I didn't have a word to spare, because words are weapons and I'm saving mine for self-defense, thank you very much.

My stomach grinds. Dust cakes my throat.

I need water. Food. A beacon.

I limp to the wreckage. Tau Ceti's cold rays filter through the ribboned metal like specters. My cockpit is vomiting a trail of ruptured insulation. The payload tube hangs eviscerated. No food. No supplies. Just a blackened husk.

I pick my way through shrapnel teeth. The chill wind bites at my face. I'm already regretting the busted helmet, the lack of a backup suit. But my patrol was basement priority and my ship a throwaway. Every gram of payload requires a thousand times its weight in fuel. Transplutoniums don't mine themselves—

I taste bile, can't bite back the memories in time. Mines cramped with Skinners and cave-ins and poison gas. A silent, cluttered apartment. Dirty bootprints to the fridge. Tears wetting Eri's perfect lips, as if I was supposed to know what to do with that vacant look in her eyes. As if any permutation of words would bring Raul back—

I squeeze circulation into my hands. *Get a grip.*

Liquid slicks the payload's inner shell. I crawl inside the busted hull, pop my shoulder lamp, and wait for my eyes to adjust.

There. Nestled between the panels. A water bladder. It's leaking from a split nozzle, but it's almost half full. I angle the nozzle, let the stream paint my throat. It's frigid. Gloriously wet.

I tug at the bladder's straps. Stuck. Can't risk bursting it, so I settle for a quick tape-job to stop the leak. Now to find some food—

Metal grinds nearby. I hold my breath.

There it is again. Not metal—wood.

Or flesh.

I crawl outside, creep around the perimeter—and freeze. Shadows churn inside the alien ship. Tentacled shadows.

It survived.

I backtrack around the other side of my ship, where the shredded thrusters are fused to the alien probe. The ground is hard and my clomping footsteps are anything but silent. Halfway to the far end of the probe, pumice slices my exposed ankle, draws a thick trail of blood. I stifle a whimper and creep to the probe's gaping end.

The personnel shaft is my height, maybe twenty meters from end to end. Shadows crowd the interior. A flickering LED draws crimson light across a sprawling, maimed body.

I've only ever seen a dead squid, and that must've been an adolescent. This fucker is big. Five tentacled limbs sprawl from its sweat-slicked body, a trunk half as tall as a man but twice as wide. No visible eyes, ears, mouth—nothing resembling human anatomy. Its tentacles are twice as long as my body and some kind of moss clings to their underside. A faint, exotic scent—ginger?—tinges the air.

I retreat around the corner. My gaze settles on a chunk of fuselage as long as my forearm with a wicked edge. I hoist it, test its weight. Should work. I glance inside to gauge the distance.

The squid's body heaves. It sags against the interior wall. A gash runs the length of its trunk, seeping black sap into a puddle on the floor. Its tentacles quiver.

It's dying.

I let the makeshift weapon slip from my grasp. Sure, our species are locked in a decades-long war spanning three solar systems and amassing millions of casualties, but I've got too much to deal with already without having to worry over whether squid sap is poisonous.

That's my reasoning. Not because I feel sorry for the damn thing.

I turn my back on the squid. If I'm going to survive this place, I need to find food and I need to find my beacon.

* * *

My beacon's dead.

My hands tremble as I rip out the battery, but not from the temperature. We're still only three-quarters of the way through the thousand-hour local day. It's going to be a long evening. And without calories, I'm going to have to get used to the shakes.

Eri always told me the hypoglycemia was all in my head, that I never got hungry until she told me what time it was.

"Wrong again, babe." My voice is harsh from disuse. Not from crying or anything.

The wind stopped dead a few hours ago and the silence is all-consuming. Like my old apartment when Eri and I were home at the same time. My reflection flits across shards of obsidian.

I stumble through the wreckage with one eye on the squid ship. Haven't seen movement for ten hours, now. Must've bled out.

My muscles are leaden, but at least my lungs are acclimating—the dark spots that crowded my vision now drift only in my periphery. I trip over a mass of melted cables, nearly face-plant on a three-foot claw of pumice. The rock slices through my glove, digs into my flesh. I wince, pull back—

Under the cables, the glint of waterproofing. A battery pack. Must've gotten chucked from the cold-storage on impact. It's battered on one side, but it's worth a shot.

I jam it into the beacon and flip the big red switch. It squelches to life.

Shadows thrash from the alien ship. I nearly drop the beacon, now slick from the blood of my hand-wound. Goddamn squid's still alive.

I put some distance between us, hope to God that thing isn't mobile. Then I turn my attention to the beacon, flip through every possible distress channel. No pings.

"Hello!" My voice is parched, alien. "Liang. Ajax." My shoulders slouch. "Come in."

Still nothing. They're either dead or think I am. Based on the location of the crash here on the blind-side of the moon, I'd wager it's the latter. All I can do is keep pinging command, hope the interference from the planet's ionosphere isn't too strong—and that someone up there's bothering to listen for the likes of me.

And in the meantime, survive.

The equatorial geysers represent the closest source of surface water and organics—a two-week trek if not for the five-hundred-foot chasms that lacerate the landscape between here and there. Not that it would matter much: the water's too sulfur-heavy to drink and I'd waste more energy scraping lichen from the rocks than the calories they'd provide.

No help from surface stations, either—not since Terraforming shut them down to wait out the dispute. This barren rock is the consequence of humanity at its best: Tango Mining demands exclusive rights to maximize profits, Population pushes the union ticket to maximize votes, and everyone screams into deaf ears just to hear the echo. It's no wonder the squids are kicking our asses.

A half-kilometer's stumble from the crash site, I find the jettisoned payload, still smoldering. It's a weak fire, but it's been eating the payload for the better part of twenty hours now. I stomp and stomp until my legs give out.

The ash slips through my fingers like the feathers of a phoenix, which is wishful thinking packed into a questionable metaphor—there's no resurrection happening here.

My food is gone.

* * *

Slowest sunset ever.

The shadows of our entangled ships stretch to the horizon.

It's been two hundred hours since my last meal. Pain lances my gut. My fingers twitch. I've gnawed the canvas weave off the ejection harness, chewed my fingernails to the quick. I drink more water than I should, try to trick my body into feeling satiated. It doesn't work.

In the darkness, the creature lurks.

We've been watching each other for eight hours straight. I've learned some things.

First of all, that stuff on its body isn't sweat, it's some kind of mucus that it can suck inside itself. I think it's using it to try and heal, although it isn't doing a very good job. The little cuts on its tentacles are gone, but that main gash in the trunk is still pretty deep.

Second, that moss is photosensitive. Its tentacles jut from a fissure in the ship's hull and the parts facing Tau Ceti are all frothy and green. It's sucking down sunlight like a fern.

My stomach growls. Lucky bastard.

This thing is more Venus flytrap than fern, though. I didn't sleep through all those bootcamp science vids. Back on their home world, the squids suck nutrients—lactic acid and nitrogen and whatnot—from the blood of the local fauna. Sometimes even from their own kind. They can't survive on sunlight alone.

And the sky's going dark in another few minutes.

"What then, fucker?"

I stagger inside the probe, wave my arms. The scent of ginger teases my nostrils.

"I said—"

My words devolve into a haggard laugh. It's like Eri berating me those last years at the station. Talking at me. Through me.

Truth is, nobody knows how the squids communicate. I'm not sure we even know how humans communicate—other than poorly.

I lean against the interior, near my makeshift weapon and not two tentacle lengths from the squid. The thing hasn't moved since we crashed—can't move, probably. And pretty soon its sole source of calories is going to slip beneath the horizon for a very long time.

Maybe I should kill it and eat it.

My stomach turns at the thought.

* * *

She had the best lips. Not juiced and puffy, like the style is these days. Thin, tight, serious. She even smiled serious. It's how I knew Eri loved me, the first time I got her to smile. Mission fucking accomplished. Hallelujah. When are you moving in?

But no smile lasts forever, especially on Mining Station Tau-B12.

"What's wrong?"

She was back from a double-shift in the arterial mine, caked in soot with a cloud of body stench. I used to love the smell. Somewhere along the way, around the time she started digging in those talons about *trust* and *letting her inside*, it started to sour. That had to be how it went down. Couldn't have been my nose that changed.

I stared at her. Tried to summon that spark. I knew if I just forced a smile and a kind word everything else would fall into step. Emotion's ninety percent physical, they say. Just gotta kickstart it. And god damn if we didn't need a kickstart.

I didn't smile. Couldn't find a kind word in sight. Eri was just leeching off my pay grade anyhow. Why else would she stick around? The only meaningful words we said anymore were in the bedroom, and god only knew who she was imagining then.

"You're making a mess." Every word was a barb. A weapon that hurt as much to stick in as it did to get stuck by. But we both kept sticking away.

She was rooting through the fridge, black finger marks all over the door. She didn't look up.

"I said—"

"Raul's dead."

My skin went cold. "Mr. Careful? Bullshit."

"Not on the clock. At the Landing."

The Landing was the station's smallest, seediest pub. And Raul—

A chill traveled down my back, didn't stop till it hit my toes. "Skinners?"

She didn't answer. The fridge was closed, her back against it, the first carton of beer already empty on the counter. Her eyes were bloodshot, her jaw clenched. Months later, I'd remember that expression when I grilled her about sleeping around. I even accused her of screwing Raul; felt like shit about it for weeks. That's all we were good at by then: making each other feel like shit.

I paced. This was bad. Real bad. The Skinners were just one faction of a whole neocon movement sweeping the station. Low birthrates and a nasty Eck outbreak had the personnel department on edge, which trickled down into a slough of homophobia. As if the breeders' infertility or the medical blockade were even remotely our fault. But facts don't mean shit to bigots. So people like us, like Raul—we had to be careful.

Raul was Mr. Careful. But put a finger of whiskey in him and he didn't know when to shut the hell up. And if the Skinners got to him—

"Say something." Her perfect lips quivered. She didn't look at me.

I opened my mouth.

Should've kept his goddamn mouth shut.

Give someone a glimpse of your insides and they'll eat you alive.

I shook my head, didn't say anything at all.

And then she fell apart like a scene from a silent movie. Her eyes jeweled. Her eyebrow twitched. Tears streaked down, one after the next, gouging rivulets through her soot-stained cheeks.

I pulled her into my arms, too strong at first but she didn't care. Her body gave out. I kissed her tears, her soot, her stench. She tasted like she used to. It felt, for just a moment, like those tears would wash away everything between then and now, all the bitterness and suspicion and indifference.

We stripped off each other's clothes in a panic, fucked on the kitchen counter, then again on the bedroom floor between a pile of coveralls and the thrumming air purifier. Neither of us said a word. It was like standing under a waterfall after a year in the desert: so much emotion I didn't know what the hell to do with it.

As my body slowed to a sweaty halt against hers she caught my gaze and, between blinks, something traveled between us—as if some piece of her soul had cracked into my own and crept inside. It was warm and dark and more than a little familiar. And it scared the shit out of me.

So I turned away.

And just like that, everything iced over. I felt her body shiver in the darkness at the exact moment my brow knotted and my thoughts turned again to our petty quibbles, my tongue-locked complaints, her unsmiling lips. We lay there, consumed by silence and regret, until we fell asleep.

* * *

I wake in the dark to a slurping sound, like grease through a half-clogged drain. A spicy scent flares my nostrils. My pulse thumps in my ears. When did I fall asleep?

The floor of the alien ship chills my back. Starlight filters through the fuselage. Something moist glistens near my right leg.

I try to scramble away, but my leg resists. It's stuck, inside—

Oh god.

The squid has dragged itself closer, wrapped its tentacle around my leg. I pummel its shimmering flesh. It releases a groan from somewhere inside its trunk, so close I can feel the breeze against my face. My leg won't move.

I flail my arms. My hand clangs against something metal: my makeshift weapon from forever ago. I bring it down hard onto the tentacle. The metal cleaves through its flesh to the midpoint. I yank it loose, swing again. The serrated edge slices clear to the fuselage beneath. Black sap oozes from the severed limb.

I wrestle the now-dead tentacle from my leg, stagger into the open. Sweat mats my face despite the chill night air. I probe my leg. Other than the gash I earned from my landing and a fresh slick of mucus, it appears uninjured.

Behind me, the squid doesn't pursue. Rather, it writhes in slow motion.

What just happened? It wasn't attacking me: the squids are smart enough to run an interstellar invasion, they're sure as hell smart enough to know where my jugular is. One twist of that tentacle around my neck and I'm dead. My leg feels fine—better even than before. So then, what—

I scan the darkened horizon. No sunlight.

It's weak. Starving. Just like me, my ribs and hips already jutting, body incapable of moving for more than a few minutes at a time. Just like those vids said, the squid was sucking nutrients from my blood. Its saliva must've numbed my injured leg.

The squid shifts its body with slow determination. It extends its abridged limb into the starlight. I backpedal, but it isn't reaching for me. The tentacle hangs in the air, repairing itself. Pink flesh unravels from within, slowly compiling into a stump—the beginnings of new growth along the severed end.

It extends a second tentacle, wraps it around the severed segment and extends it toward me. I'm pretty sure I'm not breathing anymore. I can't hear anything but my heart hammering in my ribcage. The thing stops a half-meter away, deposits the severed segment of alien flesh—no longer than my own body—at my feet.

I stare, horrified.

It nudges the severed limb toward me. Beneath a layer of mottled skin: meat. Calories.

I shiver.

It nudges the limb again, then retracts. Gives me space.

The scent of ginger is intoxicating.

I drop to my knees and devour the alien flesh. It tears easily against my gnashing teeth, tastes bitter in my mouth. I chew, swallow, try not to think about what I'm doing.

Impossible. I gag and retch. My stomach heaves. Sweat beads on my brow. And yet, my hunger only grows.

I wipe my lips. The second bite goes down easier, as does the third. Strength slowly returns to my muscles.

I hardly notice the alien approaching. When its tentacle wraps around my exposed leg, it's as if a circuit's been completed. A warm darkness traverses my body. Guttural tones resonate, deep within my bones.

* * *

I wake with a surfeit of energy. A suspicious amount.

My eyes flare. I sit up. The lunar air chills my skin. Around me lies the carnage of my evening feast. Bile creeps up my throat.

What have I done?

I scramble backward—and freeze. My leg is glazed in mucus and half-numb, tingling like I slept on it wrong. Or like I just let an alien—

Nausea clutches my gut. I vomit. The spicy scent persists. I pound on my dead leg. The blood courses and some feeling returns—enough to stand, at least. I stagger to my feet. Stumble away from here. Anywhere.

A panicked glance over my shoulder reveals the alien, huddled at the edge of the fuselage, swathed in shadow. It wraps its tentacles around itself, bows its trunk, and slinks into the ship.

* * *

I am alone.

The beacon stopped working some time ago thanks to the damaged battery, though it wouldn't have mattered either way. Piece of shit never picked up a signal. Nobody's coming for me. If they do, it'll be too late.

Hunger gnaws at my gut, though this time it's tempered with disgust. What the hell did I eat? And what did I let that monster do to me? The bastard tricked me, used me for sustenance.

I scrabble across the desolate landscape, weighed down by the water-bladder on my back, the heavy gees, the burden of aloneness. The thin air makes every breath long and unfulfilling. The silence hangs heavy. The Milky Way bruises the night sky. My gaunt reflection haunts every obsidian shard I pass. My only companions are my memories.

Eri.

I spend four hours counting the things that went wrong. The boozy nights at the Landing that devolved into petty arguments. The weeks of her incessant bickering and my indifferent silence—each of us orbiting the other like rogue asteroids, aliens that shared a common language but had forgotten how to use it. The Skinners. The fear of being outed, of winding up like Raul. The fear of being alone when it happened.

She cut her hair short once. I didn't compliment her, didn't say anything at all. A week later she shaved it off. I asked her why she did it and, with one foot out the door, she said: "Conversation starter."

It was the last thing she ever said to me. The curse-breaker. We loved each other, but no matter what your mama tells you, sometimes love isn't enough.

That evening, war came to Tau Ceti. I enlisted. Wrote a note telling Eri I'd been forcibly recruited because of my education. Chickened out even with that, ended up leaving without a word.

A year later, I checked the personnel logs while on leave at the station. Eri was dead. Tanner's Disease. Takes three years from onset to kill you, and you know you've got it from day one because of the ringing in your ears. One of the side-effects is hair loss.

I stop at the lip of a crater. Shadows tangle the depths like a valley of thorns. I kneel, run my fingers over my leg. The feeling has completely returned, and with it a crushing guilt. Why did I run? What was I afraid of?

Movement catches my eye overhead. There, just beneath the Pleiades. A pulsing light creeps across the sky.

I stagger to my feet, wave my hands. "Hey! Down here! Hey, you assholes—"

My voice catches, devolves into laughter. Tears streak my grimy face. Like Eri, mourning a friend or a long-dead love affair.

The pulsing light plunges beneath the horizon.

I glance over my shoulder, to the unseen wreckage.

Conversation starter.

I'll be damned.

My body trembles with recent memory, of resonance piped into my bones, so fine-tuned—so purposefully shaped—they had to be words.

The squid wasn't just sucking nutrients from my body. It was communicating. That's how the fuckers talk.

And I didn't so much as cock an ear. Instead I did what I've always done: I turned away.

Give someone a glimpse of your insides and they'll eat you alive.

Maybe that isn't always a bad thing. Maybe being eaten alive is what Eri was always asking for. She wanted to share my vulnerability, my weakness, my dirty insides. All those years, I couldn't believe anyone would want such an awful thing.

That night, when Raul's death and Eri's tears had routed my defenses, she almost got her way. She almost snuck inside. The whole thing terrified me so much, I walled it off for good. Without trust there's no common language, Eri always said. Maybe she was right all along.

Three years later, I've still never visited her grave. Never told her I was sorry.

Three years later, a squid's asking for my trust. And goddamn it all, this is my last chance to get it right.

I stumble back to the crash site. I have no idea how long it's been. Days. Weeks. At the sight of the crimson fuselage my legs pump faster. I lose my footing, collapse. Blood greases my hands. I haul myself standing, limp closer. Shadows consume the fuselage. Was I gone too long? I creep around the corner, step inside.

The alien ship is empty.

I sink to the ground and lean my head against the hull. I close my eyes. The stinging distracts me, though only for a moment.

"I'm sorry." The tears on my lips are salty and stale and I can't tell who I'm talking to—Eri or the damn squid. "I should've said something. I should've let you in."

I curl fetal, hug my knees—

And touch something foreign. My eyes flare open. The alien's trunk lies on the rock outside, heaving, in bad shape. A pair of tentacles extend through the fissure in the ship. One hovers near my leg wound. The other extends across the ground to my side. Like an offering.

Its scent envelops me.

Slowly, with trembling hands, I draw the flesh to my teeth. Warm sap floods my mouth.

The alien doesn't flinch. Its tentacle approaches my leg. I choke back a laugh at the absurdity of it: sure, we might salvage trace nutrients from one another's bodies, perhaps enough to string out our pathetic lives for another week or two. But it's a closed system— without external energy we'll still die.

Its tentacle touches my leg: the circuit completes. Deep, resonating tones carry through my body. Words. I don't have the slightest clue what they mean, but now I get it: it isn't the words that matter.

It's the talking.

So I talk back. I talk about Tau-B12 and the stench of stale beer and vomit at the Landing after second shift. I talk about the Skinners and their deadly blame games, and the unwavering human propensity to fear and loathe those who are different from ourselves. I talk about transplutoniums and mildew-encrusted rebreathers and the sharp pang of first light over the cold horizon that invokes just enough serotonin to drag us kicking and screaming through one more shift in the mines.

But most of all, I talk about Eri. Her thin lips. Her serious smile. Her unwavering trust.

We talk until we run out of regrets, me and the squid. And when we're done, all gory and wet and glutted, the silence doesn't sting quite so bad anymore.

* * *

I'm falling.

My hands grope for purchase. Pumice digs into my palms, halts my fall. I crane my neck.

The alien clutches the lip of the gully overhead. The gulch bottoms out a few meters down, where the rock walls converge into a wedge.

It's trying to bury me. Bastard of a squid must've shoveled me over the edge while I was asleep. But why now? I bare my teeth, reach out to grapple its extended tentacle—

That's when I hear it. The distant hum of an air purifier or— stabilizing thrusters.

The hum gets louder, quickly. The alien waggles its tentacles.

I loosen my grip on the walls and let my body slide deeper. My boots touch down. Darkness consumes me. The alien disappears over the edge.

The engines roar. I clamp my hands over my ears. The ground shakes.

Then silence.

I hold my breath. Pneumatics hiss: a hatch opening. I crouch lower and stare at the sliver of stars overhead.

A familiar slurping sound persists: alien tentacles. A lot of them.

A shadow passes overhead. I scramble out of the way. Something thumps to the ground. It's not moving, but I'm too terrified to approach. I cower in the shadows and wait.

The thrusters fire up again. The alien ship howls away. I wait for as long as I can—an hour, maybe more—but the silence persists. Then, slowly, I creep toward the object. I prod it with an outstretched finger.

A tentacle lies at the bottom of the gully. Sap oozes from its freshly-severed end.

* * *

The Protectorate ship finds me huddled in the alien fuselage, clutching the remains of the tentacle like a chunk of driftwood in the open ocean. Hugging it like a dead lover, trying in vain to squeeze one more word from its lifeless flesh.

They tell me everything's going to be all right, that I'm lucky they were running recon through this hemisphere when I pinged them a few hours prior. They say they didn't think it was me at first and ask me how I managed to work the alien beacon.

I clutch the tentacle closer to my chest and say nothing.

When they say they need to get me back to command for debriefing, my lip curls. Nothing that happened here is going to change the war, even if command decides to believe me. Which they won't. Besides, I've got someone far more important to talk to first.

I throw one final glance at the wreckage, my ship and the squid's entangled in their clumsy union. Then I stagger onboard and tell them to drop me off at Tau-B12, to hell with the debriefing.

I have a grave to visit.

THE ALL GO HUNGRY HASH HOUSE

Andy Duncan

The All Go Hungry Hash House was easy to find because dozens of buzzards circled it overhead in a perpetual column visible for miles, a landmark like Clingman's Dome or Chimney Rock.

Two ridges away, three travelers stopped to regard the spectacle. They had known each other a long time, had rambled many a mile together, and yet they all still spoke to one another. Now, a three-man musical act communicates mostly nonverbally, just from sensing one another's presence, one another's needs, one another's place on the beat. But these three all liked the sound of their own voices too much to stop talking altogether. One of them, especially, liked to talk more than anyone else in North Carolina.

As the three travelers watched, one buzzard swooped too close to the boardinghouse chimney, faltered, fell out of formation, and plummeted to land head-first and half-buried in the earth, quivering like a spear. The dead buzzard did not exactly call for comment, but comment they did anyway.

"He must have got a whiff," said Roy, who carried the guitar, an instrument of complex origin. He was famed across the Piedmont as "the one with the glasses."

The bandleader, the most talkative of the three, rubbed his hands together and said, "Yes, sir, they're cooking today, no doubt about it. Step up the pace, boys. We best hurry or there won't be none left for us."

"Please, Jesus," Posey murmured, "let there be none left for us, Amen." As always, Posey brought up the rear, on account of his limp. He carried the fiddle, another instrument of complex origin. He was famed across the Piedmont as "the one with the foot."

Roy cast a wistful backward glance at the exposed talons clutching the air and said, "We'll wish we had some good buzzard by time we're done."

The bandleader just laughed. "Quit your bitching. Remember, it's my treat."

The bandleader carried the banjo, yet another instrument of complex origin, though not as complex as the bandleader himself. He was famed across the Piedmont simply by his name, which was Charlie Poole.

While much has been said and will be said of Charlie Poole, all that need be said of him here and now is this: when Jimmie Rodgers and the Carter Family and all the other unknowns went to Bristol, Virginia, in summer 1927 to record their first discs for the Victor Talking Machine Company, they all shared the same dream—to be just like Charlie Poole.

Seen only fitfully, frightening in his implications, and approachable by few, Charlie Poole was legendary, a marker of treasure, like a spook light in the woods. He also had a clawlike, painful-looking right hand, and broomstraw hair that broke every comb; spoke with a one-man accent; and, when he smiled, revealed a dimple so deep that souls could fall in and be lost forever.

He smiled often. He smiled when things were good and he smiled even wider when things were bad. On this pitted, twisting, single-file track along the ridge, his smile was as wide as the New River Gorge, for the three travelers had seen nothing but ill omens since they left the trailhead. The buzzard that fell from the sky was less a surprise than a mile marker, one in a series.

"Charlie, don't you think we ought to turn back?" asked Posey, because it was his turn to ask.

"I agree with Posey," said Roy, because it was his turn to agree. "From what I hear, there ain't nothing at the All Go Hungry Hash House that I need."

"Me, neither," said Posey. "If we turn back now, we can skip dinner and eat supper in town."

Charlie just laughed and smiled even wider. "The point, boys, ain't the *dinner*. The point is the *experience*. The All Go Hungry Hash House is something every wanderer should experience eventually." He dropped his smile long enough to give them each a grave and fatherly look. "But it ain't nothing to risk without a trusted guide and your trusted guide is me! Why, boys, taking you there, it's my duty to you. Besides," he added, as he reached the crest of the trail and headed downslope, "*I've* been there and lived."

Roy and Posey were not at all reassured by this, but they followed Charlie downhill anyway, as he knew they would.

Charlie did not tell them his real reason for doing most things, even crazy dangerous things, was boredom. But they were beginning to realize that on their own.

The Hash House was one of a cluster of thrown-away-looking buildings of gray clapboard at the foot of the ridge, all leaning into one another like drunks on the watery bank of a clay-red stream. The dirt track winding among the buildings was deserted.

As Charlie, Roy, and Posey approached, the double doors of the Hash House flew open with a bang and a man in coveralls emerged, carrying one end of a stretcher. "Make way, make way," the man cried as he walked across the empty porch and down the empty steps and into the empty street. As he went, more of the stretcher became visible. There was a lot of it. The man kept on walking, and the stretcher kept on coming out the door. Lying on the stretcher was a prone figure entirely covered with a sheet. Whether the figure's head or feet had come out first was impossible to determine, but as more and more stretcher became visible, more and more of its sheeted occupant became visible, too. The occupant was just as long as the stretcher, and a damn sight more improbable. The man carrying the first end of the stretcher had crossed the street and passed out of sight behind another building by the time the other end of the remarkable stretcher emerged from the Hash House doorway. The man holding that end was the mirror image of his partner. In a way, this was anticlimactic, but it was also profoundly unnerving, in a way that was downright mathematical, and the three travelers stood frozen, watching. "Make way, make way," the stretcher-bearer or bearers cried, as the stretcher finally was borne out of sight, past a sign that said, "Tan Yard in the Rear."

In front of the swaybacked building next door, which would have collapsed long ago if not for the Hash House's support, a crooked man dressed formally in gray hunched over a couple of sawhorses. He was sawing planks by hand, his top hat ticktocking back and forth as he worked. All around were partial coffins of varying size. Behind and above him hung a signboard that said, in faded cursive script, "Pritchett and Scrye, Undertake." Someone had scrawled an "R" and an "S" at the far right of the sign, as an afterthought and in an entirely different hand, like a child's.

Charlie called out, "What happened to your sign painter, brother?"

Mr. Pritchett, or maybe Mr. Scrye, didn't look up from his work. "Knocked off for lunch twelve years ago. Warned him not to eat next door. Had to finish the job myself."

"Why not finish off these coffins?" Posey asked, kicking at one with his club foot. "Some of 'em lack only one board, or a lid."

"No coffin is finished," Mr. Scrye or Mr. Pritchett said, "till it's claimed and occupied." He adjusted his sawdust-crusted glasses and squinted at each musician in turn. "And these will be, directly."

There was no reply to that, so Charlie, Roy, and Posey turned back to the Hash House—just as the first stretcher-bearer stomped back into view around the corner. He was eventually followed by his double, by which time the first man had reached the Hash House steps. The stretcher that connected them was just as long as before. So was its sheet-covered occupant, though from the bearers' pained expressions, this one was heavier. Maybe it was multiple occupants, laid end to end. Or maybe it was the same occupant, getting heavier over time, as burdens tend to do.

"Make way, make way," the stretcher-bearers cried.

Charlie held the doors open for them as they toted their burden back up the steps and into the boardinghouse.

"It's a wonderful cycle of life," Charlie said.

"See you soon," the undertaker called. He had dragged forward three coffins of varying lengths and was sanding their corners, humming a tune that, though wordless, sounded dirty. One of the coffins was Charlie-sized, one Roy-sized, and one Posey-sized; but this caused the men on the porch no serious alarm, as each noticed only the two coffins not sized for him, and entered the Hash House reassured. Such is human nature.

The boardinghouse's narrow, cold, silent front parlor contained only an empty elephant's-foot umbrella stand, a spavined deal-topped table that held a thimble-sized container of toothpicks, and a framed tintype on the wall of three children wearing Halloween masks. At least, Posey thought they were masks. Where the stretcher-bearers had gone was a mystery, but there were only two interior doors. The one on the left had a sign that said "Eat" and the one on the right had a sign that said "Ate." After only a moment's hesitation, Charlie pushed open the door marked "Eat," revealing a scene of such raucous noise, such brilliantly lighted confusion, that the still and chilly parlor was immediately forgotten, like a distant, small mistake.

Stretching into the misty distance were scores of round tables, each ringed by eight chairs, and every chair full of people talking to one another at the top of their lungs. Pale, hollow-eyed waitresses careened between tables, platters in their hands and balanced on their forearms. The heat was stifling.

A gap-toothed, broad-faced old lady in a gravy-clotted shirtwaist hobbled through the crowd to greet them, waving a ladle. She moved slow but got bigger fast, as if she was out of perspective somehow; by the time she finally arrived, she was easily seven feet tall, her ladle the length of a table leg. "Charlie!" she cried.

"Duchess!" he cried. He reached up to hug her wattled neck and she stooped to accommodate him. "You know my friends, don't you? Roy with the glasses and Posey with the foot? Sure you do. They wanted something good to eat, so I brought 'em here instead."

She cackled, her dimples tunneling into her head. "Ah, that's sweet of you to say, Charlie, but I got nothing for you. You can see for yourself, every table full."

At that moment, a bald salesman several tables away clutched at his throat, shrieked, and toppled backward. He was out cold before he hit the floor, his wingtips pointing at the embossed tin plates of the ceiling. The salesmen on either side of him looked at their fallen companion with horror, then at one another, then shrieked in unison, clutched their own throats, and flung themselves likewise onto the floor. All three lay there like dynamited trout, openmouthed and still.

"Well, ain't you in luck?" the Duchess continued. "We just had three places open up."

She wedged two fingers into her fishlike mouth and emitted a whistle befitting a steam locomotive, at which signal three young flappers scurried out of the crowd shoulder to shoulder, tittering like birds. They wore cloche hats and bobbed hair and shameless spangly dresses that bared their knees, almost. As each flapper grabbed a salesman by the collar and dragged him away toward the back of the room, toward the kitchen, the Duchess bussed the table through the simple expedient of sweeping all the salesmen's plates onto the floor with a crash.

"There you go, boys," she cried. "We serve family-style around here. Make yourself some new friends. They'll pass you whatever you want."

Indeed, the instant Charlie, Roy, and Posey sat down, stashing their instruments beneath the table, the other men and women around the red-and-white-checked oilcloth—all of them glassy-eyed, slack-jawed, and reeling from exhaustion—began passing them pots, pitchers, plates, platters, jugs, mugs, tureens, bottles, cups, saucers, salvers, samovars, bread baskets, salt cellars, pepper mills, finger bowls, trenchers, trays, teapots, coffeepots, coasters, crocks and casseroles—anything within reach, really, on their table and neighboring tables. In moments, every liftable object and consumable was piled in a jumbled arc around the newcomers, like the wall of a playground fort.

"Hey, whoa, whoa!" Roy said. "You passed all your food to us and look at your own plates. Empty as the night train to Gibsonville. Y'all must not be hungry."

"We're starved!" a woman wailed.

"You will be, too," a man said, "soon enough."

Posey lifted the lid of a butter dish, revealing a stick so moldy that it had grown a tuft of waving red tendrils, like a polyp beneath the sea. As he held the lid aloft in horror, the longest tendrils reached upward, wrapped around the lid, and slammed it back down where it belonged with such violence that three tendrils were severed by the impact, spurting purple fluid that singed the tablecloth. The survivors slurped back into the crack between dish and lid, which settled into place with a click. Then came a slithering, as the mold resettled.

"No telling what you'll find, lifting lids willy-nilly like that," Charlie said. "Best to make sure they ain't moving first. Let's try this one here. It seems calm enough."

He lifted the lid of a large tureen to reveal, splashing among the ice cubes, a singularly unattractive baby of uncertain sex, its swollen doughy expanse of head interrupted by an ancient face that was fisted into too small an area not quite in the center. The baby's eyes crossed in ecstasy as it rubbed cold soup into its armpits. A sprig of parsley was draped behind one snaillike ear, suggesting a poor attempt at half a bust of Caesar.

"Oh, *there's* the baby," the Duchess cried, seizing its throat in both hands and lifting it. This didn't bother the horrid child, which cooed happily as blue-green soup poured from its diaper's every orifice.

Once it was clear of the tureen, the Duchess set it onto the tablecloth three times in succession, *squelch squelch squelch*, as if the tablecloth were blotting-paper.

"There, now," she said. "Wookums has sure enough got something in its die-dee—and it ain't just soup, neither!" she shrieked into Roy's ear, cackling as if she had made an all-time funny. She wedged the squirming, sodden creature beneath one vast arm and bustled away among the tables, the baby clutching at diners' clothes and hair as they went.

Charlie, having given a charred beefsteak a practiced appraisal, hitched back his chair, dabbed his dry lips politely but needlessly with his napkin, stood, and walked to the nearest wall, where a selection of swords, bayonets, cleavers, and other edged instruments hung in a rack like billiard cues. He selected a broadsword that might have been left by an Ottoman harem eunuch in lieu of rent. He raised it overhead and swished it around in practice arabesques, nodded with satisfaction, returned to his untouched steak, and from a standing position used a single vicious downstroke of the broadest part of the blade to cut the steak, and the plate beneath, cleanly in two. A pinkish stream gouted from the center of the otherwise coal-black meat.

Charlie cried, "Aha, dead! I thought so, you rascal, you," and sat down, retucking his napkin beneath his chin.

Roy reluctantly selected, as the least of many available evils, a bowl of gray biscuits, hooking one finger over the ceramic rim and dragging the bowl toward him, tensing every muscle in case something should leap forth. He gingerly lifted a biscuit, using only his fingertips, and was surprised by its weight and density. It was like lifting a baseball.

As he brought it nearer his twitching lips, he saw that it was striated with odd markings. Peering through his glasses, he realized that words in various hands had been carved onto the top and sides of the petrified biscuit:

LEVON WAS HERE, 1868
GOD HELP US ALL
MAISIE DOES IT IN MEMPHIS
THE DUCHESS IS COMING

And sure enough, the aforementioned crone was hobbling toward him, bearing a platter that held four lopsided eggs, which rolled and clicked together as she lurched along. When she set down the platter, the eggs paused only for a second before they resumed their rolling and clicking.

"Never too late to hard-boil an egg, I say," said the Duchess.

When Posey tapped one with the butt end of his butter knife, it cracked open and a reptilian bird with greasy feathers shouldered its way onto the table, scattering shells and squawking harshly.

One of the other diners, blinded by hunger or perhaps by the Brilliantine in his hair, made for the bird with his fork, but speared only tablecloth as the creature darted out of the way, skipped across the surface scum in the baby's bath-tureen, launched itself from the table's edge, missed the window entirely, and dropped to the floor with the grace of a dead frog.

As Posey and Roy watched, the other eggs dutifully rolled along after their adventurous elder sibling, tumbling one by one off the table's edge in a series of wet reports.

Charlie, having given up on the steak, now plunged his fork into a sausage that barked in response. Without the slightest sign of surprise or unease, Charlie yanked back the fork, returned it to his plate, and sat smiling pleasantly at no one in particular, like a small boy determined to look innocent.

Having failed to do more damage to his pickle than gnaw dents that immediately filled back out, as on a pneumatic tire, Roy decided to test its rubberlike qualities further by flinging it against the wall. It ricocheted about and smacked another diner in the eye. Before it could fall, Mr. Brilliantine lunged with his trusty fork and speared the pickle, though fortunately not the eye beneath. The eye's owner reacted not at all to any of this, merely stared dumbly forward, having unwisely tasted the liver.

Charlie jerked backward and cried, "Get away, there," kicking something under the table that yelped. The figure that rose into view, top hat first, was a fat man dressed formally in gray, rubbing his jaw and looking at Charlie with reproach. He was the long-lost undertaker.

"You know," Charlie said, "I had a premonition you were going to show up."

"Why get all shirty, then?" retorted Mr. Scrye or Mr. Pritchett. "I was only measuring your inseam."

"Thank you kindly," Charlie said, with a wink, "but my inseam has been measured by experts."

"Want seconds, boys?" asked the Duchess, looming over them again. Her grin looked less friendly this time, more feral; one canine tooth glinted in the fading light. Though the room had no visible windows, the overhead lamps were dimming and the samovar in front of Posey cast a long shadow.

"I couldn't eat another bite," said Posey, loudly, which was the truth, except technically he hadn't eaten even one bite yet.

"Me, neither," said Roy.

"I reckon we're ready for the check, Duchess," said Charlie.

The old lady whistled again, but the flappers were already there, had already surged around her as floodwaters surge around a stump. Each held a tiny silver tray that held a single folded piece of paper.

"Here you go, Posey," said the flapper nearest Charlie.

"Here you go, Roy," said the flapper nearest Posey.

"Here you go, Charlie," said the flapper nearest Roy.

This took some sorting out, but eventually each man had the right tray, as was evident when they unfolded their chits. They bore no sums, no writing of any kind, just drawings of men's faces, like the sketched-in kissers on wanted posters. They were very good likenesses of Charlie, Roy, and Posey.

"What the—?" asked Posey.

"Oh, Lord," said Roy.

Without moving, the flappers, the Duchess, everyone in the place, all seemed to surge forward, to close in.

* * *

Some argue that in moments of crisis, human beings surmount themselves, become better than they were. This is untrue. In fact, in moments of crisis, we all become, not someone else, but fully ourselves, unhidden, exposed. Outer layers are shucked away, like dry husks. Charlie Poole understood this and what he said next required no thought, no emotion, no faith, only this understanding.

* * *

Charlie yelled, "How about some music!"

And the crowd whooped and roared and leaped in joy, the way crowds always had for the banjo player, ever since he was a boy.

The damned were no different. Besides, in that joint, dancing was preferable to eating.

Automatically, too, Roy reached for his guitar, Posey for his fiddle. Charlie already was holding his banjo, though Roy and Posey knew that could not be right; it had been under the table, just like theirs, hadn't it? They sometimes felt that Charlie's banjo was other than a mere instrument, more like a familiar.

"What you gonna play, Charlie?" Mr. Brilliantine yelled.

Mr. Liver croaked, "How about 'The Man Who Rode the Mule'?"

"Or 'Honeysuckle'?"

"Or 'Budded Roses'?"

The horrid baby, now standing bowlegged in a green puddle and smoking a ten-cent Sullivan cigar, suggested a title so obscene than even Charlie was taken aback. He recovered quickly.

"The number's a hot one," he said. "It's the most appropriate-est song I can imagine for you good folks, because you're all in it. Ever' damn one of you!"

The crowd roared again. Only the Duchess looked suspicious.

"Hold on there," she said, but no one heeded her.

"Yes, boys, it's 'The All Go Hungry Hash House.' Let 'er rip!"

Charlie's crippled right hand landed on the strings like a sack of meal landing in a wagon, and his sidemen laid right in with him, as they had done so many hundreds of times before, and everyone in the place broke into an orgiastic frenzy of dancing. Chairs tumbled sideways. Tables crashed to the floor. Bottles shattered. No one cared. The dancers whooped and hollered and howled like beasts. The St. Vitus had hold of them all, from the knees-up flappers to the diaper-shaking baby—even the Duchess, though her broad fat face was clenched in a rictus, as if she were the only one trying to resist the spasms irresistible.

The raucous song that Charlie hollered out had many verses, some ancient and some extempore. Only a few were audible.

From our hovels and our cells
And our precious private hells
That have worn all our dreams down to a nub
We have hobbled and we've crawled
And have fetched up here with y'all
At this All Go Hungry Hash House for some grub.
These gray biscuits have got names
And we aim to get them framed
Like we hang pics of dead babies on the wall

All the sausages are marked
If you bite one it will bark
At this All Go Hungry Hash House where we trawl.
We all shiver like the crew
Of an iceberg-sunk canoe
And we cry the directest prayers we can shout
Cause we're dying from the breeze
Off that ambelonious cheese
That the All Go Hungry Hash House dishes out.
There will be no fighting free
This bacterial nursery
Will shovel us ever one into our graves
We'll writhe and grovel on the floor
But sup on only metaphor
To this All Go Hungry Hash House we are slaves.

During all this, the atmosphere in the room was becoming less like a dance and more like a riot, as first one, then three, then a dozen people started jerking and wincing and clawing at themselves, as if something unseen were swarming over them. In moments, the no-see-ums had seized everyone in the room, save only the musicians. Charlie gave his sidemen the one-eyebrow high sign that meant Big Finish, that meant We're Done, that meant Save Yourselves.

Now hark, you sons of bitches
As you scratch off all the itches
That you caught off all the bedbugs in your seats
This song has been a spell
That will bind you just until
Our three shitasses flee into the street.

"Let's go, boys!" Charlie yelled, and he, Roy, and Posey somehow made it back through the doorway at the same time, three abreast—instruments, goozlums, galluses, and all—which was not the least of the impossibilities in that cursed boardinghouse that day. But folks always had to take their word for it the rest of their lives, because the only potential witnesses were so frenzied dealing with the bedbugs Charlie had conjured that they plumb missed the miracle, and even if they hadn't, how would they have spread the word, being nailed to that starvation-spot until the final lamp is doused in the final window on that final hill, Amen?

Also, the door they came through was now the one marked "Ate," but not even the musicians noticed that.

The miracle was not repeated at the front door in any case, as Charlie lagged just long enough in the entrance-hall for Roy and even Posey to get ahead of him; he could not resist snatching a toothpick off the deal-topped table as he passed. But like the other two, he burst from the front door and landed in the middle of the street with scarce attention to the intervening porch and steps. All three fled into the hills like jackrabbits ahead of a fire.

The undertaker, who was still at it, whose ticktocking top hat is still at it even as you read this, did not even look up from his labors. "No coffin is finished," Mr. Scrye or Mr. Pritchett repeated, "till it's claimed and occupied." When he sneezed, fresh lung-ground sawdust flew out his nose and fanned onto the planks before him like silt in a delta. Compared to the older sawdust, the fresh was brighter yellow and better withstood the breeze. "These coffins, too, will be claimed, directly," he added to us all, to a wide and heedless world.

* * *

"I wouldn't want to eat there *ever'* week," Charlie said, when they paused for breath several miles away, "but for special occasions, it cannot be beat."

He removed the souvenir toothpick from his mouth and admired its small, drab perfection, wholly unblemished by food.

"Special occasions, my ass," Roy said. "You dragged us there just to show off, and play Posey and me for fools, and damn near got us killed."

"That ain't so," Charlie said. "First of all, boys, ever'thing is material. Anything you live through, you can make music from, and that's a fact. Besides, I like to pay the All Go Hungry a visit now and then just to remind myself how bad it is, so that no matter what food I get served any other place on the road, I know it ain't the worst in the world, and that way I can choke it down and call myself lucky."

Posey snorted. "I'm so lucky I'm clubfooted and starving and I work for a crazy man. When we getting some actual dinner?"

Charlie looked thoughtful. He patted himself down two-handed, as many peace officers had done. "Come to think of it, I just might have...Ah! Here we are." From a jacket pocket, he flourished a flask, steel-shiny like an unfired bullet, and spun roulette with the cap.

"Looky here, boys. Dinner is served!" He tossed aside the toothpick to make way for a burning slug of Wilkes County's finest, which singed his tongue and set his palate alight.

Forgotten before it hit the ground, the toothpick was trod upon first by Roy, then, unintentionally but more emphatically, by Posey. Mashed into the rich Carolina earth, it lay fallow as the three men rounded the bend in the trail, laughing and drinking. As they vanished between the trees, the toothpick twitched once, twice, then split, and sprouted first a stem, then a leaf, and finally a single wine-dark blossom, which might have been right pretty in the daytime, but in the evening just lay there like a hole.

PICKLED ROOTS
AND PEELED SHOOTS
AND A BOWL OF
FARFLOWER TEA

Chaz Brenchley

there's rue for you, and here's some for me

Just that morning, she'd had a novice shave her head. He was a promising lad—no, more, he was a promise halfway to being realized—but still all awkwardness and angles, nervous of his own body let alone anyone else's. Let alone hers.

Of course he'd cut her. She'd felt the cold bite of the blade before he gasped and snatched his hands away, then the tentative touch of a cloth. She raised a hand and laid it over his, pressing firmly, teaching him not to be shy. Not with her body, not with her blood.

When she released her grip, he kept the pressure on a minute longer. Swift to learn, yes, the promise made actual. When he peeled the cloth away, he held it within her line of sight, because she still hadn't turned her head, she still hadn't moved at all except to give that lesson, and she needed to be shown what he had done.

She bowed her head, acknowledgement of his part and of hers, that she had bled on his cloth. One hand lifted to say *that is behind us now* and she straightened her back and knelt as steady on her heels as she had been before, so that he could finish. It was a precept here, a fundamental, that no task was ever left half-done. Readiness, focus, detail: everything in order, and every one thing completed before the next could be approached. That much he had learned already, and she felt the razor on her skin again; but this was to be a morning of lessons for him, seemingly.

Well, it would do a boy no harm to learn how to take blood out of fabric. Anyone here could teach him. It was not her task today, though it was now certainly his to seek the lesson.

Freshly scraped, she bowed to him as he to her, and he scurried away with his blade, his bowls and cloths. She would sternly have suppressed the smile that rose at his puppy clumsiness, except that too was something to be embraced and examined. Nothing in her rule preached solemnity, but mockery was not to be tolerated, even in herself. Especially in herself. She considered that smile, determined that it was rooted in love and hope, anticipation of the man he would become, and let it stand.

She moved outside in the wake of his turbulence and stood quiet and receptive on the steps below the shelter. The planet turned beneath her restful feet, bringing the sloth sun up above the mountains. This would be a good morning to gather and glean, out on the slopes, under the trees' canopy; she could work her garden later, once the hammer heat had passed.

* * *

She collected a sister-adept, because her rule preached both solitude and community, and a companionable silence was the finest realization of both. To that small party she added a brawny novice— not Pamien, because she kept no favorites here, and besides, no one could ever have called him brawny—and a pair of netting sacks.

Down to the river, and they took the boy out between them along the stepping-stones that led across the bitter, hurrying water. Halfway over, she held up an arm to stop them all. He did—just—manage to keep his balance and his feet, neither careering into her nor tumbling helplessly into the water. She had known both in earlier years, with earlier novices.

She faced downstream and settled herself cross-legged on the stone. Beyond him, her sister-adept did the same.

"Is, is this a teaching?" the boy stammered, hurrying to follow suit, too large to fit easily on the wet and narrow stone.

"Of course. Have we taught you nothing yet? First, tell us everything you know about current and flow, about strength and power and source." That would not detain them long; this lad was the opposite of promising. In truth, they had kept him more for his strength and willingness than for any more hopeful potential. Nevertheless: no teaching was ever entirely wasted. And they kept no mules here, and it was a long, long walk down from the mountain, and a longer one back up when you were burdened. A broad back and tireless legs were not to be lightly dismissed. "And then, when you are quite done and we have meditated on your words awhile, plunge your hands into the water. You will find a fish trap on either side of your stone."

At this time of year, the spratlings should be hatching high above, and not so much swimming as being hurled downstream to the great still lake below. The stepping-stones were only the visible end of a system of underwater walls that steered the little fish through to the traps. There was teaching in everything; come late summer, when the stream was lowest, the novices would be wading thigh-deep in the still-chilly waters, learning the patterns of flow and thrust as they rebuilt walls damaged in these surging currents now.

Today, though, two teeming traps meant a lesson on everyone's plate tonight: structure and similarity, potential, growth. Oh, and not to get caught in a trap.

An hour later, Borin's face and hands might be badly scratched and his robe smeared with blood and lichen in more or less equal measure, but his second sack was heavy with the tender shoots of twistangle vine, gathered from high in the canopy. His seniors discoursed helpfully on the nature of spiral climbing, the virtues of energy and range. He was perhaps paying less attention than he might, under his double load; even so, his young ears were the first to catch the sound echoing up from the valley and feeling its way through the trees.

"Forgive me, sisters—but isn't that the bell?"

They paused to listen, and now it came more clearly through the forest's noise: a low throbbing call and nothing natural, entirely the work of man. The work of men, indeed, who had carried bars of bronze all this way and then built themselves a furnace to melt them down, dug a pit in a dry paddy, and cast the bell right there: a gift, a love-offering, a blessing to the wise.

Three strokes, and three, and the three that all but he had missed: "Visitors," she said.

"Yes," said her sister-adept. "Perhaps we should hurry back?"

"No." It was important not to hurry, only to arrive in time. "They can be welcomed without us. And I want to dig fallonroot from the bell field, now they're here. I believe we will need that tonight."

* * *

So, they had come at last. They were certain to come in the end, so why not now? It had taken them long enough, in all conscience. Now was the moment, then. Now was always the moment.

Out of the trees, through her rampant garden and toward the compound below. Yes: there between the scattered roofs of the compound, down on the lowest terrace, men—and they would certainly all be men—stood in strict ranks, five and five, with two more facing them. An officer and a sergeant, perhaps, with ten troopers to make assurance doubly sure. In jungle uniforms, no doubt. They would be hot under the sun and horribly uncomfortable, heavily equipped and certainly armed. Not expecting trouble, surely, but armed anyway. And treating the compound like a barracks, standing on parade. Demonstrating their hardiness, dismissive of a community in retreat, refusing to seek shade or the simple comforts of the guesthouse.

Well. She could do nothing about them from up here.

"Borin, take the roots and twistangle to the well-house and scrub them thoroughly before you bring them to me. Scrub yourself, too, and change your robe. Just give me the fish now, I'll clean those myself."

She heaved the damp sack onto her shoulder and headed toward the separate gather of roofs that she liked to call her kitchen.

"Should we not go down to speak with them?" her sister-adept asked.

"We? No. You certainly should, if none of the others have thought to do so yet. Me, I have a meal to prepare."

It wasn't fair, perhaps—it would be she they had come for, after all—but even so. They had sought her this far; they could seek her a little further. She would not go to them. Not even this least little distance, another flight of steps.

* * *

He came to her alone, out of uniform, as far as she could see unarmed. Perhaps he meant to be disarming.

He was young, and hence unfamiliar, but she knew him nonetheless. She knew his type: privileged, ambitious, powerful. Political. She'd

need to be careful around this one. What he wouldn't—couldn't—
know was that he needed to be careful around her.

"I am Major Halder," he said, with that stiffly military little bow
that officers liked to affect in lieu of a salute, when they were out of
uniform or dealing with civilians. "And you are the pilot Mirielle, I
believe?"

"Here," she said gently, "I am known as Lanaya. We leave our
worldly names behind, when we come to this place."

"Of course. Lanaya, certainly. Should I say Sister Lanaya?"

"There is no need. We have little use for titles here. Or for rank;
your men will be no less welcomed than you are yourself. I hope you
have not left them still out in the sun?"

"No, no. I dismissed them to wash and change; they'll be doing
their laundry by now, I expect. It took us some days to get here. We
were told it wasn't possible to fly."

"That's right, yes. Some magnetic peculiarity of the mountains,
perhaps? Airborne vehicles tend...not to survive."

"And yet pilots thrive, I see." After a moment's pause—an absolute
silence, on her part—he went on, "You seem very well. I am relieved;
I had worried that—what is it, twenty years?—of meager rations and
little exercise might have seen you...diminished. Or worse."

She laughed. "Is that what you expected to find? A collection of
half-starved hermits hiding in their huts? Let me assure you, Major—"

"I thought you set no store by titles."

"No, but you do. There is no life I have found more healthy than
the way we live here. I scour these mountains for our food, and that
is exercise enough for anyone; and no one goes hungry under my
watch. As you will learn this evening. If you will excuse me now...?"

A gesture of her arm toward the great pots steaming over charcoal
fires. She thought he would leave her then, with another of those crisp
little bows—there was little that the military class valued above good
manners—but he paused, with an expression of genuine curiosity on
his face. "When did this happen, that you became a...cook? You, of
all people?"

"When I couldn't be a pilot any longer," she said, "and I needed
something actual to offer."

"I see. I...see. Well, we can recover you from this, I believe. I am
here to call you back, you know. You can be a pilot again. We will
welcome you home."

"I know you would," she said, "but of course I cannot come."

A momentary hesitation, and then, yes, that brisk salute. Not quite one soldier to another—she had been a pilot, after all, which meant never military—and nonetheless there was something comradely in it. Combative and comradely. He wouldn't dream of taking no for an answer.

* * *

There was a technique to gutting and filleting these little fish, one-handed and without a knife, just with thumbnail and fingers. She let her mind dwell there for a moment, and then decided to leave them whole this day. They could be fried crisp and eaten entire; the young liked them better that way and they'd appreciate the guidance of bones and fins and belly, when it came to the teaching. Which it would. She knew this man; he'd bring her to it soon. Soon enough. Over dinner.

The fish could wait, then, floating in a bowl of cool water refreshed with slices of shem. The fruit was too bitter to eat in hand, but its sharp juices would infuse the flesh with flavor, cleanse the gut and soften the bones. Meanwhile, she reached for the basket of scrubbed fallonroot. These she would peel and slice and set to pickle quickly in separate bowls, separate liquors, pink and green and purple. Color was always a lesson in itself.

And then the vineshoots: young as they were, those too would need peeling. They were thick as a man's thumb already, even at the tip. Another month, they'd be too tough to be worth the harvest. Borin could save his skin for another season. If he were still here, and anyone who might send him climbing.

* * *

Those tasks behind her, more lay ahead. That was too obvious even to be a teaching.

She was on her knees when he came a second time, reaching down into one of the great half-buried earthenware jars, drawing tangles of fermented greens out of their pungent brine. These leaves were last winter's crop, hot on their own account and hotter now after steeping so many months, packed down in salt and spices.

She coiled them into a bowl, wiped her bare arm with a cloth, and peered up at him, where he stood against the sun. That was deliberate, surely. He was the type to make a bold silhouette of himself, to look down his own shadow, to have her squint into the light.

"May I help you, Major?"

"It was a compliment to you and a cost to us, that we hiked all through this country to come find you. When they told us not to fly, that it was not *possible* to fly, no one spoke of magnetic abnormalities. They said it was forbidden, no more than that."

"Ah, yes. Certainly, we are a community that treasures the peace we find here. Rotor-blades and engines... Well, they would not be welcome."

"No. That was my understanding. So we came as we did, out of courtesy to you and your...community. I might hope for some courtesy in return: not that you would walk with us, perhaps, but at least that you will help me to understand why. Why not."

"Major, I walked away from you long ago."

"You did. Our need for pilots was great even in those days and it is greater now; you are a rare breed, hard to find and hard to train and hard to keep alive. Our losses have been brutal. We can build ships in plenty, and we have, but they are useless without pilots to helm them. You were always exceptional, even among your cohort—a leader and a teacher, a legend even now, when none of our surviving flyers know you. And yet here you are, in hiding from the world and from the war, seeking shelter in a slew of monks."

"Say in rejection, rather than in hiding. I have come a long, long way not to fight with you. I was a merchant pilot, not a soldier. Never that. I flew passengers and cargo, all through human space. I had all the reach and breadth of the Limb at my fingers' ends, I had the shift and flow of n-space in my head—which is the greater loss, and which you will never understand, and I tell you anyway in courtesy, yes— and your war took that away from me. There is no trade now, except in weaponry and death. You want me to deal in such matters on your behalf and I will not. Am I plain?"

"Admirably so; and—in courtesy, again—I will match your plainness with my own. I was sent to invite you back, but I mean to take you in any case, willing or otherwise. My men...could cause great harm here, and do great damage to something you hold dear. I dislike to threaten you, but—well, as you say. We are at war. And— plainly—a little desperate for strength. We will use what we have. And we do have you."

"Not with my consent."

"No, seemingly not. Though that may change. We must talk more."

"Of course," she said. "At dinner."

He bowed and was gone again. She went to her sauce jars and stirred, and sniffed, and considered. The recent, or the aged? Or the ancient? Everything builds to a narrative; everything has its part in the teaching.

* * *

As the sun dropped down to the mountains' rim, so too did the cold air of the mountain come down in its turn, to mingle with the still-hot air rising from the valley. Now was the perfect time to sit cross-legged at one long table, all the community together and their guests among, and eat and learn and practice, while the sky slowly darkened above.

She set the major on her one hand and his sergeant on her other, at the center of the table, to have them close when trouble came. There would be trouble: that was the point and purpose she'd been working to all day, all these years. The troopers she scattered among the adepts and the novices, trusting those to deal when the crisis came, but these two she wanted for herself. That might be vanity, or greed, and even so. Some tasks were hers to do.

As was the meal, hers to describe, hers to explain:

* * *

"Here," she said, using chopsticks to unfold a budding flower where it floated in a bowl, where it had been steeping for hours now, "this is farflower tea: a lesson in perspective, for we who hold ourselves apart. It lends so little of itself to the water, it almost might as well not be there at all; and yet without it, the water would be a solitude, an emptiness. Instead it is touched by presence. As we all are, here or beyond."

She dipped a ladle, filled a cup, passed it to the major; another to the sergeant. Then she handed the ladle to a brother-adept, to serve all the table else.

The major sipped, and frowned, and sipped again. "I...see exactly what you mean," he said.

No, you don't, she thought, *you really don't*.

"The flavor is...almost nothing, and yet it sings in my throat. I could drink this all day."

"Please," she said, gesturing. "We have plenty."

* * *

Novices brought plates to everyone, the freshly pickled fallonroot: a slice of each color on every plate and every slice showing the same swirled pattern of holes spiraling in to the center, like a galaxy revealed.

"One hot, one sour, one bitter," she explained to the curious major. "They remind us first to be cautious, because the world is rich and deep and dangerous beyond our knowing, and yet never to be tentative as we reach out. Touch your tongue to the pickle and the concentration will overwhelm your senses; bite through boldly to the sweet raw root beneath and the one will temper the other and you will experience the whole. Still potent, but not to overmaster."

Fumbling a little with unfamiliar chopsticks, the major lifted a slice to his mouth and bit boldly. His eyes widened a little, but he chewed and swallowed, considered a little while, and then nodded. "Yes. It takes me to a limit, but it doesn't push me through. And the experience is...deliciously unnerving. Unnervingly delicious. Yes. Thank you for the guidance."

To judge by the low buzz of humor from her people up and down the table, others among his men had been less well advised, or else less heedful. She was aware of gulping, of gasps, of calls for more farflower tea. She didn't look around. She kept eyes and focus on her own plate, and on the men on either side of her. The sergeant had bulled his way already through his serving, and was sweating profusely but showing no other sign of weakness. Nor, blessedly, any sign of interrupting. He was content to leave the talking to his officer. He would listen, and hold himself in reserve as a good subordinate does, all his attention on the major. Which left her free to do the same.

* * *

"I shall be sorry," he said, "if you don't choose to come with us voluntarily. Obviously, I am prepared for that contingency." And far too mannerly to gesture toward his men: no conflict at the table. Unless she precipitated it. No doubt they were all well-briefed. And poised at trigger-point, ready to act at a word.

Not armed, though. They had left all their weaponry in the guest-house. That again was his courtesy, and her relief. Sometimes the simplest solutions were the best.

Cautious but never tentative, she said, "You are only a dozen. We are three times as many."

He snorted. "A dozen soldiers, at the peak of fitness. They have little to fear from monks. Did you imagine that the long march here would leave us weak, or weary?"

"I had supposed you might like to rest a day or two, before you start for home," she said mildly.

"No. We leave in the morning. With you."

"I think not. You do remember, I am sure, that there is a long tradition of martial arts in...secluded communities like ours? The discipline here is as physical as it is philosophical. I would pit my youngest novice—see her there, between those two hulking brutes of yours?—against either of those, any of your men. Against the sergeant here, if he likes."

"Just say the word, sir," the sergeant growled.

"A wrestling match, to entertain us as we eat? I don't think so, no. My men are also disciplined and trained to fight bare-handed, and I shouldn't wish to see anyone hurt, from either camp. Besides, I think you're bluffing."

"Do you? Well. By all means, let us leave the matter untested. I believe we are done with this course."

* * *

"These greens speak to us of time and immersion, of depth, of maturity and wisdom tempered by the fires of youth. The sauce I used is as old as this settlement; it has been brewing in its jar since all this was bare-stamped earth and hope and a few willing hands to do the work. The greens themselves had half a year in brine, to let the flavors wake. Those jars you saw lie deep in the earth, for equilibrium. The passing seasons barely register; neither heat nor chill will touch them. I believe you'll find a calmness at their core, to echo that."

"You have...an odd approach to thinking about food," he said. "Indeed, I begin to wonder whether you're actually talking about the food at all."

"Oh," she said, "there are lessons all around us. Meaning in everything. But trust me, I am very much talking about the food. We do not trade in metaphor here, but hard reality."

"Well." He ate distractedly now, learning nothing, something on his mind. His free hand toyed with something in his pocket: not a weapon, she thought. Not directly a weapon.

"You drive me to this," he said, as he took it out at last, being plain again. Honestly, she thought, she could almost like this man, though never anything he stood for.

A button, on a box. That was clear enough.

"It sends a signal to a satellite," he said, "that we have set overhead to watch you. There is no way else to thread a message through these mountains, but this will bring an aircraft straight to me. Another dozen men and heavier weapons than we could carry. Enough to destroy this place entire, and all in it. All but you. I will fly you out tonight."

He pressed the button and a small light flashed.

"It is done. They will be here shortly. I hope you will be ready and make things easy. For all of us. It would be a shame to leave all this in flames and sorrow."

"It would," she agreed. "Is there another button, to send it back again?"

"There is not."

"Ah, well. That does seem a shame."

* * *

The fish were crisp and hot yet on their plates when the first sound of engines came sliding seemingly down the mountain slope to find them. Word had spread, all up and down the table; everyone looked.

"There!" One of the soldiers pointed and, yes, there was a light against the darkening sky, a solid shadow behind. Moving, coming closer.

She said, "Pamien."

The boy stood, nervous and certain in himself, both at once. As he should be. She was almost amused to see that he held one of the tiny fish between his fingers. He might be a promise half fulfilled, but he was young yet; he needed the reassurance of touch. Not of figure, not of metaphor. Sometimes the map and the territory share the same reality.

He waited for clarity, for purpose, to be sure: until the twin rotors were clear to be seen in the craft's own light, the shape of weapon pods below. Yes, this was all that had been promised, plenty large enough to

take the major away with all his men here and all his reinforcements and her besides. Well.

She might have nodded to Pamien, instruction or consent, but there was no need. With a twist of his fingers, he tore the spine out of the little fish.

She had time, just, to be surprised. *Did I teach him that?*

Then the craft exploded.

* * *

After the racket of its motors, the explosion itself was almost quiet: an abrupt flare of light and color, a dull heavy sound, a chaos of disintegration, falling.

The silence after she took care to use.

Speaking quickly, loudly, clearly, she said, "There is no point any of you running for your weapons. You would find them gone. I suspect my novices have thrown them all into the river. Similarly, please do not think you can assault any of my people and survive it." She didn't need an actual twistangle vineshoot in her hands to let every one of the soldiers feel it around their throat, tightening. And then—to make assurance doubly sure—inside their throat, climbing up from their belly, filling their airway, rising into their mouth, reaching for the light.

When the last of them had subsided, choking and frantic, she lifted her control and gave them ease, while ensuring that each one had two of her people standing over them. Let them wonder, if they cared, whether she had been bluffing earlier; they knew she was not bluffing now.

To the major, she said, "You thought this was a monastery I ran to, seeking refuge? This is a school. I built it. We did, my first pupils and I." Her first generation of novices, her adepts now, the seniors at this table. "It was their first teaching, first steps on their path to pilotry. You have no idea, none, what it takes to steer a spacecraft through n-space, the mental disciplines they have to learn, and then learn to apply. Most pilots cannot teach it at all. I found a way, an exercise of years. You have tasted a very little of it today—and seen a very little of the side-effects. I beg you will not have me show you more."

At first, he didn't answer, he only breathed. Then, at last, he looked up to where she was standing over him. "I thought you were people of peace."

"Oh, no," she said. "I said only that I would have no part of your war, that I would not be a soldier for you. My people and I, we stand opposed to your government, your military, your philosophy entire. We have to. The training, the teaching here, the ways we have to guide ships safely from one planet to another: all those militate against your ways of thought. We cannot but resist you, tooth and nail."

"How, then? By hiding here, where there are no ships?"

"Until now, yes. But you have built us ships, and my people are ready for them now." Well, perhaps not Borin. There would be a place for him, though. A place for them all. "We will go to take them," *and you know now how we can do that, from a guarded military base,* "and fly to join those who fight against you. With luck, with work," *with focus and stretch and immersion; with everything I teach these children every day,* "we will soon enough have the peace I treasure, all along the Limb of human reach. Without you and your kind breaking everything to dust as you march by.

"We will be gone within the hour. Don't think to follow us. Rest here, as I told you, major; take the time you need, recruit your strength before you tackle the path back. Eat whatever you can find, drink tea—and think about it as you do. That above all."

He might even do that, she thought. He might. That was a leaven of hope, to season all her regrets about this day and everything it brought her, everything it took away. Then she set her palms neatly together, bowed over them like the monk she never was, and led her people away.

COURSE OF BLOOD

Howard Andrew Jones

1

Outside the battered feast hall door Myrikus checked to ensure the skull-faced cloak tabs on his shoulder were upright, then pushed the black garment back so it was clear of his arms. A glance at his companions assured him their gear was in order, from ebon horsehair helmet crests to dark leggings. There was nothing to be done about their muddy boots, but Demian scraped specks of mud from the musculature etched into his chest armor. He finished, then nodded.

Myrikus pushed the door open. The aromas of roast boar and wine overwhelmed the lingering stench of the mountain town's hot springs and the dull throb of voices they'd heard outside rose to a din.

The feast of Acarcia was well into its second day. Likely many of the patrons crowded about the benches were on their third day of drink. They clapped and sang boisterously along with the trio on the cramped circular stage. Serving girls wove among them carrying platters of ham, bread, and cheese, and the ubiquitous pitchers.

Myrikus left Demian at the door and advanced confidently toward the stage, Telian at his shoulder. He couldn't contain a smile at the silence following in their wake and spreading before them. Some were sober, others were well inebriated, but their expressions were similarly apprehensive. He thought it proper that the legion's most elite order be regarded with fear and respect.

The music ground to a halt and the drummer, piper, and vocalist retreated to the stage's back wall.

Myrikus eyed them briefly before climbing the single step to face the crowd. Telian executed a pivot at the same moment, just short of the stage, hand on the hilt of his gladius.

Apart from one drunken woman shouting about cider, silence dominated the feast hall. Myrikus savored the crowd's rapt attention and palpable anxiety, while the woman's companions struggled to silence her. The serving women backed to the kitchen doorway.

Myrikus smote his breastplate. "Hail the Emperor!"

The revelers fumbled to repeat the gesture and echo the phrase.

He bared his teeth in a smile, their sloppy movements pleasing him. "It is good to see so many people give reverence to our emperor." Myrikus indicated the low bar, where two ashen-faced cooks watched. "I wish we had come solely to enjoy your festival. But we hunt a fugitive. Descriptions vary, but he's a fit older man with graying hair and a military bearing."

The patrons searched the benches. Those who fit the loose description looked nervously among their fellows.

Myrikus doubted their quarry would be found so easily, but scanned the throng, knowing keen-eyed Telian would be looking with him. "He's a murderer, and a necromancer, and has sometimes claimed to be Hanuvar Cabera."

The name of the infamous Volani general prompted whispered exclamations. No man was more feared throughout the empire than Hanuvar. He'd fought it to a standstill and led an invading army within sight of the Dervan gates.

Hanuvar's city was reduced to ashes and his people sold into slavery, but his name still evoked terror. Myrikus thrived on fear, but only when he controlled it. He raised his hands.

"Hanuvar himself is dead. This man is an impostor. We will capture him and punish him for his crimes." Myrikus paused. "You're going to help me. I will sit over there—" he pointed at an occupied table in a corner "—and my fellow soldiers and I will eat some of this fine food. Anyone with information can seek us out. Things can be easy. Or, if I don't hear anything, matters might get uncomfortable."

Myrikus didn't have to say more; all who heard him knew the Order of the Revenants could arrest anyone they cared and subject them to extraordinarily persuasive procedures.

As the three Revenants neared the table he'd indicated, the festival goers already seated there scrambled to depart with their platters and bowls.

Myrikus sat, brushed crumbs from the table, undid his helmet, and placed it on the bench. While his companions did the same across from him, a flushed serving woman arrived with slabs of meat, bread, mugs, and wine pitchers. Beefy Telian slapped her on the bottom as she scooted away, laughing at her discomfiture.

Demian, a recent inductee, was some five years Telian's junior, and still in his mid-twenties. The dark-haired youth used a knife to leverage a slab of meat onto his plate. Telian used his hands.

Myrikus set to with his men, relishing the cool wine and cooked food. They'd eaten road rations for most of the last week.

Telian wiped wine from his broad chin, scanned the room, and quietly addressed Myrikus. "Why do you keep saying it's not the real Hanuvar?"

"Because it can't be him. You still believe he's alive? What do you think, Demian?"

"I think that's highly improbable."

"You heard him," Myrikus said. "High horse shit improbable, especially since Hanuvar's bones are resting on the ocean floor."

"But the witch said she was certain he was here," Telian objected.

Myrikus washed down a bite of ham with a swig of wine. "People say things all the time to get out of trouble. You know what we're going to get here? A free meal, gossip about some local problems, and a whole lot of worried nonsense from idiots with grudges. If we're lucky, we'll find a lead on some witches, or bandits. But we're not going to find Hanuvar, because he's dead."

"If Hanuvar came back from the dead," Demian said, taking another slab of meat, "he'd be after vengeance. He'd go hunt the emperor, first thing."

"You afraid to touch your food with your hands?" Telian asked him.

"I'd be afraid to touch it with *your* hands."

"Well," Myrikus said, "I don't care what the trivon or his little witch said. Hanuvar's not going to be hiding at this little horse shit mountain festival. What's up here but meat and stink?"

"It has its attractions." Telian watched the slender serving woman, who nervously set another pitcher on their table.

She bent to wipe the table with a damp rag and let slip a piece of paper. "I was asked to bring this to you," she said, and scooted away.

While Telian followed her departure, Myrikus surreptitiously held the note open against the table. The message was short and blunt. *I know where he is. I'm in the alley back of the inn with a red scarf.*

Myrikus frowned and pushed the note across the table to his companions.

"Do you think it's a trap?" Demian asked.

Myrikus chuckled. "Who would dare attack Revenants in the middle of an empire town?"

"Whoever wrote that note seems pretty certain it's actually Hanuvar," Telian pointed out.

Myrikus sighed. "That's probably what the impostor's telling his associates. Telian, head out. You're searching for anyone watchful or sober who fits our description. Ask at the stables. Word's probably out we're here and our quarry may be making escape plans."

"You want me to send word to the trivon?"

"No." That spoiled aristocrat would only get in the way. Besides, if there was glory to be gained here, it would go to his trio, not the trivon. "Demian, head to the far end of the alley. Find a spot where you can watch and not be seen. I'll give you a few minutes to find your place, then head to the meeting."

Both men saluted informally, donned their helms, and started to leave. Telian doubled back for a final swig of wine, then followed Demian from the hall.

Myrikus forced calm as he finished his meal. He didn't want the onlookers to think him excited. It would be wonderful to show that smug trivon that he and his boys knew how to run an investigation. He and Telian had been hunting witches for four years; they didn't need any patrician—especially one with a pet witch—telling them how to root up a fugitive. Myrikus could guess why the trivon really kept her around.

He downed his wine, pulled on his helmet, and stood, adjusting his cloak over his shoulder.

The stench of the hot springs hit him as soon as he left the feast hall. His breath vapored in the evening air and he was once more glad for the leggings and boots he'd donned before they started into the highlands. The skies were gray, for winter was closer here than in the valleys below. To the west, inns sprawled around an open space filled now with great bonfires, around which crowds of celebrants drank and sang, no matter the chill. Through the screen of pine trees directly north lay the road to the hot springs and the actual temple of the old mountain god, along with a cluster of villas overlooking the Ardenine range that loomed on every side.

He cornered the building and headed into the wide alley between the feast hall and a windowless wooden storage building. The deeper into the alley he walked, the more the side farthest from the feast hall sloped, until it was almost four feet lower than the half along which he strode. Barrels and crates had been wedged in between the drop off and the building. Discarded tarps, broken wood, and detritus were piled against the feast hall's edge.

Alert for ambush, Myrikus put a hand to the hilt of his short sword and stepped past a huge open barrel that caught runoff from the feast hall's roof. At the alley's end, a dark-skinned man waited beside the drop off, a dark red scarf at his throat. A curly-haired Herrene. The impostor had been seen with just such a man.

Myrikus didn't care much for anyone from the Herrenic coast, for they prided themselves on their ancient culture, soft and feminine though it was. Patrician decadence—like theatre, and complicated singing—resulted from their adoption of Herrenic customs.

He eyed the informant as he drew close, then looked past him to the cluster of small homes and sheds beyond the alley's end. He didn't see Demian; likely the Herrene didn't see him either.

The Herrene appeared young, fit, clean-featured, and sober. He shifted nervously as Myrikus approached.

The Revenant got straight to the point. "You know where the man who calls himself Hanuvar is?"

"I do." The answer was soft but certain, and the Herrene's dark eyes were intent.

"Who are you?" Myrikus tried to look over the man's shoulder, but the Herrene shifted, as if to hide something.

"It doesn't matter, does it? Look, he's dangerous, and you've got to be quieter. If he finds out I'm talking to you—"

"He's not going to sneak up on us. I have people watching."

As the black man shifted again, Myrikus' suspicions flared. "Step aside." He pushed him with his off hand and the Herrene jumped as if touched with a hot poker.

Myrikus saw nothing behind the Herrene but another large rain barrel set into the hillside, its rim rising only ankle high. But might there be something or someone within? With a final snarl at the Herrene to stay, Myrikus peered into the dark water.

A pole lashed at his shins. He sprawled belly down in the dirt, his helmeted head over the barrel. He fought to push himself up but something heavy slammed into his upper back and a hand drove his face into the water.

Pressure on his legs told him that two people sat on him. The Herrene, probably, and someone else. He pushed up with his arms, then felt a dagger driven through one bicep. He opened his mouth to cry out and sucked in water.

He struggled to break free. His lungs strove and failed to find air. He wondered where Demian had gone, but suddenly dying was much easier than he'd ever guessed.

2

Hanuvar levered the body into the rain barrel and pushed the Revenant's booted feet down until the dead man was fully hidden. He looked up and down the alley, his gaze lingering only briefly on the dirty tarp under which he'd hidden.

Antires, panting as though he'd run a long distance, eyed him accusingly.

"They're Revenants, Antires. Their job is hunting midwives and burning them as witches."

The Herrene nodded but his gaze was dark. "I still don't like killing a man."

"He'd have slain either of us, given the chance. And he'd have been slow about it."

"He said he had someone watching."

"I left him in that storage shed." He nodded toward the cluster of small buildings beyond the alley.

Antires' dark eyes widened. "How did you—"

Hanuvar shook his head. There wasn't time for discussion. While Antires had been in position, Hanuvar had simply weaved drunkenly toward the other Revenant. Often a direct approach worked best. His spinning attack had caught the Revenant off guard. Success came down to knowing the habits of your enemies and knowing the ground you were about to fight on.

"So, what do we do now?"

"I need to know how they found us."

"You couldn't have talked to these?"

He shook his head. There'd been no time to question the first, not when he'd known he would be placed to watch for the leader. And Hanuvar had needed to dispatch the second quickly, in case the third had been sent on rounds.

"You can explain later," Antires said. "Shall I ready the horses?"

"I want you to look around. There may be more. Sometimes they travel in multiple groups of three."

"So six."

"Or nine. Or twelve."

"Or three hundred," Antires said dryly. "I get it. You sure we just shouldn't count ourselves lucky and leave?"

"No."

"Very well," his friend said reluctantly. "Where shall we meet?"

"Our room. If I'm not there by nine bells start on your way."

Hanuvar heard the usual muttered protestations as he drew up the hood of his cloak and stepped into the street. He approached the bonfire, where an impromptu dance was underway. Wisps of frosty air rose from the mouths of the crowd as they sang together. Somewhere outside he expected to find the third Revenant.

3

Vennian enjoyed the warmth of the hearth at his back and the fine wine in the goblet; the duck had been deliciously seasoned, its skin crisped to perfection. The reek of the mineral springs, though, marred everything, and he was astonished by the mayor's claims that one grew inured to it. Even as he sipped the fragrant wine, Vennian was aware of the stench of spoiled eggs. It was enough to put a man off omelets for weeks.

Beyond the cluster of couches where he lay with the mayor and his family, his two men had set aside helms and cloaks to mingle with the patricians gathered around the banquet tables. His two officers weren't rough and tumble louts like Myrikus and his band, but proper Revenants, raised in ancient homes and destined for high office. The odd dozen guests in this most exclusive of the banquet halls had initially been cautious of them, until they'd realized that beyond their polished armor these Revenants shared a similar background and reverence for the finer qualities of life.

Beyond them lay wide windows looking onto the steaming hot springs. The villa had been built beside the best of them. The mayor had told him that the more oddly shaped or dangerous lay to the east.

The darkening sky touched distant snowcapped peaks with a dull blue, though enough light remained to highlight an occasional frosty sparkle.

Evara lay on the couch to Vennian's left, garbed in finely-tailored stola decorated with the black and gold of the Revenant order. She looked deceptively at ease, a slim noblewoman gracefully sliding toward middle age. She picked at the duck leg on her plate with seeming concentration, but he knew her black eyes might be focused far beyond mortal affairs. Moments ago he had seen her surreptitiously nibbling at a black root she had removed from a hidden pocket.

The mayor finished his discussion with an older, dignified slave. The man bowed before turning away. Some, Vennian thought, believed all slaves were to be pitied, but those accorded status in a rich man's home lived better lives than many a freeborn man.

The mayor favored Vennian with an unctuous, gap-toothed smile. "My apologies. There was some confusion about the timing of tonight's sacrifice. Do you know that it was only a few generations ago they actually sacrificed a virgin during the festival? Ghastly, wasting a good virgin like that!" He laughed tightly, giving Vennian the sense that he'd told this joke before. "I'd think the gods would tire of virgins. More seasoned bed partners are far more interesting!"

"What do you sacrifice now?" Evara asked without looking up.

"A bullock on the first day, but every evening we prepare the finest of meals and send it into the abyss, the same way we used to hurl youngsters. Acarcia must like it, because our winters have been short since we took up the custom."

Vennian had little interest in the mountain god or his festival, and the mayor must have sensed this, for he cleared his throat and changed topics. "You were telling me about this Hanuvar impostor of yours. What do you think he plans to do?"

"Wherever he's gone, destruction and death have followed," Vennian said softly.

"The fire at the amphitheater," Evara suggested without looking up.

Vennian shot her a dark look she could pretend to have missed.

The mayor's watery eyes widened. "He's an arsonist? You think he might burn down the villa?"

"With your guards, and my men, inside and outside, there's no real danger," Vennian said. "In any case, we don't think this was his destination. We believe he's headed over the mountains, toward Derva itself."

"Retracing his steps," the mayor mused.

"Except that he's an impostor," Vennian reminded him.

"Maybe he thinks he really is Hanuvar. It's a wonder he hasn't tried to scare up some elephants."

Evara's head whipped up, as though she meant to rise. Then she sat still as a statue, apart from her eyes, which closed. Her expression had been the same those nights Vennian had forced her. This, he knew, was tarva root at work. He turned from the mayor and addressed her softly. "What's happening? What are you seeing?"

"Hanuvar... He knows. He knows we're here." Her voice was low, though every vowel she spoke was stretched to twice its standard length.

"I thought you said it wasn't Hanuvar!" The mayor's voice rose in alarm.

"Where is he?" Vennian demanded. He swung off his couch and loomed over her.

"He's..." She shuddered. "He's killed them."

"Killed?" the mayor asked. The nearby nobles looked up from their knot of conversation and stared in alarm. "Who has he killed? What's going on? Is she some kind of seeress? Is it really Hanuvar?"

"No, no," Vennian said over his shoulder, inwardly cursing Evara. He'd been instructed never to reveal that some feared they pursued Hanuvar himself, lest the populace panic. Rumor had it one of the most frightened was the emperor himself. Vennian gripped Evara's right arm. "Pull yourself together and report."

She remained entranced, even when he shook her. "Dead, dead, all three are dead and he will not flee until he kills us all." She let out a strange, tittering laugh, her eyes rolling. Vennian slapped her.

She gasped, blinked her eyes, felt her reddened cheek.

"I've told you to control your outbursts," Vennian snapped.

Fire blazed briefly in her dark eyes before she resumed her inscrutable demeanor.

Vennian's rage boiled close to the surface. "What did you see?"

"A moment. Let me sort my thoughts." Evara's speech was slightly slurred from the root.

"She is a seeress, isn't she?" the mayor asked, his voice climbing. "Have you brought a witch into my villa?"

Vennian had no patience for this sort of nonsense. Teeth gritted, he looked over his shoulder at the fat mayor, his sluggish wife, and their slack-jawed son. "She recanted and puts her powers to use for the emperor. Do you question the judgment of one of the emperor's officers?"

"No, I—"

The old slave ran in and bent at the mayor's side, his calm shattered.

"Master, there's a body near the sacrificial platform. A man in a uniform." His gaze flicked toward Vennian. "A Revenant."

While the mayor asked for more details, Vennian snarled at Evara. "Do you have anything that's useful? At all?"

"If I can touch something Hanuvar's touched," Evara said, "I might be able to find him."

Vennian brusquely bid farewell to the mayor and gathered his two officers. Once more garbed with helms and swords, wrapped in heavy cloaks, he left with them and the witch and the alarmed old slave. Some of the mayor's guard turned up, so unnerved by the presence of the Revenants they looked uncertain if they wanted to help or run. Vennian sent them to keep the crowd back and look for suspicious people.

Snowflakes swirled through the dusky sky as the old slave led them. His dignified manner gone, he babbled about how he'd been carrying the first platter when he spied the corpse.

Between the villa and the cliffside lay a grassy sward and dozens of smoking pools of water. Five hundred feet away, the cliff edge had been fenced with stone so drunken guests wouldn't stumble off the mountain.

Pertian, the more seasoned of Vennian's two officers, spoke gruffly. "I still don't see how he could sneak around without being seen. Until the guards called guests away, this place was crawling with people."

"Not so many," Vennian objected. "And most were well drunk and keeping to the mineral baths or the firepits."

"There it is, officers," the old slave said, pointing to the cliff's edge.

Near one of the wooden decks that projected out from the cliff, the headless body of one of his men was stretched out on the ground with a hand aimed toward the view. Sitting on a chair upon one narrow projection was what Vennian first took to be an empty helmet.

It wasn't empty, though, and the old slave knew it. He bent over and retched.

Pertian considered the body with casual interest. "This is Telian. Look at those hairy knuckles."

Vennian squeezed Evara's shoulder. "You said you could gain information if you touched something the impostor has handled. He's clearly handled this body."

She shook her head. "I want that." She pointed to a placard now visible against the chair legs on the platform. "Touching the body might overwhelm me with the pain of Telian's last moments and then I'd be useless for at least a quarter hour."

Vennian bit back a retort suggesting she was already useless and barked for Garnan to retrieve the placard. The younger officer grunted his assent, flexed hands in his fingerless gloves, and started forward, hand to hilt.

"Watch to the left," Vennian ordered Pertian. "I'll watch to the right. Let's follow on his heels in case the impostor's lying in wait. Old man, cease your vomiting and head in."

As he, Pertian, and Evara followed Garnan toward the cliff side, Vennian heard music and laughter rising from the main street. The common folk had let nothing interfere with their own celebrations.

Garnan stopped just beyond the projecting wooden deck and its chair, contemplating the slack-jawed face framed by the helmet.

"What does the sign say?"

"I can't quite make it out." Garnan stepped onto the planks and bent to retrieve the placard.

The wood creaked ominously, then splintered. Garnan rose, started to turn, but the entire projection dropped out of sight, taking him with it. Garnan's scream of terror receded for a long while.

Vennian spun on Evara, hand raised to slap her. "Why couldn't you see that coming?"

She cowered, lifted a hand to block, then lowered it. "The effects of the tarva don't last long! You know that!"

"There's someone moving over there," Pertian cried. "You! Stop!"

Looking away from Evara, Vennian spied a figure dashing into the mists to their left.

Pertian sprinted after, unsheathed gladius in hand. Vennian followed, threading through drifting snowflakes and wafting smoke from the mineral pools. Pertian still shouted for the figure to halt. Vennian had lost sight of their quarry and simply followed his soldier.

Suddenly Pertian dropped from sight with a cry. Vennian slowed to a jog, fearing a pit lay hidden amongst the grounds. But Pertian lived still and called to him. The officer was being jerked backward on his stomach by some unseen force. He clawed for purchase in well-trimmed grass as he was hauled toward a smoking mineral pit.

Dashing after, Vennian perceived a rope wrapped about his companion's ankle. A snare. He also saw the wooden barricade emblazoned with skulls and a red warning sign lying face up as Pertian was dragged past it toward the smoking pool. The mayor had told them a handful of the mineral pools were scalding hot, or worse, and used only for special sacrifices.

Vennian saw Pertian's eyes bulge in fear as the rope dragged him over the crusted ledge and into the wide circular pool. He screamed as his legs hit, and then the whole of his body dropped in with a splash and a soft sizzle. No other sounds followed.

Bile rising in his throat, Vennian stepped back from the searing steam, searching the grounds. He started at a sound behind him. The witch approached, panting from the run.

"Can you manage anything useful now?" Vennian demanded. "If you can't, you'll regret it for the rest of your days!"

"He's over there." Evara pointed toward a little outbuilding on the edge of the mineral baths, near a smoldering firepit. "On that roof."

"Go get the guards," Vennian snapped. He closed on the shack, stopping at the firepit to grab a torch. As he hurried forward, an arrow from the roof narrowly missed his throat. He varied his course, teeth gritted. Two more arrows slashed down from the dark-cloaked figure atop the shed, each perilously close. But his luck held. Reaching the side of the building, he dropped the torch at its base. He dove away as another arrow quivered in the ground at his feet.

The wood was old and dry and flared up instantly. Red flame soared heavenward and a rush of heat spread. Here, too, there was a single scream.

Vennian backed away, searching the darkness. If the scream had come from the impostor, his fate had finally caught up to him.

The witch drew up beside him once more. "I thought I told you to get the guards," he said, watching the flame.

She put a hand to his shoulder. "I was worried about you," she said, which was pleasing, and a little surprising. So was the sword she drove into the back of his neck.

His arms flailed and his legs collapsed beneath him. He fell sideways and glared, scrabbling for one of her booted feet. She stepped out of range, her eyes shifting back and forth between him and the villa. As he died, he saw the snarl of hatred on her lips, though he couldn't hear her words. He was dead by the time she drove one of the arrows into the wound where she'd stabbed him.

4

The cave was very different from the soft beds they'd known for the last few days, but the fire near the cave mouth was warm and the supplies they'd brought from the feast were wonderfully fresh. Survival would grow more challenging as they advanced into the mountains and were reduced to dry rations. Though Hanuvar had never expected to retrace his old route through the Ardenines, he well knew the way, just as he knew that they attempted a crossing later in the season than advisable. It was possible, it just wasn't simple. But then little he had accomplished had ever been simple.

Antires jotted notes on a parchment in the code he'd devised. Hanuvar had discouraged him from committing anything to paper, lest their identities be revealed if they were ever searched. But Antires insisted on recording the most important details as they took place.

As ever, Hanuvar chafed at the delay and wished he were the sorcerer his enemies thought him so he could magick them both over the mountainside. His greatest fear was not his own death, but that the remnant of his people, held in slavery by the Dervani, would perish in the long days before he could cross the Ardenines, reach Derva, and carry out his ambitious scheme. Likely some died every day. But those who could hold out might stand a chance, so long as he kept moving. Each day, each week, took him a little closer.

At the tread of footfalls outside the cave, he put hand to a spear. A woman's voice called softly above the moan of the wind. "I know you're in there. I've come alone. To talk."

He stepped from the firelight. He'd never heard Evara's voice, but he guessed her identity on the instant. The Revenant he'd questioned had said the witch was like a magical bloodhound.

"Come forward." He held the spear ready in both hands.

She stepped into the cave mouth, cloak-shrouded shoulders hunched against the cold. She was small and of early middle-years. The firelight harshened the lines of her face. She pulled a dark scarf from her chin and mouth. Her eyes held the weary, hunted look of someone worn down by combat or great stress. Hanuvar nodded to Antires. The scholar threw on his cloak and stepped past her to peer outside.

The woman came forward and he lowered the short spear, though he did not drop it. Her eyes met his, their deep honey brown reflecting the flickering scarlet flame. She started, then blinked in surprise. "I didn't..." her voice trailed off.

"No one's out there," Antires said as he stepped back inside. "Not that I can see, at least."

Hanuvar considered the woman. "Are there others with you?"

"No. They think you were killed. Who really died in the blaze?"

"I left one of the Revenant's bodies." He'd wanted one or two witnesses to think he'd died and had been much obliged when the Revenant trivon supplied the flame. "Why are you here?"

"I thought..." She shook her head.

Curious. He stepped back, gesturing to their little fire. "Come. You look cold."

She hesitated, then walked in and put her hands above the blaze, continuing to stare at him.

"I saw you kill the Revenant," he said.

"Yes. I told the mayor and his guards you'd been killed."

"Well, that's good," Antires said.

She paid the playwright no heed. "I steered them toward you, you know. To make sure you got them. I don't know that they would have advanced onto that outlook if I hadn't pretended I needed something you had touched. How did you manage to pull it down?"

"He climbed down the face," Antires explained, his pleasure in his friend's cleverness manifest. "He found some weak support beams. He tied a rope to the last one and looped it around a winch, then concealed himself and waited for their arrival. Choose the ground where you mean to fight, and lead your enemy to it," he added, quoting Hanuvar.

"And you had a snare readied," she said to Hanuvar.

"You're staring at him," Antires said. "Is that because you just now decided he really is who they feared?"

"No." She spoke without hesitation. "I knew. I think Vennian might have known, but he didn't want to admit it."

"Then why do you keep staring at him?"

"Because..." Finally she looked to Antires and addressed him directly. "His aura's all wrong. The Revenants—there was so much red and black... It's what I see now when I look in the mirror. But him." She pointed to Hanuvar. "I don't understand." She took a step closer and stared into his eyes. "You're a killer. Thousands, tens of thousands, died in your wars. The men you murdered today...I don't understand."

"What does my aura look like?" Hanuvar asked.

"It's almost completely golden," she said as if doubting her own words. "How can a murderer have a golden aura?"

"You're asking the wrong man. I'm a killer because I'm a soldier. And I was a general because I found no one who could manage better."

"Manage what? Killing?" Sword-sharp challenge rang in her voice.

"No."

"He means fighting to keep the Dervan yoke from his people," Antires clarified.

Hanuvar had no interest in justification. "Why did you seek me out?"

Her answer was a while in coming. "I've seen things. They've done things to me... I've done things. I've had to." She shook her head. "No, I didn't *have* to. I could have let them kill me, but it would have been a terrible death and I was afraid." She continued bitterly. "I've revealed the hiding places of women who knew nothing of any kind of magic, just the miracle of childbirth and a little herb lore. Many of them died horribly, after terrible treatment. All so I could keep on living."

Hanuvar understood then. "You thought I would kill you. Quickly."

"Yes."

Antires mouthed a curse. "You want to die, but meant him to take your life, so you wouldn't go to the afterlife of the suicides."

She nodded.

Antires's handsome face twisted into an ugly mask. "Did you think to fool the gods?" His voice was heavy with scorn. "Do you think they don't know what lies within your heart? That they couldn't know you engineered your own death?"

Her expression sagged. Perhaps she hadn't considered that.

"You're free now," Hanuvar told her. "We mean to cross the Ardenines. You could come with us and begin a new identity in some little town. Practice your gifts as you will."

Her head drew back. "Closer to Derva?"

"There are many remote places, even there."

"The Revenants will find me."

"Something will find us all, in the end. We can make long term plans, but face each day's obstacle as it presents itself."

Antires nodded. "Come with us. We've need of friends."

"What is it you mean to do?"

Antires looked over to Hanuvar, then answered for him. "He won't tell me. He can't, in case we get separated and I get captured. But I know it's going to be fit for an epic."

"You're going to kill the emperor."

Hanuvar laughed, though without humor. "No, that wouldn't help my people."

"He's going to do something that will aid the survivors. I'm not sure what, but I'm sure a woman with your gifts could help."

She shook her head and backed toward the cave mouth.

"You don't have to do anything," Hanuvar said. "But you can join us on our trip over the mountain. Come back to the fire."

"No. It's too late for me. The hand of doom's been on my shoulders for long months. I'm glad I could bring Vennian down before me, and by my own hand." She met his eyes resolutely. "If I go with you, it will make it easier for them to find you." She took a single step backward. "Farewell, Hanuvar. May the gods watch over you."

She turned and sprinted from the cave.

Hanuvar darted after, only to meet a gust of icy snow. He stepped back to grab his cloak, threw it over his shoulder, and headed into the storm. He stopped as a white swirl blinded him, for he knew the trail's edge loomed near. His vision cleared and he stepped forward, only to see her scarf, blowing free down the mountain side.

A REAL LLYWELYN SCONE

Mike Jack Stoumbos

Dafydd squinted at the plum pit pinched between his thumb and forefinger, whose wrinkles had been painstakingly cleaned of every bit of stick and slime that could alter its flight. It had been a tasty plum, not the stuff to inspire songs and stories perhaps, but it had served its purpose by supplying nearly symmetrical ammunition. All Dafydd needed was a target and a bit of luck.

The approaching clack and crunch of wooden wheels on the hard-packed path signaled an incoming target, an unsuspecting merchant and his wagon, traveling along the peninsula's coast road toward the mainland. Dafydd and his cousins Brynn and Bronn prepared for yet another round of the only sport in the little village of Gwynned.

His mouth still messy with plum nectar, Bronn took three steps and heaved his pit, shoving it like a heavy stone. It sailed through the air and struck the trotting horse on the bottom. The horse twitched in irritation but continued to pull its cart and driver. "Ha!" exclaimed Bronn. "Beat that."

Brynn, typically loath to follow the directions of her brother, obliged. She slung her plum pit in a practiced arc, like a precision spear, and struck the carriage itself. The driver looked in their direction.

Both Bronn and Brynn dropped to the ground, invisible behind the crest of the hill, leaving only Dafydd, ready with pit in hand.

The driver raised his fist at the boy and exclaimed some unflattering things in a thick dialect, then urged the horses a little faster, cursing Dafydd to miss by virtue of an unthrown pit.

"Tough break, 'Fydd," said Brynn. She had already selected another plum to munch.

"You can always try the next one," suggested Bronn.

Dafydd turned his eyes to the road. As luck would have it, another carriage approached from the opposite direction, this one much bigger, which meant it would be easier to hit. Having never succeeding in making contact, Dafydd would take any advantage afforded him. And he was confident that today would be different. He had been training, meditating, and drinking awful herbal teas that were supposed be good for nimble fingers. He had listened to the encouraging remarks of his Aunt Ffion that he was not uncoordinated but merely distractible; he had purposefully *not* internalized comments from his Uncle Olwydd that he was cursed by a bit of the bad luck on his departed father's side.

He tried to draw inspiration from the tales of his ancestors' dragon-facing daring-dos, of which he knew every allegedly-true word.

Dafydd prepared to combine the forms of both cousins—to use the force of Bronn and the form of Brynn—which was easier than trying to invoke the heroes of old, whose descriptions were always too general to emulate. Sure, they were mighty or clever or profound, but not one of them had left a manual of *how* to actually do any of the things that had made them famous. Despite memorizing the stories, Dafydd wouldn't know the best method to assault a mighty beast or brew an alchemical poison or even to bake an allegedly life-changing pastry. But he was almost certain he could learn to throw.

The boy was all set up to land the pit right on the red scrub-brush of the driver's shiny bronze hat when Brynn interrupted him.

"'Fydd, wait!" Brynn had noticed that the driver wore a helmet and cape, and that the carriage flew a golden lion flag.

"It's a soldier!" warned Bronn.

Any child knew better than to throw at a foreign soldier. Without a standing army, the people of Gwynned feared any casual campaign into their homeland. They survived by paying the occasional tribute, having little of value, and not antagonizing those with bigger swords.

Dafydd, however, was already mid-stride. He tried to halt, but his foot slipped on the dewy hilltop. He flailed his arms to catch his balance and let go of the pit, which sailed up high toward the road. Dafydd, still slipping, tried to jump and reach for the innocent projectile and lost his footing completely.

He skipped, stumbled, tripped, tumbled, and rolled down the hill toward the road, landing in a jumble.

The driver called "Whoa!" and the horses cantered to a halt.

Dafydd lifted his face from grass and dirt and whatever else had made its way to the sides of the road just in time for the plum pit he had thrown to knock him on the head.

The driver scowled down at Dafydd from under his helmet, but then the scowl twitched, broadened, and turned into a laugh. Seeing that Dafydd was no threat to anyone but himself, the well-armored driver continued forward along the coast road, toward the tip of the Llyn peninsula and the heart of Gwynned.

Bronn and Brynn skidded down the hillside to help Dafydd to his feet, all of them keeping their eyes on the carriage, which was quite a bit grander than most of what they saw sail or drive by their village. It was drawn by six horses, layered in metal for decoration as well as armor, and must have been big enough to fit twelve strong men.

"What do you suppose they want?" asked the incredulous Dafydd, for he had never before seen such a display of wealth or weapon come to their forgettable village. After all, it had been generations since anyone from Gwynned had done something worthy of song.

* * *

"There was a time," grumbled his Uncle Olwydd, "when the only people we had to fear came from the coasts we could see. After a minor scuffle or two on the borders, we'd drink, shake hands, and act like neighbors again. But *now* we have these strange boat people in fancy metal tunics. Gwynned is at the mercy of the whims of foreigners and all of their confusing appetites."

"It could just be a hospitality call," said his Aunt Ffion, as she continued to scrub at Dafydd's muddied shirt. "Or maybe they lost their way and need to be pointed north or south."

"No, I can feel it," Olwydd insisted. "It's going to be a tribute call. Bigger than the others."

"But they can't think that we have much to give!" With a splash into the basin, she added, "And I can't work through this stain.

Dafydd, you're gonna have to borrow something of Bronn's tonight. Everything else is dirty or torn."

The shivering boy did not protest that Bronn's things were all too big for him, or that an oversized shirt could look quite a bit worse than a torn one.

"It's just rotten luck that I tripped," he grumbled.

Ffion caught the comment and turned a sympathetic eye. "Yes, but count yourself fortunate that the soldier passed you by. Often with some bad luck comes some good. You just have to be willing to see it. Tell him so, 'Wydd."

Olwydd, the pap of the family, had been doing his best to spy out the window, but he had no choice but to agree with his wife. "True! Very true, Dafydd."

Ffion placed one fist on her hip and cocked her head in annoyance. "An example, 'Wydd?"

"Right, yes!" floundered Olwydd. "We all miss your mum, but we got you!"

Ffion put the other fist on the other hip. Olwydd sensed a bit of bad luck coming his way later, but that would have to wait until after the assembly at the Grand Lodge.

* * *

The Lodge was the largest building in all of Gwynned and could host the whole populace—not that this was much of a feat. At its highest point, however, it barely stood taller than the impressive foreign carriage.

Dafydd, whose borrowed sleeves hung well past his wrists, couldn't help but gawk at the fine metalwork on the contraption, right down to the wheel covers and the armor on the horses. Fancy metal was a rarity in the little village of Gwynned these days, though he had been told it was once as abundant as cause to use it.

The people of Gwynned milled inside the Lodge.

The village elder, Treffor, wore his beard wispy, his 'stache bristly, and his head bald, and he communicated with furtive smiles and worried eyes. He did not give answer or introduction to the imposing figure in the center of the room, whose appearance would make the people rethink the term *grand* and no longer apply it to their Lodge.

The foreign Lord wore red and gold and looked neither weary nor stained by travel. His impressive jaw was clean-shaven and supported a grin. He stood in front of rather than behind his guards and addressed the congregation of Gwynned.

"Hello, my new friends!" he called in a warm, brassy voice. "I come to you today as an outsider, but I hope in the near future to be a protector as we unite our lands."

The people of Gwynned shifted nervously.

"Upon my first visit to the Llyn peninsula in the shadow of the three peaks, I have but one humble request."

Gwynnedians braced for the worst. Would it be a trial by combat? A wedding to the loveliest daughter of their people? Four-fifths of every product produced and ten-tenths of every penny earned?

"It is my wish to try..." he curled the corner of his mouth into an almost sinister grin "...a *real* Llywelyn scone."

A ripple went through the crowd—undoubtedly everyone who had been holding their breath either inhaled or exhaled. Most felt relief, some were surely plagued by confusion, and only a select few had any traces of dread. A rare few felt excitement, but Dafydd was one of them. Every Gwynnedian, from tiny tot to ancient relic, knew the secret ingredient required in a real Llywelyn scone.

Elder Treffor spread his arms magnanimously and covered the short distance between himself and the foreign Lord. At such close proximity, it was abundantly clear that the Lord stood at least a whole head taller than the little villager. But with the confidence of years and wisdom behind him, he declared, "Of course! Of course, we shall make you a real Llywelyn scone."

"Excellent!" announced the Lord, as if it were a sweeping proclamation. "I have heard stories of this fine delicacy for which your people are famed. Why, my father said it was the best thing he ever tasted from coast to coast."

There were some murmurs and nods of *yes* and *of course*. This time, Dafydd was not one of them.

"I will be traveling across the channel and back this way over the next two days. But on the third day, I shall return. Is that enough time to prepare a Llywelyn scone?"

"Of course!" Treffor gesticulated wildly, attempting to rouse enthusiasm from his neighbors. "Of course, we shall have a Llywelyn scone when you return."

The foreign Lord flashed a toothy grin, which glinted nearly as brightly as the reflections of his armored chest. "I look forward to it!" He gave one curt hand-signal, and the visitors marched out without another word.

Soon the sound of a whip led to hoofbeats and the clacking of wheels on stone. After even those drifted away, the Gwynnedians were left alone in their slightly-less-than-Grand Lodge, with only the noise of drafts and distant seabirds to keep them company.

It did not take long for the silence to turn into whispers, then grumbles, and finally into all parties yelling over one another. To an outsider, it might have sounded like random rabble, but the locals, especially the old ones, knew the question on everyone's mind:

"How do we choose who to send to Y Draig Aur?" They fretted, they sobbed, they bellowed—all different variations of the same question. Who would be sacrificed for the sake of a Llywelyn scone?

A loud note through a freckled ram's horn silenced the people. Treffor took a deep breath and swelled his ribcage as big as he could—perhaps to recover from blowing the horn. He wrung his hands and regarded his shoes. "Well then!" Now that he had the floor, he did not quite know what to do with it. He attempted a weak smile. "Um... does anyone have any suggestions?"

The suggestions were so plentiful that the horn had to be blown again. A little order was restored, but not much agreement, as each idea could be shut down with a rational remark.

One fisherman might say, "The life of one of our people is too high a price to pay for a scone!"

A shepherd would reply, "But it's a small price for the protection and good graces of well-armored Lords."

Then a carpenter could say, "Why not bake him a scone without dragon tears? He'd never know the difference!"

And a tailor would ask, "Do we dare risk the ruse?"

"Impossible!" As one of the few who had been around for every one of the Brothers Gruffydd, Treffor explained, "You cannot fake a Llywelyn scone! You cannot shortcut it and hope it will succeed. The dragon tears are more than a minor seasoning or icing, they are essential for the process.

"First, you need the tears to churn into the butter, making it richer than any mere dairy. Second, the dragon tears activate the flour, causing it to ripple and rise. Third, the dragon tears melt the sugar into a glaze, finishing the scone as the gods and Llywelyn kings of old intended!"

After that, no one objected to the objective: Gwynned needed a real Llywelyn scone to appease the real foreign Lord, which meant that they needed the tears of the terrifying Draig Aur. Although they couldn't agree on the steps or the methods, it was difficult to argue their way out of a human sacrifice.

Perhaps because they were not yet worn down by the winds and salts of age, the children and the nearly-adult had a different course in mind.

Dafydd and his cousins were keen on the idea of sending another champion.

Even though it wasn't her turn, Brynn said, "Don't be daft! No one needs to be sacrificed."

"That's right!" added Bronn. "We'll pick a champion like in the songs and stories."

Despite doubtful murmurs, Treffor took the opportunity to regain the floor.

"Well, why not? After all, it's been done before. As descendants of the Great Gruffydds and tellers of their tales, our village is most apt for the task." He held up his hand with three fingers raised and declared, "Three times in living memory have our people gathered the tears of Draig Aur without a sacrifice. And three times, we have made the most wonderful, authentic, traditional Llywelyn scones to be smelled and loved along both coasts and well into the mainland.

"Back in the early days of songs and heroes, our noble leader, Gruffydd the Mighty, broke the cycle of sacrifices. As the strongest man in the lands, he strode right up to the golden dragon and popped him so hard on the nose that he cried out two jars worth of tears. The people made enough Llywelyn scones for days of feasting."

Nods and murmurs of agreement rippled through the crowd.

"Then his brother, Gruffydd the Clever, continued the legacy. With his superb wit and knowledge of every herb, he whipped up a poultice so potent that the dragon's eyes watered out five jars of tears and kept the people in Llywelyn scones for weeks."

A few hardy *"Hear, hear!"*'s were heard.

"And then *his* brother, Gruffydd the Profound, topped them all. As the finest orator the coasts have ever known, he recited *The Incomparable Tragedy* with such conviction that the dragon wept out *ten* jars of tears. The people made Llywelyn scones for months."

A *"yip"* and a *"whoop"* sounded from the inspired throat of each Gwynnedian, of whom Dafydd may have been the loudest.

But then Treffor's eyes blinked out glistening tears of his own. His shoulders dropped and his head drooped in shame.

"But after the success of the Great Gruffydds, the people didn't want to go back to sacrifices for scones. And when the last of the Great Gruffydds set off on the sea in search of greater glories than could be found in Gwynned..." The elder sighed.

The people had not known a real Llywelyn scone in years.

None of the children who wanted a champion had any memory of the fruits of those labors. After all, the Brothers Gruffydd had left for more interesting shores before many of their parents were born. And since that time, no one from Gwynned had dared wake Y Draig Aur.

Dafydd searched the Lodge. He did not see anyone mighty, clever, or profound enough to coax tears from a dragon, especially not a very old dragon with, most likely, very high standards.

Sure, Bronn was big and Brynn was quick-witted, but could they be the stuff of legends? And Dafydd himself—well, even if he could recite most of the stories by heart, he was far from profound.

Treffor cleared his throat. "Do we have a...volunteer champion?"

The silence was much heavier, thicker, and harder to endure this time. It was the kind of silence that could make men faint and women miscarry if allowed to last too long.

Then Dafydd had an idea—not to volunteer, for that would be absurd. His hand shot up and he expressed one syllable: "Ooh!"

"Yes? Dafydd?" wondered Treffor. "Are you...volunteering to be our champion?"

Dafydd quickly withdrew his hand. "No. That would be absurd." But now that all eyes were on him, he gave out his idea. "We could cast lots. After all, even the first Brother Gruffydd was selected by lot to be sacrificed."

It was not so much that people agreed with him. Rather, they could not come up with any alternative on short notice.

With some reluctance, Treffor waved his approval and indicated that Dafydd should go collect the large clay pot from the pedestal. Even an elder could fear his own name coming up, but he could not outright dismiss so old a tradition as casting stones for scones.

The pedestal at the edge of the room was probably the fanciest thing there, made of some kind of imported, polished stone. And the pedestal held a pot, an ornate ceramic container that may have been closer to a jug or an urn. As no one knew a more technical name, they simply called it a *pot*.

The pot contained a few dozen flat stones, each marked with the name of every able-bodied Gwynnedian. Only a few decades ago, this would have been used to determine who would be sacrificed. For all of Dafydd's life, casting lots from the pot was merely a way of selecting who would have to do the jobs that no one wanted to volunteer for.

Dafydd picked up the pot in both hands and pivoted to return to the center of the Lodge. That is, he *tried* to pivot, but one of the overly long sleeves caught the decorative carving of the pedestal and jerked him back. The pedestal was too heavy to move more than a wobble, but the pot, held by only one hand, continued forward, tipping and slipping with glacial speed.

Dafydd yanked his arm free from the captive sleeve and tried to reach his hand out from under the tunic to assist him in catching the slipping pot. Though tangled in the folds of fabric, his hand found an opening and pushed. A loud *rip* sounded as Dafydd's fist widened what would have stayed a tiny hole in the fabric, with enough force that he lost control of his own arm and swatted the pot not only off-balance but into the air.

Apart from gasps and a few furtive shouts, the crowd stood too shocked to react, with none willing to disrupt the flying stones.

The pot hit the ground and split, spraying its contents across the floor.

By remarkable chance, every stone landed facedown, so that the individual's mark was not visible. All except for one: a small, smooth, recently-painted stone, which continued to spin and wobble, until it came to rest face-up right between the split halves of the pot.

Dafydd, still tangled in his cousin's tunic, only needed to see others' faces to confirm the name on the stone.

"No! Not Dafydd!" said Ffion. "He's far too young!"

"Aye! Not Dafydd!" echoed Olwydd. "Did you see what he just did with only a sleeve to worry about?"

In truth, it would have been hard for anyone to see Dafydd as the champion of their village, but it was much harder to argue against such a display of fate.

Bronn tried to assure him. "You know the stories! You can just do what the Gruffydds did."

Brynn took the more logical approach. "If that doesn't work, human sacrifice is a solid backup plan."

There were nods and murmurs of agreement.

Before Dafydd could protest that it was rotten luck, Ffion tried to reassure him that something positive could come of it.

Olwydd remarked, "Good thing there's no time to overthink it."

***

A trip to the mountain and back with enough time to prepare a perfect Llywelyn scone with dragon tears demanded a tight schedule. Dafydd would have to leave as soon as possible. While Ffion prepared the boy's travel gear, Olwydd, Brynn, and Bronn rapidly scoured the village for any items the boy might need in order to coax a tear from the great Draig Aur on the top of the middle mountain Eifl that loomed over Llyn peninsula.

"I'm sure it will be just like the stories," Ffion said, putting the last stitch in one of Dafydd's torn shirts. "And you know the stories so well, Dafydd. Isn't it fortunate that you have the examples of the Gruffydds to follow?"

Dafydd shrugged. "I don't know if I can punch a dragon or brew a whatever-it's-called."

"But you know every word of *The Incomparable Tragedy*, and you say it so well!"

"What if that doesn't work?"

The answer came in the form of Bronn tromping into the room, bearing a dusty collection of leather and crude metal.

"Here!" he said, handing over the large, armored glove. "I found you a goblet from the old Gruffydd stuff."

"Isn't that a gauntlet?"

"Yes, you can wear the goblet when you punch the dragon."

Dafydd accepted the gauntlet, noting that—like most things he got from Bronn—it was too large for him. But it was heavy enough that it might be able to make a dent in a dragon, so he accepted it graciously.

Brynn strode through the door a moment later, with the next offering, which grew suspiciously in smell as she got closer.

"Here," she said, pinching the smelly, wrapped poultice between two fingers. "You can hurl this at his nose and make him cry."

"What is it?" Dafydd lifted one flap of the fabric covering the poultice. His own eyes stung with tears. "Where'd you get that?"

"I asked the worst gardener and the best chef in the village for the stinkiest and spiciest thing they had."

"This is an onion."

"Yeah, it's an onion, but it's doused in spices and starting to rot! It might not be a magic eye-stinging potion, but it's pretty close."

Dafydd was not keen on accepting the spiced, rotting the onion, but Brynn clearly wasn't taking it back.

The clinks and clacks of ceramic jars accompanied Uncle Olwydd's return. "I managed to get a clean jar from almost every family," he said.

He opened the sack for Dafydd to see.

With both hands full, Dafydd peered inside. "There's got to be a dozen!" His elation was cut short by a realization. "I'll be lucky if I even get one."

"Not necessarily," said Ffion. "Why, you have three methods going for you, where the Gruffydds each used one."

"First, you crack him hard with the goblet," advised Bronn.

"Then, you assault his nostrils with the onion," added Brynn.

"And if that doesn't work, you hit him with the *Tragedy*," finished Ffion.

So Dafydd gained a sack of jars, a final addition to his quest.

Bronn and Brynn eagerly agreed to help him carry the vessels there and back—to the opening of the tunnel and not a step further.

* * *

As they journeyed up the peninsula toward the mountain, Dafydd practiced reciting *The Incomparable Tragedy*. He moved Bronn to tears first with the power of the story itself, then Brynn when she got sick of hearing it.

As they snaked their way up the foothill slopes of Mount Eifl, Brynn and Bronn took turns speculating about the true size, shape, color, and ferocity of Y Draig Aur, whom none of them had seen apart from vague illustrations and commentary from the elders.

The path to the tunnel was easy to follow and clearly marked by people who had gone before, sacrifices and heroes alike. Once they reached the entrance, Brynn and Bronn arranged the necessary items in the sack and roped it over Dafydd's shoulder.

"If you're going to get gobbled," Brynn said, "your best bet is to make like you're a fish and slip right down his gullet, missing the teeth altogether."

Dafydd only needed to consider this for a moment. "But then I'd have to wait to die slowly, starved of air, in his belly, while the acids and toxins pickle my skin!"

Brynn paused to consider. "On second thought, 'Fydd, better to make sure your head gets chomped by his molars so you get it over with quickly."

"Thanks, Brynn," said Dafydd, not feeling at all comforted.

"If you do get gobbled up, I'll write a song about you. A really, really good one," promised Bronn.

"Thanks, Bronn," said Dafydd, with a little more sincerity.

"You got everything in the sack?" asked Brynn.

Dafydd checked and confirmed. He did indeed have one gargantuan gauntlet, one pungent onion bomb, and several irregularly sized jars, just in case. "Yep."

"And you got all of *The Incomparable Tragedy*?" asked Bronn.

Dafydd indicated his skull. "Yep."

That, as they say, was that. Everything that could be prepared was prepared, and there was nothing to be gained by stalling.

Dafydd made his way into the tunnel on the side of the mountain, wondering how long it had been since a person had traveled through it. The passageway was wide enough for one man, or one boy with one bulky sack.

Dafydd squeezed around the bends and down the passage, but began to marvel as Y Draig Aur's gigantic cave opened before him. Once free of the crevice, he spent several full minutes staring slack-jawed at the beautiful stone dome, with rings of color and sparkling stalactites from uncountable years of housing the dragon. Dafydd could not begin to fathom the science and magic that made such compositions possible, but he could acknowledge that this mighty work rendered even the sky plain.

Dafydd felt like a mouse, or even an ant, as he imagined the golden dragon lying in wait.

But as he stared at the piles of old treasure, he realized that these riches were not nearly as rich as he had assumed. The sheer mass was beyond question, but this horde was covered in rust and dust and smelled like must. Clothing and armor which may once have been fine had fallen to the passage of time and lack of care. Dafydd resolved he would thank Ffion and tell her that she had been correct about hygiene—if he survived to journey home.

Dafydd reached into the sack and took out one jar he had brought to collect the dragon tears. He set it on the stone floor, where it emitted a tiny clink. He froze, but neither heard nor saw the great Draig Aur approaching.

Next, Dafydd unwrapped the onion, which immediately prickled his nostrils and tear ducts. He held the onion behind his back.

With his other hand, he reached into the gauntlet—the heavy, oversized, armored weapon thing—presumably worn by a Gruffydd.

But as he withdrew this weapon, Dafydd disrupted the jars enough that one toppled out of the sack. He had no way to effectively catch it, and so it clinked, clunked, rolled, and plunked along the cave floor, until it stopped against one of the piles of treasure.

Dafydd didn't dare breathe. He could hear someone else's breathing though, and the sound of old, rough scales grinding against one another and scratching the stone.

"Who goes there?" asked a low, rolling voice, composed in a throat too big to find a boy like Dafydd a satisfying meal.

Even so, Dafydd scrambled back, leaving the jars behind. He wedged himself into the crevice, just as he saw Y Draig Aur's wings approaching from behind one of the piles of treasure.

"No need to deny it," the dragon went on. "I heard your footsteps before you dropped the jar, and I can smell Gwynned all over you."

Dafydd was aware of the onion behind his back, but neither confirmed nor objected. A clawed foot, as long as Dafydd was tall, came into sight.

"You have come for my tears, have you not? For the missing ingredient for a pastry..." The dragon's face moved too quickly for Dafydd to rightly track, until his sharp eye was just an arm's length away from the opening of the crevice, looking directly in at Dafydd. "So trivial a thing for which to offer your life."

Dafydd probably ought to have been terrified, but his voice found him and he blurted, "I'm not here as a sacrifice!" He gasped at his own audacity and braced for the worst.

Instead, Y Draig Aur chortled, a throaty chuffing sound that was too soft for a roar. The eye withdrew from the opening, and the dragon positioned its face so it would be fully visible to Dafydd. "Indeed? Well, I'll say this for you, little one, you have courage. Even if it is contained in so small a package." The lizard lips drew back from its fangs in a smug smile, reminding Dafydd of the foreign Lord.

"So you're not here as a sacrifice," hummed the dragon. "Perhaps that is best. I cannot promise I would shed a tear over a snack such as you anyway."

"But wasn't that the deal? If Gwynned sacrifices a villager, you exchange a jar of tears?"

"And why," wondered the dragon, "would the death of a lowly Gwynnedian, trembling under the mountain, cause me to weep?"

"Um..." Dafydd wracked his brain, but he was pretty sure he had never heard an answer for this one. "Because you feel sympathetic?"

The dragon gave a short roar, so startling in volume that Dafydd did not initially realize it was a laugh.

"Sympathy! For the barbarians of Llyn peninsula? For the descendants of dragon slayers? No, tiny creature. I pay with tears because the taste of human flesh—especially that of a Gwynned, dusted with sea salt, smoked by cooking fires, and stuffed with mutton—is so unquestionably, incomparably wonderful that we dragons cannot help but weep for joy. That you find the taste of my tears to be equally incandescent is incidental. And exchanging jars of tears as part of the arrangement was a...gesture, if you will, for purposes of good relations, you understand."

"I don't think I do..."

Y Draig Aur sighed, a rumbling grumble made of leather drums and distant rolling waves. "My predecessors were foolish. They ate too many people and found themselves hunted. The longest-lived dragons are those who learned how to play with their food, how to seem like the beneficent gods in the mountains. Because if humans willingly sacrifice themselves—once, twice, thrice a year—there's no need to hunt, and no need to be hunted. To the greedy, who scrape through a finite resource, it soon disappears. But to the sensible and patient, the resource could continue to be replenished. Do you now understand?"

"I think so. But you haven't had a chance to taste a human for a really long time."

"True, ever since those cursed Gruffydds!" he snarled. "But I have been patient, and I can continue to be patient. After all, *you* are here. Tell me, insignificant Gwynnedian, how do you propose to gain my tears?"

"Well, by the methods of the great Gruffydds. I'll use my might, my cleverness, and my...my...profoundation."

"Profundity," the dragon corrected, amused. "But it does not matter. Perhaps, once you fail, the cycle of sacrifices will begin again. So, what will it be? Are you brave enough to face me?"

Dafydd stood in quiet contemplation, protected in the crevice, outside of the giant dragon's reach.

"Go home, little Gwynnedian. Tell your village that I will accept their future sacrifices." Y Draig Aur slowly began turning away, taking his eye off of Dafydd. "Perhaps when you grow up properly, you can be one of them."

Dafydd would not have been able to explain what precisely possessed him in the next moment. Perhaps it was the dragon's casual disregard, or maybe it was some sense of pride in his village or dread of the foreign Lord. In any case, Dafydd had made the decision and was moving before he had a chance to think himself out of it.

He charged out of the crevice with a bellow, scraping his shoulder against an errant snag of stone, hearing his own voice reverberating from all sides.

He pointed the oversized gauntlet straight ahead like a lance, ready to strike.

He drew the spicy onion back like a catapult, ready to lob.

And his yell began to form words, the opening phrases of *The Incomparable Tragedy*, which he was determined to recite correctly, without dropping a syllable or tying his tongue.

Dafydd should have put more focus on not tying his *feet* while running with gauntlet, onion, and oratory. His right foot found a loose coin, his left a scrap of leather. As each tried to recover for the other, both splayed, then skated. He tried to use his arms to find balance, but the heavy gauntlet pulled one side of his frame farther off-course, away from the genuinely surprised dragon.

When Dafydd finally lost his footing entirely, he began to tumble head over heel. He tried to swing toward the dragon, knowing that he was past the point of being able to pop him on the nose. The gauntlet caught and stuck in something that felt a lot more like rotting wood than dragon flesh.

Dafydd saw the stone floor racing toward him, so he used his other hand to guard his head from cracking open like the pot in the Grand Lodge. He had completely forgotten that the other hand was equipped with a slightly softened, very spiced onion, but a nose-first landing quickly reminded him.

To his credit, even when he was facedown in onion, Dafydd never stopped reciting *The Incomparable Tragedy*.

Y Draig Aur let loose a mighty roar that made every spider and worm in the cave tremble and could be heard halfway down the mountain.

Just outside of the tunnel, Brynn and Bronn regarded each other with worry.

"At least there will be a jar of tears for Gwynned," Brynn said.

* * *

The Grand Lodge looked a little grander when the foreign Lord returned. The fires were lit, and the few Gwynnedians blessed with some musical talent played their instruments. Most importantly, there were fresh Llywelyn scones—the dragon-activated flour, the dragon-churned butter, and the dragon-boiled glaze all doing their jobs precisely.

The foreign Lord was pleased, to be sure, but not half so satisfied as the Gwynnedians, many of whom had heard stories of the scones for a generation without having tried them.

Gwynnedians sat or stood in family groups. Uncle Olwydd, Aunt Ffion, and the cousins Brynn and Bronn clustered together, but Dafydd was not with them.

Instead, the boy stood on the small stage, with a work glove on one hand and a raw-but-not-overripe onion in the other. "But when I swung at the dragon," he explained, gesturing with the gloved hand, "I missed and stuck the gauntlet right into a rotting wooden shield!"

Snorts and barks of laughter rose up from his audience.

"When I fell, I tried to cover my face. I had to make sure I'd land in something soft." Dafydd only needed present the onion to elicit more and louder guffaws.

"Red-eyed, red-faced, and muffled by steaming onion, I kept right on reciting *The Incomparable Tragedy*," Dafydd told them, grinning at his own misfortune. "Well, even Y Draig Aur couldn't take any more. He let loose a roar like nothing I've ever heard before. He hooted and howled and flopped over onto the floor. Unable to contain himself, he laughed so hard he cried, spilling so many tears that even a dozen jars weren't enough!"

At this, the laughter turned into cheers.

There would be more stories to be told and songs to be sung, but Dafydd's tale and the scones he helped to fetch had put the foreign Lord in very good spirits. It seemed as if the people of Gwynned had laid the foundation for a wonderful relationship with a heavily-armed and well-moneyed outsider.

At the end of a long evening of merriment, the foreign Lord continued to praise the scones on his way out of the Grand Lodge and for much of the carriage ride back along the coastal road. "The stories were good too," he said, "especially that yarn about the dragon tears. Shame it's not more believable."

TENDER

R.S. Belcher

I had twenty-three minutes or less to get the gorgon her dream-marrow or it was going to be no charge and my manager was going to be pissed. It would come out of my pocket. No way! It wasn't my fault the contact at the hospital had taken longer than usual to siphon the marrow from the patients in the coma ward. Not my problem, brah. My Civic screeched around the corner as the light went from yellow to red—maybe it was orange. My nearly bald tires scrambled for traction on the wet road and I almost slid into a parked minivan. I corrected at the last second and kept on keeping on.

The navigation feature on the app pinged as I got closer and closer to the delivery address. It was a part of the software that only a driver or someone in management could access. The users just downloaded the app off the dark-web site and then placed their orders and paid in bitcoin. No-fuss, no muss.

I made turn after turn, delving deeper into a mostly dark residential neighborhood. This part of Saint Louis might be showcased in Better Homes and Meth Labs. Faded "for sale" signs jutted up among the uncut, trash-strewn lawns like weeds. Condemned notices shivered on doors in the autumn wind. Thirteen minutes left. My phone pinged again as I slowed. It was on this block. I had a .380 pistol in my jacket pocket. It wasn't for the customers—most of them wouldn't even be scratched by mortal steel—it was for the local predators, with a small "p." The company frowned on us carrying a piece, but there was no way in hell I was going to creep around the neighborhoods our customers tended to frequent without some kind of insurance policy.

The app informed me that I had reached my destination. It had been a beautiful home ninety years ago. Now, its roof was caving in and the great brick columns that lined the entrance patio were slowly turning to dust. The whole place was dark, uncontaminated by a hint of light. I parked and killed the engine. I did my usual gut-check. You'd have to be out of your mind to approach a place like this, knowing what was in there waiting, hungry, and not feel ice water in your stomach and bladder.

I did the quick calculation in my head that I always did: how much was I making for this run? How much would I lose if I punked out and didn't deliver the goods? And then there was the spiel they gave us at orientation. That usually cinched the deal for me, which of course was one of the reasons they had hired me in the first place. I climbed out of the Civic and retrieved the medical cooler from the trunk. It was always heavier than I expected it to be. Some dreams held more weight than others.

I started toward the door and then stopped, doubled back. I had almost forgotten the glasses. I fumbled around in the glove compartment and finally found them among all the junk that had accumulated in there over the years—a pair of old Ray-Ban sunglasses, wire-rims with big mirrored teardrops lenses, cop-style. I slipped them on, picked up the cooler, and checked the delivery app. Three minutes until I was out of time.

The stone path was strangled by weeds and with no light and the damn sunglasses on it was hard to see more than a step or two in front of me. I almost tripped, but I righted myself and made it to the patio. There was a tangle of broken, ancient garden equipment piled a few feet in front of the door. I side-stepped it and knocked on the door. It sounded like a hammer striking the gates of Heaven. I glanced down at my phone. One minute. Yes!

The front door flew open and I kept looking down at my feet. It was hard to do. Most fears diminish when confronted; this one killed you with a stray glance. I heard hissing, imagined the tiny forked tongues of the vipers darting in and out, spitting droplets of acid as they sensed me. Their breath reminded me of the stale air of ancient caves.

"The mirror thing doesn't work," she said, her voice like burbling water whispering across creek stones. "It's a myth."

"Yeah, I know. Better safe than sorry, right?"

"It does piss me off, though." All the S's were drawn out, like air escaping through a leak. If a gorgon saw its own reflection in a mirror, it didn't turn into stone, but it was painful to them, and it made them avert their own petrifying gaze from soft, non-ingenious, little, old me. "That the marrow?" I nodded. "You're late!"

"I'm not," I said, holding out the cooler. "Check the timer on the app." Hard nails ticked on a screen. The gorgon snarled and then the cooler was pulled from my hand. Cool, dry, smooth skin brushed against my own.

"No tip, asshole," she spit as the door slammed shut. Shocker. Gorgons were notoriously bad tippers.

By the time I got back in my car, the app was chiming a new order for pick-up and delivery. I glanced back at the dark, ramshackle house and imagined long, scaly hands ripping the lid off the cooler, fumbling with the semi-tangible stuff dreams were made of, frantically gobbling up bits of the claustrophobic, smothering nightmares of those trapped inside their own immobile bodies, like marshmallow fluff, sweet with voiceless screams.

I tossed the gorgon glasses back in the glove box and scanned the details of the order. My stomach churned as I read, full of biting eels. I cussed under my breath and pulled away from the curb. The clock was ticking again. "Fucking gods."

* * *

I'd needed a gig, anything to pay the bills. I'd lost my delivery hustle at Uncle Enzo's Pizza for smoking too much weed by the dumpster with the prep cooks. I tried my hand at a fast-food job and I lasted two days under a hair net and there was no way I was cutting my hair. Someone, a friend of a friend—I couldn't tell you who it was—had told me about this courier job they had heard about from a friend of a friend. You applied online, so I did. Then I got a strange message request a few days later. I accepted it and it told me to go to this site that was on the dark web. I started to get a bad feeling about this job, but I was intrigued, too. My only excursions on the dark web had been to occasionally buy some smoke. I got too paranoid about the whole thing though and soon stopped buying that way.

So, I booted up my Tor browser and went to the address the message directed me to. It was a black screen with a photo image of a dirty, rusted fork with a few of the tines bent. Beneath it was a white text box. I typed in my application code and then waited. Ten minutes later a message appeared on my screen: "Plug in your webcam. Let us see you." I felt the hair rise on my neck and I swallowed hard. Every Creepy Pasta I had ever read about human trafficking, serial killer hunt clubs, and organ harvesters swirled in my skull. But, like a dumbass, I did it. I stared into the camera and tried to look cool. After several long, uncomfortable, moments, a graphic of my Missouri driver's license popped up and I saw the electronic measles of points of recognition dance over my face and my three-year-old photo. How the hell had they got that? The screen went blank and I seriously had to fight myself not to shut the computer off, unplug it, and go hide under my bed. After five minutes, a message scrolled across the screen: "Verified. Good evening, applicant."

"Uh, hey," I said. That's how it all started.

* * *

I had forty-three minutes left to deliver. I pulled into the parking lot of a closed convenience store in Hyde Park. A locked, steel shutter had been rolled down over the store's doors and windows. A white work van waited, idling, its headlights catching the misting rain as it fell. I pulled up beside the van and the side door slid open as soon as I put the brakes on. A big guy in black whose hood obscured most of his face climbed out and helped a young girl down. She couldn't have been older than sixteen. She wore a white gown covered in red embroidered symbols. If I looked at the symbols too much they made it feel like snakes were slithering through my brain's grooves. I tried to just look at the kid's face and her menacing escort. He opened the passenger door and leaned the seat forward, struggling into the back. "The compact is fulfilled. Your masters have agreed to deliver the anointed one to her betrothal, to the faceless god's feast, as has always been the tradition."

"Yeah, I see on the app you're a long-time account. Gold card. Hop in and we'll get this over with."

"What is that stench?" he sniffed.

"Beer, pizza...mostly. Hey, watch that stuff in the back, man." The big goon shoved a bunch of boxes and some wadded-up clothes aside and sat, pulling the seat back into its normal position.

"The Vessel of Arruule shall sit here," he said to the girl. She smiled and nodded, sliding into the passenger seat.

"Cool," I said. "Shotgun!" They both looked at me like my head had just popped like a zit. Cultists, am I right? She closed the door, but it drifted open again. "You...you got to really slam it," I said to her. She had big green eyes and dark blonde hair. No makeup, no piercings.

"If you do not proceed in haste to the ordained site of the ritual, then Arruule, the Unseeable, the Duke of the Forgotten Second, High Lord and Creator of Anti-Time, He Who Is Hidden From the Tyranny of Causality, shall synchronize with this space-time and all that is, was, or ever shall be, will be annihilated!"

"Okay, cool," I said. "We have an hour or less or it's free guarantee and we've still got, like, thirty-nine minutes, right? So, no worries. This A-hole, or whatever he is, will get his grub, okay, man?"

"Arruule!" the big guy nearly screamed.

"Right, right." I looked over the girl. "Just give that door a really good slam this time okay?" She nodded, smiled, and slammed the door shut. I hit the gas and we spun out of the lot.

The drive was deadly silent, with only the app on my phone dinging every so often to remind me of the countdown. Finally, I glanced over to the girl. "You...uh, you good with all this?" She seemed to come out of a trance and glanced over at me. Her brow furrowed in confusion. "The whole human sacrifice to some weird-alien-god thing?"

"Oh, yes," she said, her smile growing wider. "I've been prepared by my parents for this since I was born at the appointed time and place. It's my purpose for existing—to feed the clock-eater and sustain the universe for another cycle until the next vessel is born. He devours me instead of time, itself." No doubt, no questioning, not even a trickle of fear. I figured I'd try again.

"You, uh, you ever been to a birthday party? An all-ages show? Tried on makeup when your mom told you you were too young? Had someone you loved in an 'all-crazy and fuck you, dad' kinda way? Any of that?" She looked confused again. "A pet? A puppy? A gerbil? A cat? A snake? Snakes are really freakin' cool!"

"Really?" the girl said, her face brightening at the notion of a snake.

"Silence!" the imperial buzzkill in the backseat bellowed. "Do not trouble the mind of the vessel with your secular nonsense. Her sacrifice will ensure the continuation of this space-time and your ilk's miserable existence along with that of the faithful."

"'Ilk?' Really? Why the fuck would you guys worship some cosmic pucker-nut that makes a rule that says kids have to suffer so it can chow down?" Before Darth Douchebag could answer, the girl spoke up.

"Oh, it's fine," she said. "I won't suffer at all. My glorious husband-to-be will pierce my chest with one of its stasis-edged tentacles. I won't feel a thing. And then he will liquefy and digest my heart. At the same time, he will generously fill me with venom that causes absolute euphoria." She patted my hand and I felt like throwing up. This poor kid. "I will die enraptured—far happier than I would ever have been if I had lived out my life."

"Says every heroin junkie ever," I said. "What if all that is bullshit, dogmatic propaganda? Why would some alien super-god give a shit if its lunch was a happy meal or not?" I saw a shadow cross the girl's face and discovered it was possible to feel worse than I was already feeling. I was most likely her only contact with the rest of humanity in her entire life not affiliated with the whack-a-doodle cult. I was the first dissenting voice she'd ever heard...and the last. I carried some weight despite the lifetime of indoctrination and dogma.

I glanced back. Her handler looked pissed at me and worried at her. There was emotion in that worry, maybe even love, in a really fucked-up way. I suddenly saw the resemblance for the first time. This was probably her dad or her uncle. I snapped my head back around. "Of course," I said, "nobody likes to eat meat full of fear and stress toxins, right? Free Range all the way! I bet the big guy does pump you up with some serious happy-juice."

"Really?" she asked, the cloud lifting from her innocent face.

I nodded. "Oh yeah. He's a god, right? Not just some sketchy, alien poser. He only gets to eat every, what, twenty years, so yeah! Top shelf all the way." She was smiling again, at ease. The universe was exactly the way she had been taught it was. Squiggly-tentacle-Jesus-Santa was real and benevolent and all was well in hentai heaven. Poor home-schooled kid.

The ritual site was inside a boarded-up old building in Riverview, north of the city. More big guys in hoodies stood near the entrance. They cradled assault rifles and scanned the darkness. I pulled up to the curb with ten minutes to go. One of the gun-guys opened the passenger door for the girl. She gave me a final, peaceful glance and climbed out. "I'll pray for you," she said, and she meant it. The hooded men hustled her away toward the building and her date with her groom.

The seat flipped up and dad, or whoever he was, climbed out of the backseat. He reset the seat and looked at me with red-rimmed eyes. "You have served your masters well and I shall make sure you are compensated well for your service." Thunder, echoing strangely, pealed across the storm-filled sky. Purple lighting danced among the brooding clouds and for a second I thought I saw a massive, writhing form illuminated against the bruised night.

I looked at the father and shook my head. "Only thing I want from you, pal, is a promise to stop having kids." I pulled the passenger door shut, made sure I slammed it real good in his face, flipped him off, and drove away.

Since the universe didn't end, I decided to celebrate by logging off the app for a little while and getting something to eat myself. I ended up at the Peacock Diner and got what I always got, the Loop Slinger with chili. I hung with the usual suspects: a bunch of off-duty bartenders, waiters, hacks, Uber, and Lyft drivers. We bitched about customers and tips and work schedules and management. I didn't mention I had been active for the last forty-eight hours. Ortiz, one of the independent hacks—a real solid guy—asked me again which food delivery company I worked for.

"Nobody you ever heard of before," I said with a dismissive wave. "They got what they call an exclusive clientele. Exclusive pain in my ass."

The old cabbie laughed and nodded. "Need to get you a *real* job, boy! You don't want to be my age making food runs for people too lazy to get up and at least walk to their car to fill their bellies, do you? You need a job with a future!"

"*Convenience*, Ortiz, old buddy, not laziness." He laughed. "Way of the future, man," I said. "Never underestimate the power of *Convenience*." I ordered one more cup of coffee for the road and got back to it.

* * *

"I've heard of you guys before," I said to the smarmy HR guy I met for the second round of interviews. Honestly, he gave me the creeps more than the anonymous interviewer on the dark web. "But it was spelled with an 'i,' not an 'e,' and isn't it like a hook-up app or something?"

Mr. HR laughed. It sounded prerecorded. "That's a very different company," he said. "No, what we do here is provide a premium, intimate, customized, gourmet experience to a very selective clientele on their schedule. We bring the banquet to them."

It sounded like corporate BS. The kind of thing only management and the dipshits on the training videos said. The word that stuck with me, even now, years later, was *intimate*. Dead on. It was intimate. That word used to evoke in me notions of sexy-time and words whispered in the darkness; soft sheets and softer skin. Now, whenever I heard intimate, something inside me trembled uncontrollably. Some things you didn't want to get too close to, ever.

* * *

The app chirped as soon as I went active. There was a backlog of orders. Fabulous. Enough to keep me busy until the end of my shift at dawn. I saw who was first up and I groaned a little. It was Genta. I pulled away from the curb and headed for the pickup.

Sato Genta lived in a long-closed old water-treatment plant over in Bissel Point. He was 472 years old and didn't have any friends as far as I knew. Given his habits, that was no surprise.

I had picked up the order from the Johnny B Goode Porta Potty compound. They were one of the legion of companies that worked with my employers. I struggled with two heavy, black, plastic, sloshing bags—industrial-grade debris sacks—with one hand and used my flashlight app on my phone with the other to navigate the underworld. The old treatment plant was a dark, cold maze of crumbling concrete tunnels and thick clusters of old pipes. To me, it seemed to change every time I delivered here. The place smelled of mold and the ghost of methane.

"Yo, Genta, it's me! I got your order, man." My voice echoed through the corridors. The only reply was the chorus of drips from the aging ceiling and the pipes. The darkness seemed to swallow everything, including my voice. I kept walking. "Don't pull that shit where you..."

A demonic face leered out of the darkness into the beam of my phone-light. Bile-green, pebbly skin and saucer-sized eyes of red loomed above a swollen bulb of a nose. A wide mouth filled with crooked, yellow fangs yawned open and a thick, rope-like tongue slithered toward me. I jumped and cussed, dropping one of the big black debris bags. Fortunately, it didn't burst. The devil-thing laughed, a high-pitched nasal sound. "Gotcha again!"

"Damn it, Genta! You made me drop your dinner." I patted my chest over my heart with my suddenly-free hand. "I hate it when you do that." Genta, who stood all of four and a half feet tall, chuckled. The laugh had a few snorts in it. He picked up the fallen bag and sniffed the plastic surface.

"Lighten up. Mmmmm, smells great. It fresh?"

My stomach clenched at the thought of the contents of the sack.

"Ugh, I guess." I handed him the other sack. "I try very hard to not think anymore about what you eat than I have to." That elicited another chuckle.

"You don't know what you're missing."

"Like I said, I don't want to know, my dude."

Genta was an Akaname—one of the Yokai, a low Japanese ghost-demon-thing. They were filth eaters, specifically, the filth that accumulated in bathrooms.

"Stay," Genta said. "I just got Disney+ and we can watch..."

"No offense man, but I cannot chill out with you while you, y'know...eat."

"Oh, come on, I'll share!" Genta began to slip one of the bags open. I started walking faster toward the exit. He stopped. "Wait! Wait, come on. I was just kidding. Stay for a little bit...please."

I stopped and looked at my phone. The next delivery was already cued up. I was going to be slammed till morning. I didn't have time for this. On one delivery, Genta had told me that he hadn't been out of this building in seven years. Compared to most of the horrible, terrifying, inhuman things I feed on a daily basis, Genta was a pretty decent guy. He said his existence after death as an Akaname was his karma for leading a shallow, evil life. He was a monster by pretty much anyone's definition—he sure looked the part—but he was just a lonely, awkward dude afraid to leave his home. On a level I hated to admit, I understood him. I think a lot of people could. I sighed and keyed the app to show me unavailable. "Okay, one episode of *The World According to Jeff Goldblum* and then I got to go, man." Genta gave me a wide, sharp, yellow smile. "And no eating until I'm gone!"

* * *

I got the gig, obviously. The training was unlike any job I'd ever had. It was a little more complicated than pizza delivery or Chinese take-out. Rode along with this space-case named Dan for six months. Dan had been a food delivery guy for the company for over ten years. Riding with Dan was like a cross between *Training Day* and *Taxi Driver*. He showed me the ropes, got me familiar with the territory and the clientele.

"It works like this," Dan told me on our first outing. He had picked me up at my apartment in a beat-to-crap old, blue Chevy pick-up. When he opened the glove box to grab something, I saw vials of weird powders, charms, a wooden stake, a bag of weed, and a .45 pistol. "The customers that management wants, they approach online or by mail. They get an invite to a dark web site kind of like the one you applied on. They fill out a profile, agree to the terms and conditions, and we add them to our customer list."

"Why all the weird secrecy, dude?"

"Don't call me 'dude'." Dan slid an unfiltered Camel between his cracked lips and lit it up. "Our customers value their anonymity and they don't eat out much anymore. Thank god."

"So we're like Meals on Wheels for a bunch of rich, old weirdos?"

"A lot of them are old, older than you can imagine. Many are rich, but not all of them. You'll be surprised, and maybe a little sad, when you see how some of them live." He looked out into the night, his face washed out in the headlights of a passing car. "Weird? Not sure that's the word I'd use. You'll see."

The first time I laid eyes on a client I lost my shit. It was a thing called a Meti and it was 450 pounds of intestine-colored Jell-O covered in the faces of all the victims it had ingested over its century of life. The slack, dead-eyed faces all moaned and gibbered as we approached it with the body bag.

"Be cool," Dan said.

"What the fuck is that thing?"

"That thing *is* the job," he said. "Be. Cool. It's got the munchies and we're delivering. This is how we get paid, man." That shut me up. My legs were wobbling like there was an earthquake as we slid the packaged human corpse toward it. The Meti oozed toward the body as we backed away and ghosted once the app said that payment was complete.

"We bring food to monsters," I said, still in shock. "*Real* monsters."

"*Clients*," Dan corrected. "'Exclusive clientele,' remember?"

"Are they all big face-blobs?"

"Nah, you name it. Vampires, Werewolves, Gaki, The Skinless Choir, Succubi, The God Fish, Leechkinder, Breath Thieves, Red Caps, whatever, they call us for grub or transport, but mostly grub."

"Monsters are real? No shit?"

"Yeah, I know. It's a little hard to wrap your skull around at first. A long time ago the founders of the company approached the Night Diet and proposed a solution to coexist with as little drama and bloodshed as possible. Over time, that became the company and now, the app."

"Little bloodshed?" I had nearly jumped out of the moving car. "Dude, we just fed that thing a human being!"

"A *dead* human being. *Already* dead. We just picked up the corpse from one of the company's contacts in the morgue, a John Doe no one claimed. When the Meti eats it, another face won't appear on it, because it won't be absorbing another *living* human being. Compromise. Less bloodshed. They don't hunt us and we don't have to hunt them."

That was when he gave me the spiel, the words that sealed the deal for me. It changed my life. For good or the bad, the jury is still out.

* * *

The rain had stopped by the time I left Genta's. I arrived at the next delivery. It was a mnemovore—an asshole who called himself Quentin. Pretentious bastard. I had picked up his dinner—a whacked-out meth enthusiast called Bootie—who made a supplementary income by selling his memories. Bootie got paid at the end of the transaction, to make sure he didn't rabbit with the money before he gave up the gray matter.

Quentin didn't live in some abandoned castle with bats flying around it or something. He had a condo in a nice area of Soulard. The night had a threat of dawn far off but approaching, inevitable, beautiful, and terrible.

Bootie spent the entire trip explaining to me about the roaches digging under his skin. A few times, early on, I had tried to get him help, get him into a program, a rehab, something. It was strictly against company policy and my manager and I had a "could you please step in here and shut the door" moment over it, but I figured I had to try. Even if he hadn't had some inhuman horror feasting on his memories, he had something far worse eating him alive. He was done. His soul had vacated the premises a long time ago with no intention of getting its security deposit back. Bootie was a skin robot waiting for his battery to run down. Once, it made me sad. Now, it was just an observation, like the rain had stopped and the sun was coming.

I rang Quentin's doorbell and Bootie and I waited. Bootie shook a lot and mumbled while we did. When Quentin threw the door open, he looked in as bad a state as Bootie, only better dressed. He was paler than his white bread ass normally was and he had a sheen of sweat. His eyes were large and his dark, red-rimmed pupils eclipsed the white of his eyes. He reeked of spoiled milk; he always did. Apparently, it was some kind of unconscious sense projection. "It's about fucking time. You have any inkling of how much I pay your superiors for this? I shouldn't have to wait this fucking long."

"Well, here he is now," I said, guiding Bootie across the threshold. "Bon appetit."

"Wait!" Quentin barked. He pulled Bootie in and pushed the junkie back onto the leather couch. Bootie let out a belch and a whoosh as he sunk into the upholstery. "You're staying until I'm sure I actually got something palatable from you people. I'm in no mood to get fucked because my order is wrong."

"Beggars can't be choosers, dude," I remarked as I walked in and Quentin shut the door. "You look like you're hurting pretty bad, Quint."

"How fucking dare you!" he said as he stood over Bootie. "Is this what you people call customer service? Do *not* expect good online feedback!"

He leaned over Bootie and placed his fingertips at the junkie's temples. Bootie made a little "ooop" sound and then was silent and still.

Quentin, his eyes closed and his brow furrowed, began to shake his head. "No, no...come on, damn you, where is it? Anything?" Bootie began to convulse. He was still silent. Some foam formed along the seam of his lips. "Give me fucking *something*." Quentin was almost pleading but it still sounded nasty and short. He squeezed Bootie's head, like someone trying to eek the pulp out of an orange.

"Hey, hey!" I said, stepping up to grab Quentin by the shoulder and pull him off the junkie. "Stop it, stop it!" Pain filled my universe, my hands were on fire—like every time I had ever touched the eye on the stove or a hot plate; every time I'd placed too-hot food in my mouth, burning the roof, my tongue; every time the shower had scalded me—I screamed and staggered back while Quentin kept going. My eyes refocused after the haze of pain faded and I looked at my hands. My skin was smooth and uncooked. I thought about going for the pistol in my pocket, but I mentally flinched, wondering what Quentin would do to me if I did. "Yo, Quint! You're killing him, man! You're killing him!"

Quentin let go and stepped back. Bootie let out a low moan, still alive at least. The mind eater turned to me, his hooded eyes now wide and full of emotional wildfire. "There is nothing in there for me to eat, you stupid errand boy. Nothing! Decaying half-memories and vague sugar-spun recollections...no substance! I'm starving and you bring me *this*?"

"Look, look, it's cool, man."

"It is not cool, you imbecile! I'm going to have to go out now and hunt."

As freaked out as I was, Quentin's declaration that he was going out looking for a meal slapped me back to reality, hard. I remembered what Dan had said that first night when I learned monsters were real and how outnumbered and outgunned us human schmucks really were.

* * *

"We can't just let things like that run around and *eat* people!" I said to Dan, terrified and indignant with his capitulation to the Meti.

"Oh, really? Look who knows so much on his first night working," he said. "Tell me genius, what do you want to do to the scary monster?"

"Fucking kill it!"

"Okay. Guns don't work on it, sharp blades don't work on it. Gasses, bombs, acid, fucking nukes...none of that will even tickle it. Do you know what *does* kill a Meti? Did you even know that was its name, a Meti, not a face-blob?" We drove along in silence for a while. Finally, he said. "Plastic cutlery."

"What?"

"Plastic cutlery kills a Meti. It has to be blessed, of course, by a priest of Baal...reformed."

I looked over at Dan. "If you know how to kill it why..."

"Why don't we?"

"Well, yeah."

"Because just like you, most of the good folks on Earth don't know what kills a Meti.

You also don't know that there are a quarter-million of them living among us right now and another two million hibernating in craters on the dark side of the moon. That's just one—one!—of millions of species of creatures, beings, monsters—whatever you want to call them— that have shared this world with us for a really, really long time. That's not counting the gods, aliens, astral parasites, angels and demons, Id tyrants, and rogue origami space-times out there. We tried killing all the monsters way back when and we came close to getting wiped out ourselves." He paused awhile and let all that sink in. "The company we work for is the current incarnation of the humans who brokered a peace with the Night Diet and a bunch of other affiliations, guilds, tribes, and nations of non-humans. We— you and me, champ, and all the delivery jockeys that work for the company worldwide—we keep the monsters fed and quiet and not slaughtering millions of people. And you know the really funny part? Some of the customers aren't really all that bad. They're just...not us."

I was silent as we drove along. The app chimed and Dan glanced down at the details of the next delivery run. He looked over to me through a fog of cigarette smoke. I looked back at him.

"So," I said, "how good *is* the benefits package?"

* * *

"Okay, easy, easy," I said to Quentin. "Look, we got a make-good guarantee on every delivery. I'll drop Bootie off here at a hospital and I get on the horn to management and we'll get you a fresh..."

"No, no more of this bullshit. I need food and I need it now." He was looking more and more emaciated by the second, his cheeks were hollowing out, his eyes were growing sunken. "It was a mistake to ever stop hunting, to stop getting my own food instead of relying on you people. If I don't eat, I will die, and I'll go mad before that. There's...no...more...time." He staggered toward the entrance but I wasn't sure if he would make it or not. I stepped between him and the door.

"Eat me," I said.

"What?"

"Eat. Me. Make-fucking-good-guarantee, right? Go on, have a nosh." Quentin looked back to the front door. He nearly fainted doing it. He knew he was out of time, and so did I.

"You understand," Quentin said as he placed his trembling, skeletal hands on my temples, "once I devour your memory, it's gone forever."

I nodded. I was trembling, my legs had rubber bones.

"Sixth grade," I said, and swallowed hard. "Take the whole Motherfucker." I felt his icy fingers on my skin, smelled the stomach-churning stench of rotten milk around him like a cloak. Dizzy darkness swelled up inside of me and I fell into it-deep, narcotic, and suffocating.

* * *

I came to in the front seat of my car. It was morning and I was in the parking lot of Quentin's complex. Imagine the feeling of a dried-up itching scab on the roof of your brain, aching to be satisfyingly scratched and picked off. No such luck. I rubbed my eyes and my face and checked my phone. I'd been out a few hours. I started to slump back in the seat, then shot upright. *Bootie!* At a deep, long annoying snore from the back seat I snapped my head around and saw him. He was alive and deeply asleep. I relaxed just as he released a loud and very smelly fart.

"Awww, man," I groaned. "Dude! That's gonna seep into the upholstery, I just know it." He stirred a bit at that and rolled over, his back to me now. "Let's drop you off at a hospital anyway, man. Just to make sure you're good. Besides, anyone got a smell like that coming out of them needs to consult a physician."

The phone chimed. It was the app, calling up a new delivery. Some monsters only thrived in the daylight. I snorted, "Yeah, right," and logged myself off duty. Those customers were someone else's problem. The car started up and I pulled away for the curb.

There was a hole in me now. It was ragged and fresh and my perception probed it the way your tongue can't help but seek out the empty socket of a recently excised tooth. I did notice that resting-bitch-face Quentin had slipped a few hundreds into Bootie's stained shirt pocket. When I shut the app off, I also saw that he'd given me a hell of a tip and a five-star rating. I guess, come payday, I could justify selling off a little piece of myself, a few shitty memories. Meh, it's a living. Who knows, maybe I might take that tip money and see if I could coax old Genta out of his lair for a few brews. On me, of course. Neither of us gets out enough.

THAT FINAL TOUCH OF SALT

Mia Moss

I was made into a ghost by a hollow woman who could only smile when someone was looking directly at her. I have haunted her since I was an infant. Before she placed her mark upon me, I belonged to someone who once made her smile every day for a whole summer. But when he stopped looking at her and started tending to a baby, the hollow woman could not bear that he should ever find reason to feel joy again.

So she stole me from my crib and set a curse on my brow that made dark craters of my eyes and faded my skin until I had as much substance as fog across a thief's path. Then she stoppered me up in a crystal phial which she wore strung on a leather cord around her neck.

I undid this curse with a pot of good soup, but that came years later.

With my ghost at her throat, the woman fled north into shadowy exile at the heart of a dark, cold forest. Her name was Mirror, and what I was called before she stole me I did not know for decades. In the hollow woman's household, my name was Spit, or if she was feeling charitable, Girl.

Mirror settled in a lonesome glade just outside a village and kept mostly to herself, until she realized that a ghostly infant could be used to great effect for sympathetic attentions. I was from time to time set free from the phial just long enough to be put on display as a morbid pet, promptly blamed for the day's ills, then stuffed back inside when no one else was looking.

These public hauntings attracted the interest of a local sad-eyed poet who wooed Mirror with silky, rich chocolates and bottles of passionate red wine and songs written just for her. And though he said it was her beauty and wit that truly captivated him, more often than not his eyes were on my spectral form.

"It's so tragically romantic," he murmured one night as they lay tangled in each other's arms. I wish she had stuck me in the phial for those lingering evenings, but Mirror took great pleasure in making me watch her receive the affection I could never hope to feel.

"I believe you meant to say annoying, my dearest."

"It is a little romantic, though, don't you think?" the poet insisted. "This lonely little girl dies and out of all the people in the wide world, she chooses you to cling to. Why do you think that is?"

"I must give off a naturally maternal aura."

I tried to scream, but nothing came out of my raw, open mouth except soft wind.

* * *

I thought eventually she would set me free. When the poet married Mirror and she dressed herself in a white gown and invited all the villagers to a summery altar filled with flowers, she stroked the phial and I thought, *Finally*!

Instead, she set me loose among the guests and then cried and cowered and let them comfort her, as though it were my fault and not hers, as though I had a choice. The priest even tried to banish me, but banishments don't work on curse victims.

Five years later, when she bore the twins, a boy named Shade and a girl named Glory, I thought she would undo her charm. What did she need a toddler ghost for when she had two fleshy babes of her own? Instead, she kept me out of the phial more than ever.

I begged for comfort with my dead girl eyes, pointed mutely with my transparent little fingers at the cozy nest of domestic bliss. It made her babies cry to see me and then the poet would comfort the three of them and I floated there in my own little Hell, begging to be put out of my misery. Only when I turned my back to them and stared blankly at the wall, pretending to actually be dead, would she tire of the game and lock me away again.

If the twins had stayed babes forever, perhaps this might have been all there ever was to my tale and I would still be a prisoner in that crystal phial. But they grew into healthy children and Mirror had no inclination in raising them herself nor money to find a governess. So eventually she offered me a secret bargain.

"Spit, darling, how would you like to know what earth feels like beneath your bare feet? Or know the taste of water? Or smell the first snowfall drifting through the pines?"

I shrugged and pointed to the beds the other children got. *Might I have one of those?* Mirror smirked and shook her head.

I wrapped my arms around myself. *Might I be entitled to hugs now and then?* Again, the smirk and a rejection of my counter-offer.

"You can serve us or you can stay a villain, if you prefer, but you will never be loved like my children are loved," she said. "Will you make the bargain?"

I didn't want to, but I nodded my assent all the same. I wanted desperately to feel something, anything beyond static numbness.

Mirror relaxed the curse just enough that I could touch the world. She popped me out of the phial each morning and I silently swept the floors, changed the bedclothes, bathed the twins, cleaned the laundry, and saw the children off to school. When they had no school or if they fell ill, I entertained them as a mime or followed them into the woods among the cedars and brambles where they liked to play and acted as their guardian, scaring away any wolves that might draw too close.

"What a strange phantom," the poet remarked one night as I washed the windows. The family had gathered around a merry hearth to play card games. "I have learned stories of every sort of ghost, but I've never heard of any that haunt houses just to clean them."

I turned and gaped at him. Did he truly still think I had a choice? But Mirror narrowed her eyes at me and stroked the phial nestled at her bosom and I turned back to my duties, trying to shut them out as best I could.

The one task Mirror reserved for herself was the cooking. Perhaps she knew it was the chore I longed to take on as my own. Certainly, she took no pleasure in it herself; her soups were flavorless hot water in which she boiled unfortunate vegetables into oblivion. I had more substance than her pasta sauce.

Yet for all that, she flew into a rage the first time I laid hands on a skillet, thinking to make some eggs for the children's breakfast.

"Allow you to cook? What, so you can poison my children before I'm even awake? I don't think so, Spit."

"Dearest love," said the poet, who was quite happy to no longer do any chores and certainly wouldn't have minded never having to cook again, "why would our ghost poison any of us? Surely after all these years, if she were an evil spirit, she would have shown us some wickedness by now?"

Mirror staggered back as though he had struck her across the face. "Not shown *wickedness?* Do you not recall how she terrified our guests at our wedding? Do you not remember how she hovered by my birthing bed, waiting to suck the life out of our children before they could open their eyes? You would have that same monster cook your meals? This soulless, spiteful thing? You would trust it over your wife? Over the mother of your children?"

"No, of course not."

"Then what are you suggesting?"

"Ah, nothing. Nothing. You know what's best, I'm sure."

I would find no ally in the poet, less in the children. They learned quickly from their mother that attempts to befriend the peculiar ghost that haunted their house would result in wild mood swings, ferocious punishments, and a torrent of tears from their mother. Conversely, finding new and interesting ways to torture me earned them nothing but praise from her, and so naturally they both chose to follow this route.

As they grew older, they also learned that any wickedness they might lay at my feet would go unpunished.

"Nothing to say in your defense?" Shade liked to sneer at me, knowing full well I could not speak.

Still, it was not entirely unbearable. When the family went into the village, Mirror loved having me tag along—especially if she needed to play a crowd's sympathies to her advantage. How could anyone begrudge the mother of two such fine children when she was ceaselessly haunted by that hideous ghost? And while I was out, I was able to watch and listen and learn from the villagers.

Often, in those days, I dreamt of somehow convincing Mirror to let me cook for them. If she and her family could only taste what I had to offer, maybe they could see me as something other than an unwelcome pest. And so in every house we visited, every dinner table we passed, I learned how to make yeast into tangy sourdough, how to summon the moistest, fluffiest cakes from an oven, how to roast wild game to succulent perfection, and how to conjure the richest soup broths (Parmesan rinds are the secret weapon of many).

The years passed, and the children grew, and I strangely did as well, though no one could explain such a phenomenon. I think not even Mirror herself knew. Sometimes I would catch her looking at me as though surprised to find me still there after all this time.

Did I try to escape? Of course I did. More times than I can count. Once while Mirror napped, I tried to steal the phial and it burned through me the moment I touched it. I woke up several days later to the woman's smug face. I tried simply walking away from the family, losing them in a crowd on market days. I tried walking out the front gate. Each attempt was met with the same fate: back into the crystal, summoned at a later time.

But eventually, Mirror fell ill.

It happened one morning as she led the family in grace before a breakfast of thin maple porridge.

"O Lord, thank you for protecting us from all evil spirits which might otherwise seek to harm our loved ones, and for giving us mastery over their wickedness, that we might feel some peace in the shadow of the devil's endless tricksome ways, even when sent in the guise of a wanton young woman. Thank you for this bounty upon our table and thank you for blessing me with two angelic children."

She dissolved into a fit of coughing before she could get out one last spiteful amen and the poet had to help her to her bedroom to lie down. Her cough soon heralded a fever and she fell into fitful sleep. I thought perhaps it would be best if I vanished into my phial, but the poet turned his helpless eyes to my hollowed gaze and said: "Please, do you think you could cook something? I fear I know nothing about it and the children are too young..."

I looked nervously to the bedroom where Mirror tossed and turned. The poet rushed to assure me: "She'll never have to know. I promise. Please..." And he gestured helplessly again.

I realized that with all her maneuvering, Mirror had made certain that every one of us was reliant on her, in one way or another. Much as I was never allowed to cook, neither was the poet. I recalled all the times he had offered and she had disdainfully rushed him out of the kitchen. Likely, once she recovered from illness, she would wake expecting grateful tears, adulations, endless praise for the miraculous way she knit the entire family together so effortlessly.

It was enough to push me past my doubts. I nodded to the poet with grim determination and went into the kitchen to cook my first meal.

By any standard, this dinner was not great. I tried to make chicken and dumplings, a dish I had seen other villagers create a thousand times before, but there was a trick to cloudlike fluffy dumplings and thick, savory gravy that I did not know; the end result, while flavorful, was watery and the dumplings were like doughy rocks.

"I thought you knew how to do this," Shade grumbled.

"It's still better than Mother's, though," Glory admitted. "The vegetables are holding their shape, at least. And you used just the right amount of salt."

Shade glowered and said imperiously: "My sister is being far too charitable. Do better in the morning."

Later on, alone in the kitchen, I stared at the pot of leftovers. I had never dared to try to eat food before—not that it had ever been offered. No one was around to see, and I thought if I was able to touch things, smell things, perhaps I might be able to taste as well? I picked up a spoon and sampled my dish.

Warmth. Slow, soft, spreading through me like I always imagined a hug might feel. A pull at the back of the tongue, that must be savory? Then warming spices flaring my nostrils and rushing down my spine. I looked over my shoulder, feeling like a thief, and took another bite.

One bowlful later, I set down the spoon and licked my phantom lips. I felt a spark inside of me, a fortitude distant and faint, but there nonetheless, and I knew in that moment I needed to keep it going, no matter what, if I wanted to escape my prison.

Mirror was not better by morning and I finally got to try my hand at making a dish called pancakes, which always seemed to bring so much joy to others in the village. I found a recipe for them in an old cookbook that was being used to keep a side-table even and the result was much better than the dumplings the night before.

Again, I ate stealthily in the kitchen after the others left. I didn't know for certain if the poet would object to me eating their leftovers, but I couldn't shake the feeling that this was something Mirror would forbid if she knew. So it became my secret—delicious, warm, and comforting. With each bite I felt the world become a little bit clearer, slightly more manageable.

I caught a flash of pink skin beneath the soapy water as I did the washing up after breakfast and it startled me so much I nearly broke a plate. It had to have been my imagination, surely, but...was my skin less translucent? How was that possible?

Mirror's fever broke that night, but she was still too sick to move much for the better part of a week after that. I took on the cooking with ready enthusiasm, and the twins and the poet grew used to my meals. After the second day, Shade even stopped insulting them.

Eventually, Mirror was well enough to sit up and search out something other than simple broth or tea to drink. I brought her milk toast with slivers of beef sprinkled in and fed it to her one patient spoonful at a time.

To my great surprise, she did not stop me or push me away. I wondered if perhaps the sickness still had ahold of her brain.

After that, it was as though I had received some sort of official blessing to exist. Everyone relaxed more around mealtimes and I began to branch out and try new techniques and recipes. Some were far greater successes than others. All the while, that glowing feeling deep in my chest continued to grow brighter and deeper, spreading eventually through every limb.

"You probably caused my fever," Mirror said one night between spoonfuls of soup. "But my children and my husband are healthy and well-fed. Tomorrow I'm having guests over for dinner. Do not disappoint, or I may never let you out of that phial again."

My stomach sank. Less than one full day to plan and execute a menu for not just the family, but dinner guests. Guests who would be uniformly inclined (as all in the nearby village were) to believe me some demonic hellsprite who resisted all banishment.

Thankfully, Mirror seemed nervous about making a good impression. She did not summon me back to the phial that evening and so I was free to stay out all night and work until dawn, at which point I accompanied her to the market for ingredients.

That night, after all courses had been served to great accolades and I was in the kitchen scrubbing plates, one of the guests sat back in her chair and patted her full belly. "I don't remember the last time I had fresh oysters with such fine mignonette."

"And those leek and mushroom pies!" exclaimed another. "Exquisite."

"I will be dreaming of that five-layer gingerbread trifle for weeks to come," laughed the first. Then I heard her ask: "You said your daughter made all of this? With no help from anyone? You must be very proud."

I caught my breath and only barely noted that I had a breath to catch. I wished very much that she would take the compliment back.

"No," Mirror's reply was thin and sharp, like broken glass beneath the murky surface of dishwater. "I have but one daughter, and she is at a friend's house this evening. This was all simply thrown together by a serving girl. The recipes and techniques are actually all mine. All she does is follow my directions, simple thing that she is. She's useless for anything else."

I clenched my fists and watched through the kitchen door as Mirror toyed with the phial between her fingertips.

"No, not yet. I want to stay," I whispered, pleading.

A moment later I felt an unexpected spark of pain over my skin, like a hot grease splatter from a pan, and I had just enough time to think, *It's never hurt before,* as my world went black.

* * *

After that night, she always made sure to lock me away once the final dish was prepared, but she could never erase three memories from my mind. First, for that one moment, someone had mistaken me for a real, living girl. Second, I had spoken my first words. And third, that brief and inexplicable pain I had felt when she had called me back into the phial.

From then on, I ate often in stolen moments, pocketing scraps of my own cooking when Mirror wasn't watching. I nourished my strange new physicality. This came at a price, as I have learned all worthy things must. The more I filled my belly, the firmer my heartbeat, the warmer my breath. But each return to the phial hurt more than the last.

Once, when she summoned me, my skin felt raw and taut. As I set to my chores that day, I found warm blood pooling under my fingertips and felt it trickling down my face. I licked a drop that fell on my lips and was surprised at how rich and alive I tasted. When she put me back in the phial that night, it hurt so much that I nearly screamed aloud. I vowed I would stop eating then and there. Better to be a painless ghost than a bloodied girl.

But the taste of life was too rich to resist. I lasted a fortnight before I dipped my fingers into a bowl and licked up gobs of mouth-puckering lemon curd.

The days became strange and scary, each hour balanced precariously between the pain of confinement and the pleasure of secret life, always watching for Mirror's shadow in the kitchen. I pushed through the pain, stubbornly continuing to eat until I felt as though I were as reasonably strong and filled with fortitude as any mortal. That was the day I felt whole enough to confront Mirror.

On that morning, I set a plate of craggy, buttery cinnamon scones between us at the breakfast table and poured us each a cup of fragrant coffee.

She noticed the second cup and said, "My husband will not be joining me today, Spit, he's gone to peddle lyrics at court."

I sat down in front of the cup—*my* cup—and wrapped my fingers around it as though I could absorb courage through its warmth.

"Whose daughter am I?" I asked her quietly.

She froze, then set her coffee cup down with deliberate care.

"Excuse me?" Mirror asked in a tone that once would have made me tremble into oblivion.

"I know that I am not yours, you've made that abundantly clear. And you know that I am not haunting you willingly, no matter what you claim to others. You could set me free whenever you wish."

"Since when do you *speak*?"

The witch clutched at the phial that hung ever around her neck and I pressed my question, ignoring hers: "Who did you steal me from?"

Mirror stared at me for a deadly quiet moment. I thought she might curse me again, or shove my spirit back into that horrid phial. Instead she tossed her head back and laughed and laughed until she gasped for air and pounded the table with the flat of her palm and I wondered, stone-faced, if she might actually die choking on her own laughter. Alas, she lived.

"Whose daughter are you?" Mirror stood and took another scone from the plate and rolled her eyes disdainfully. "You don't deserve to be anyone's daughter. You are flotsam plucked from the sea. Trash that I was kind enough to sweep up out of the way before you could stain the world. You've no wish to haunt me and my loved ones? The power has always been yours, should you choose to depart this earthly coil. All you need do is beg for your death."

Mirror bit down hard on the scone and gave me a significant look. Then she left. I stayed at the table and tried to finish my pastry, but something had happened to the recipe after the fact. Suddenly the pastry no longer tasted of sweetness and spice, but ash. Only ash, crumbling all over the tablecloth and making a mess.

I heard the front door close. An empty sort of sadness hit me in the stillness that followed. I wanted more than anything to flee into the promise of oblivion in the phial at Mirror's bosom, even knowing how much it hurt me to do so, and that wanting made me blush hot with shame.

Don't, I told myself. I tried to dissipate anyway, and the pain made black spots swarm in my vision. When I opened my eyes and found myself still alone at the kitchen table, I felt an uncanny ribbon of relief mixed in with the terror and confusion. Never in my memory as a ghost had there ever been a time when I could *not* go back into the phial.

I didn't know what else to do, so I continued to sit at the table and stare at the empty wall across from me, where a moment ago my captor had laughed in my face and told me to kill myself if I didn't want to live there any longer. And now, it seemed, she had locked me out of even my own cursed prison.

I stayed there until the sun had passed through all the windows from one side of the house to the other and the thin golden sunset began to flood the room. Mirror's horrible children came to see what was for dinner.

"Is that this morning's breakfast?" Shade scoffed, sounding very much like his mother. "You think just because someone praised your cooking that you can just laze about all day? Look at this mess! Look at these crumbs! You shouldn't even exist, you miserable little monster. Clean this up and get dinner started, or I'm telling Mother."

He twisted his lips into a nasty smirk and I knew he was going to tell her anyway. All the same, I blinked my eyes a few times and bowed my head humbly.

"Of course," I told him. "I would never shirk on dinner."

His sister squinted at me as I straightened up to leave.

"Spit, how funny it is that I should never have noticed until now that your eyes are green!"

I frowned, having never seen my own reflection before and having only relied on the family I haunted to tell me what I looked like. I had the distinct memory of Mirror telling me my eyes were "murky and gray as a dead dog's dung." A fitting color for a ghost.

"Are you sure?" I asked her.

"Quite sure. They're as green as leaves, aren't they, Brother?"

But Shade was bored of talking to me and simply shrugged his sulky shoulders and tugged at her sleeve. "Who cares what her eyes look like? Come on, she's got work to do. Let's go outside until dinner's ready."

I was alone again, but my thoughts were louder than any crowd. *My eyes once did not have color and now they do.* It stuck with me as I swept up the breakfast crumbs and nibbled away at my thoughts as I chopped up carrots and onions and rutabagas and threw them all into a steaming pot of water along with some herbs from the garden. What else about me had changed, and why? Had Mirror actually locked me out of the phial, or was there some other magic at work?

I worked up a batch of biscuits to go with the soup, and when my plump little rows of dough had been brushed with butter and popped into the oven, I wiped my hands on my apron and scurried as quick as I could down the back hall to Mirror's bedchamber. It was the only room in the house where she kept a looking glass. I wanted to see for myself what color my eyes were.

It was a dangerous expedition. Any moment, Mirror could come home, wondering where her evening meal was. Any moment, the poet might return from his latest travels. Any moment, one of the twins might spy my trespass through the bedchamber window that looked out into the woods behind the house. I didn't care; I needed to see for myself.

Entering that foreign landscape felt as surreal as climbing a ladder to the moon. The air was warm and stifling and smelled of sleep and Mirror's soap. It clung to my skin as though it had sentience of its own, and for an absurd moment I frantically wondered if she kept another ghost hidden away in there.

But no, it was just me and my fears. I shook my head and strode quickly across the room before I could change my mind and flee back to the kitchen. I might not get another chance like this.

Before I reached the looking glass, I screwed my eyes tight so that I wouldn't get even a hint of my reflection before I was directly in front of myself. I opened my eyes when my hip found the edge of the dressing table and slowly lifted my lashes to look myself in the face for the first time in my unlife.

Green. Bright as the wild chicory leaves I had just added to the soup in the kitchen. Vibrant and bold and certainly not any color of dun I'd ever seen.

What was more, the longer I stared at my reflection, the more I realized I looked nothing like any ghost I had ever heard of. I remembered the way people spoke of my appearance, when they thought it didn't matter that I could hear them. Hollowed, they said. Wan. Dreadfully pale skin like the belly of a nightworm after the rain. None of those descriptions fit the young woman who stared back at me in astonishment.

I sat down at the dressing table and tilted my chin this way and that, exploring my newly discovered dips and curves. The length and slope of my nose; the arch of my brows and the crease that formed between them when I made a face at myself; the way my pink lips turned ruddier if I pursed them together.

A crow outside the window cawed abruptly, startling me out of my seat, and it was only then that I happened to notice the leather-bound diary sitting to one side on the table. I knew Mirror kept one, because she often mentioned how one day her poet husband would immortalize her memories into verse and sing her whole saga to princes and queens. I never imagined I would have such easy access to it.

A tremor of fear ran through me. It could all very well be a trap; she had done such things to me before, though never quite so cruel. What if Mirror abruptly leaving the house, my inexplicable inability to return to the phial, the twins' sudden casual observation of my eyes, and the unlocked bedchamber door were all sticky threads of a cruel spider's web? Was she lying in wait at that very moment?

I turned to leave but couldn't make my feet go through the door. Not yet, not without a peek. Against all my better judgement or concern for personal safety, I returned to the dressing table and picked up the book. Somehow, I could feel the warmth of Mirror's angry fingers as though they were infused in the leather. I cracked open the cover and turned to the first age-stained page and began to read.

Once upon a time, there was a beautiful girl who was so beautiful she ought to have been a princess. Ugh. Perhaps there was no punishment but the one I was making for myself by reading Mirror's diary. It was true that I did not know much about the world, but even I knew this was a peculiar way to begin a memoir.

One day, she met a handsome boy who showered her with attention. She thought he was perfect, until the day he wasn't. He had a baby to tend to, he said. He named the creature Carys, and said it was because he never knew he could love anything more than that child, which is the sort of thing idiots say when they've never known true passion.

I flipped past several pages of the diary that detailed the girl's beauty, wit, charm, and all of the injustices she had ever suffered at the hands of those beneath her.

...And so the beautiful girl used her cleverest magics and turned the babe into a spirit, which she kept in a pretty charm around her neck. Then she left the southern realm forever and went north into the woods where all the best magics grow, and never once ever thought about the stupid, foolish, terrible, selfish, stupid, ugly, awful boy ever again. And she knew that while he would never smile at her again, neither would he ever smile at his ugly, screaming baby, either.

I snapped the book shut. The blood in my veins felt like static before a thunderstorm, frizzing and grating with each throb of my pulse. Dizzy, it slowly dawned that I had a pulse at all. When had that started, I wondered?

I re-opened the diary and tried to skim, but it was poisoned candy floss from start to finish: fluffy and sweet and you didn't realize until the end that the strange taste filling your mouth was your own blood, not sugar syrup and saliva.

So that was how I had come to haunt her. I was a burden of her own design, a war trophy and a bitter reminder of a life forever out of her reach. And now her spell was unraveling. My magic grew with every meal. I set the diary back in its place and returned to the kitchen to finish preparing the soup.

By the time I was done, Mirror and her children had made their way to the dinner table in anticipation of the savory scents wafting through the house. Along with a basket of biscuits, I carried the entire pot of soup out and set it on the table with a heavy thunk that sent waves of broth sloshing over the side.

"Careful! Clumsy wretch!" Mirror chided, but she licked her lips all the same.

"Sorry," I said, and I knew it would be the last time I apologized to her for anything. "One final ingredient needed to be added tableside for best flavor."

I reached out as if to take her bowl to fill it, but then my hand kept going, moved up to the leather cord around her neck, and yanked with all my newfound strength until it snapped and I clutched that hateful phial in my palm. Mirror narrowed her eyes and I heard the twins gasp behind me.

Although I was all but certain that the spell had been negated by the meals I had fed myself over time, reaching for the charm was still a gamble. Breaking it, doubly so. But if I was wrong, what was the worst the woman could do to me? Curse me to follow her everywhere as her ghost-servant? I had nothing left to lose.

I looked her in the eyes and held her watery gaze as I slammed my hand down on the table, smashing the phial between my palm and the wood. I felt the shards go in as it burst from the impact. I felt the hot, slick drip of my blood run down my wrist and this time the wet pain did not frighten me. I lifted the ruined charm and sprinkled it over the pot, like a chef adding that final touch of salt flakes.

Silently, I took the ladle in my bloodied hand, poured an enormous portion of the soup, and set it down in front of the hollow witch. She looked down at the bowl and looked back up at me, white lines of fury scoring her sour, bloodless face.

"You will regret that, Spit," she hissed.

The pain I felt was like a song. It hummed in my teeth and my heart beat to its savage rhythm of survival. It throbbed in my ears, drowning out Mirror's threat.

"I will regret none of this day, I assure you. And my name is not Spit. Your curse is broken."

I tossed the ladle into the pot and helped myself to a biscuit. Tender layers of care and attention between the butter and flour, salt and milk, combined to create a taste that promised me I would find a home wherever I chose to make one. I took a bite and made my way to the door, wrapping my hurt hand in a strip of apron. This time, when I tried to walk out the gate, there was no power in that house left to bind me.

ALIEN CAPERS

Gini Koch

For readers of the Alien/Katherine "Kitty" Katt series, this story takes place during the later events of Aliens Abroad.

"Dion, Prince Wasim—what are you two doing with the crown jewels of the entire Apatan solar system?"

This was, frankly, a good question, posed aloud by Malcolm Buchanan, but clearly echoing in the minds of the group of our fellow solar system travelers behind him. Sadly, neither Wasim nor I had a good answer.

I went for the truth. "It's not quite what it looks like."

This was met with shocked and stony silence.

"Ah, perhaps we had better explain more fully," Wasim suggested.

"Perhaps you should." Buchanan's tone said he was unlikely to enjoy our explanation, but fully expected to listen to all of it very carefully, with great malice aforethought.

I wanted to say that I should have left the galaxy when I had the chance. Instead, I took a deep breath, let it out slowly, and gave it my best shot. "It all started because Wasim and I both needed a break from all the pomp and circumstance, so, as you know, we went to the kitchens..."

* * *

"What are you all doing in here again?"

That exasperated question came from Buchanan.

"Spending time with the caterers," Wasim replied. "What's wrong with that? We're not on duty again for at least three Ignotforstan hours." He looked at me. "Dion, did I miss something?"

"No, you did not." Wasim was a good, dutiful kid, a Prince of Bahrain, and someone we were all supposed to watch over for his protection. Not because he was a scamp—if he was supposed to be somewhere, he would be there. Particularly in this situation. After all, it wasn't every day that a spaceship from Earth kidnapped a hundred people, traveled around the galaxy to save the day in various and sundry places, and then went to yet another unknown-to-us solar system to drop in and say hello.

The First Lady, aka Kitty Katt-Martini, was calling this Operation Interstellar. I was calling it the I Wish I'd Stayed Home Trip. I'm not really a brave man and we'd faced a lot of danger. Kitty and several others were facing even more at the moment—trying to leave our galaxy to rescue a lost solar system—but I'd chosen to stay on Ignotforsta, where it seemed safer.

Ignotforsta was made up of people who looked like, as Kitty called them, Real Naked Apes. Every ape species we had on Earth was represented here, only they were more humanoid—they all walked upright, spoke languages just as we Earthlings did, were all a bit more human-sized, and were, in many cases, far better scientists and astronomers than we were, both on the ship and back home on Earth.

The Apatan solar system was made up like the Alpha Centauri system in that there were a lot of planets, most were inhabited, and there were a lot of people who resembled Earth animals, humans included, only, like the Ignotforstans, they were all highly sentient, highly functioning, and highly advanced. They were also highly into pomp and circumstance.

Those of us left out of the Leave the Galaxy mission were tasked with attending the celebration for the return of the Ignotforstan scientists we'd rescued from one of the many distant planets we'd visited. The job had originally sounded easy and rather fun. Originally.

I was a photographer and I worked with two reporters very friendly with Kitty. One of them, Bruce Jenkins, and I were tasked with taking pictures and getting interviews. Everyone else left behind was tasked with impressing the entire Apatan system into joining our side and, therefore, the Galactic Council. We'd had no idea what we were getting into.

These people loved—no, *lived* for—these kinds of events. Everyone who was anyone within the Apatan system, and those who weren't anyone but who could afford the ticket on the shuttles that went from planet to planet, were here on Ignotforsta, partying like it was their 1999. Even in the middle of New York City at midnight in Times Square, I'd never seen so many people in one place.

And they all wanted their pictures taken.

Oh, they also wanted to be interviewed, to shake the hand of an Earth Royal Prince, to get to know the family of Earth's leadership, to talk politics with those Earth politicians here, and so on. Meaning every single one of us was mobbed constantly. We'd had to create a shift rota or all just drop dead from exhaustion within two days. And there was no end in sight.

Today's event was a gigantic gala, where everyone was in their world's version of black or white tie, males and females alike glittering in their jewels and finery. They'd provided formal dress for us, too, so we looked good and blended, so to speak.

When we'd rescued the space crew everyone was celebrating, there had been gorilla-types, chimp-types, orangutan-types, and bonobo-types. I'd naively assumed that would be it once we were on their planet. I was wrong.

Gibbons and siamangs were represented, too. They were, to a one, smaller than the other Ignotforstans. They were also treated as inferior. It was subtle, but it was there.

"Mind those people," one of the million and one dignitaries I'd photographed over the past few days told me when a gibbon came with a tray of canapes and a siamang with a tray of drinks.

"Oh, thank you," I said as I grabbed the sustenance. This earned me a cheerful, rather cheeky smile from both servers. "And thank you, Lord Sominou, for pointing out the delicious food and drink."

He sniffed rather imperiously, in what I was coming to realize was the Gorilla Way of dissing someone. "They aren't to be trusted, the Tribe of Gibb, is what I mean, Mister France."

"Ah. Um, why not?" I'd already eaten the canape and had half of the glass of liquid. "Are they poisoners?"

"No, just...untrustworthy. We know them of old."

Thankfully, Bruce called me away at that moment, so I was spared more awkwardly racist small talk.

The Gibbs, as it turned out, were those who ended up with all the nasty jobs no one else wanted. If you needed anything deemed "lower" work done, they were the go-to group. It hardly seemed fair or right, but they seemed to accept their assigned lot.

The catering crew for this never-ending extravaganza were excellent chefs and hanging out with them was a delicious and non-stuffy way to spend the time, because they were the very opposite of prim and proper.

While there was a staff of at least a thousand working this event, we'd gotten to know four of them very well. They were a family group of some kind—I wasn't clear on the actual relationships, because while they had different last names, they'd told us to call them the TCs, which stood for Top Chefs. They'd been welcoming the first time Wasim and I wandered in looking for a safe place to sit down, and they'd remained so.

I quite liked them. Because he was a bright, studious young man, Wasim was able to identify which lesser ape each of them resembled. Kram Retuals, who was the Head Chef, compared to a pileated or capped gibbon. This type was, on Earth, considered a dwarf gibbon, and Kram was definitely the smaller of the two males, by quite a lot.

Aeron Dev was the dessert chef, and she resembled a northern white-cheeked gibbon which, Wasim told me, meant she was considered a crested gibbon. I had no idea why, but she did have lovely white tufts of fur on the sides of her face and I'd made sure to compliment them, meaning I instantly became her special favorite. Aeron saved delicacies for me to try, which I shared with Wasim and, usually, no one else.

Slennug Assilem, was a lar or white-handed gibbon, also a dwarf gibbon. She was indeed tiny, and her snow-white hands were delicate, but they were also quite strong. She assisted Aeron with the desserts, but also helped Kram and the last member of the team with anything that required a delicate or intricate touch.

Speaking of Semaj Sanoc, he was a siamang, meaning he was twice the size of Aeron and a good three times the size of Kram and Slennug. I hadn't even needed Wasim to tell me this, since all the siamangs I'd seen or met were larger than all the gibbons, even though we'd been told that, on this planet, they were considered one race, regardless of size. He was quiet but also a joker, and if something went wrong with a dish, it was likely because he'd tried a different ingredient than Kram wanted.

Buchanan's glare brought me back to the moment. "We're just taking our break. We were on for the last six hours and this is our scheduled escape time."

"We are enjoying getting to try local specialties first," Mr. Ali Baba Gadhavi said. He looked and sounded like a giant bear. He'd never been anything but kind to me, but he terrified me anyway—and not just because he was the head of a giant Middle Eastern crime syndicate. That didn't matter here, across the galaxy from Earth. Though, admittedly, Gadhavi seemed like a crime syndicate all by himself.

"I am with the prince as always," Naveed, Wasim's personal bodyguard, added. "Why is any of this a surprise?"

Buchanan heaved a sigh. "It's not. I'm sorry, but we have a situation. I need you two," he pointed to Naveed and Gadhavi, "with me. It's going to require muscle and authority. I can't rely on enough of that from the politicians and all the A-Cs are busy. You two are the only ones who are available, so you're it."

Gadhavi and Naveed looked at each other. "But who will guard the Prince?" Naveed asked.

"I'm eighteen and perfectly capable of taking care of myself, you know," Wasim said mildly. "Besides, Dion will stay with me."

To the other men's great credit, none of them said what I knew they were thinking—that I was about as good at protection as a kitten.

"I'm happy to protect Wasim should the situation require it," I said. "I doubt anything will happen to us in the kitchens, however, so I feel you can handle the more important whatever it is and we'll remain here. Hidden."

"We will guard him with our lives," Kram said. The other TCs nodded enthusiastically.

None of the three men looked convinced, but it seemed that whatever was going on was urgent enough that Buchanan was willing to risk leaving Wasim without bodyguards. He nodded. "Fine. Try not to get into any trouble."

"When have we done so?" Wasim asked, rightly.

Buchanan rolled his eyes. "I like to plan ahead." With that, he grabbed a sweet roll that looked like a lump of clay but tasted like a rainbow in your mouth, jerked his head at the other two men, who also grabbed sweet rolls, and they headed off—presumably to handle whatever situation Buchanan had deemed dire, and possibly to berate anyone else they came across managing to have down time.

"Mister Buchanan seems...unusually suspicious today," Slennug said, shooting a worried look at Kram. Aeron and Semaj looked worried, too.

"He's just protective," Wasim said quickly. "Don't worry about it, it's no reflection on any of you."

"I'm sure Wasim is correct," Kram said firmly. The other three nodded but they didn't go back to their food preparations. Instead, they all stared at us appraisingly.

"Can we trust you?" Kram asked us finally.

"I don't see why not," I replied. Wasim nodded.

"Good!" Kram rubbed his hands together. "It's time to make some magic happen."

Semaj went the way the men had and was back quickly. "They're truly gone. I've secured the door."

"Excuse me?" I asked, as the four TCs took off their aprons and pulled large black duffle bags out from some lower cabinets.

"Back in a flash," Kram said. The four of them took the duffles and headed into the largest of their walk-in freezers.

Wasim and I looked at each other. I was about to suggest we leave the kitchen and find Buchanan, just in case, when the TCs came out. They were all dressed in this planet's version of formalwear for those not of high-ranking status—really fancy jumpsuits with a lot of ornamentation and far more pockets than Earth formalwear normally allowed for—and each carried a large metal tray with ornate dome covers. Aeron and Slennug handed their trays to me and Wasim, then went back in and brought out two more.

"Let's go," Kram said, as Semaj shifted his tray to one hand and opened the other kitchen door for the rest of us. My tray was heavy, yet Semaj didn't seem to be struggling to hold his. A reminder that the Gibbs might be small, but they were powerful.

"Go where?" I asked, as the ladies went first and Kram ushered us along behind them. Wasim looked as confused as I felt.

"We've prepared a very special delicacy for one of the more exclusive events this evening," Kram said as he, too, shifted his tray and closed and locked the door behind him. "We'd like the two of you to help us deliver them."

"You'll be perfectly safe," Aeron added.

Slennug nodded. "We didn't say anything to Mister Buchanan because we knew he'd tell you not to come with us."

"But it's going to be such fun," Semaj said enthusiastically, "that we just didn't want the two of you to miss out."

"Why did you lock the doors?" I asked.

"So no one can come in and tamper with my kitchen!" Kram shook his head. "I can only imagine the chaos if a miscreant got in here while we were running this errand." The other TCs nodded emphatically. I'd had no idea the kitchen was so off-limits to all but these four, and a few of us, apparently, but I couldn't argue with the logic.

"But what if they need more food or to restock the bars?" Wasim asked.

"Then they'll go to another station," Kram said firmly as he headed off and the rest of us followed.

I did want to ask why Semaj had confirmed that the other men were gone, but Aeron was prattling about what we were carrying and I figured I should be polite and pay attention. As she talked, we headed through underground corridors that allowed the caterers and other staff to navigate the gigantic celebration complex without having to pass among throngs of people.

Aeron shared that the trays held a delicacy of the highest order, a sort of concoction that was incredibly difficult to make. The TCs were quite proud of their ability to craft these things, called capers.

While passing many other Gibbs racing through the corridors on various errands, Wasim and I verified that these alien capers were nothing like the capers on Earth, being the size of, for our comparison, giant watermelons, versus the size of peas or cherry tomatoes. The taste was also described as different—less briny because these weren't pickled, for starters, and far sweeter than any caper I'd ever ingested, while still being salty, and also managing to be both crunchy and smooth. I tried to follow the full detailed description of the creation process, but my Universal Translator didn't seem up to snuff with all the cooking terminology.

"If you're willing, you can partake, too," Aeron said as she finished her cooking description. I realized we were deep within the corridor system and I had no idea where we were.

"A real treat," Slennug added while I registered that I hadn't seen any other Gibbs for quite a while now.

"Where are we going, exactly?" Wasim asked.

Kram smiled a smile that showed all his teeth. They looked quite sharp. "To a very special place."

"And that place is?" I asked.

"We're here," said Aeron, who was now in the lead.

She stood in front of a door that looked just like the kitchen door and what seemed like a million other doors we'd passed. There were no markings that I could make out.

Slennug carefully put her tray down, pulled something out of one of her many pockets, and proceeded to pick the lock.

"Is this someone else's kitchen or station?" I asked, with a chuckle I hoped didn't sound nervous.

Slennug opened the door, picked up her tray, and smiled at me. "No. It's someplace less exciting but far more rewarding."

I knew in my bones that Wasim and I should, at this moment, drop the trays, turn around, and run like hell. Only I had no idea where we'd run to and, if my instincts were wrong, insulting these Gibbs would be a terrible thing for intergalactic politics. So, instead, I followed the ladies inside, Wasim behind me, Semaj and Kram bringing up the rear.

The room we entered was mostly dark, but there was a gentle blue glow, just enough for me to see that we were in what looked like a museum. Cases lined the walls and a variety of smaller display pedestals were sprinkled all over the room. I couldn't make out what was in the cases, however.

The TCs all put their trays on the ground. Wasim and I did the same. "I don't believe I've been in here before," Wasim said, for both of us.

"You're here now," Semaj said heartily. "Aren't you lucky?"

Kram walked to a wall and flipped a light on. The room was huge and it sparkled with more ornate jewelry than I'd seen in one place. Every case along the wall, every pedestal or table in the room, was laden with jewels or jewel-encrusted things. It was as if each piece was trying to outdo the others in terms of size and glitter.

Kram returned to his tray and picked it up. The rest of us did the same.

Kram led us through this room and two more just like it, connected to each other like museum rooms on Earth. He turned on the lights for each room. Some of the other rooms had more tools than jewelry, but there wasn't one thing that wasn't covered with precious gems or shiny metals.

We reached the fourth room, which had a long table in the center. There were no chairs. There were also no cabinets or pedestals, though the walls were covered with ornamented weapons—edged, projectile, and blunt instruments of such a wide variety I had to assume they were covering the weapons display of the entire solar system.

The TCs put their trays down on the table and Wasim and I followed suit.

"What's going on?" I asked quietly, wishing I'd insisted that Naveed not leave us alone. Kram had had no issues lighting up the place, no alarms were going off, no security personnel were racing in. Perhaps Slennug hadn't picked the lock so much as their keys and locks didn't work like I expected. And yet, I knew in my bones that there was no way we were up to anything other than no good.

Kram smiled at us. "What do you think is going on?"

Wasim and I looked at each other. I had zero idea of where we were, how we'd gotten here, or what was going on, but I had a very clear idea of what we were going to do next—something illegal with potentially catastrophic ramifications. "I think we're all about to commit a crime."

"I love insightful people," Slennug said cheerfully.

"You're planning a robbery?" My stomach shared that no one I could think of was going to be pleased with my protection of Wasim, starting with me.

"Oh, no," Aeron said heartily.

"Oh, good." I felt relieved. I've always been a slow learner.

"It's been planned for years," Slennug said cheerfully. "We've just been waiting for the right event. The arrival of your spaceship and the resulting revelry is such an event."

"Oh...good." My relief had already turned to a form of resigned horror. I tried to decide if I was naïve, gullible, or just an idiot. "What do you think Wasim and I are going to do?"

"And why would you think we'd assist you in committing any crime at all?" Wasim asked.

"Don't think of it as a crime," Semaj said. "We just feel that it's time for some movement of wealth, that's all."

Kram grinned. "I give you my word no one will be injured. Well, not badly injured. Minor potential injuries only. Other than, possibly, financially. But I doubt it."

"So, it's a heist?" Wasim asked, sounding far more interested than I felt was good for either one of us.

"It is," Semaj confirmed.

"Honestly," Aeron waved her hand around at the various glittering objects, "it's like they're just asking for it. I mean, what normal person brings along every piece of jewelry they own 'just in case?' And yet, everyone here has done so. It's ludicrous."

"This isn't a museum?" I asked.

"It is in a way," Kram said. "It's the display area that doubles as what I think your people would call a safety deposit box."

"People bring their crown jewels and such here and then leave them in these unguarded rooms?" Wasim sounded shocked out of his mind. If we ever got home, I imagined that he and his grandfather, the King of Bahrain, were going to have a very interesting chat about this.

"They do," Slennug said flatly. "Can you believe it?"

"Not really," Wasim admitted. "It seems…excessive for no reason."

"Exactly!" Aeron crowed.

"And the less said about all the credits they're tossing about, the better," Semaj added. "And these weapons? Who needs a jewel encrusted mallet? Honestly, tell me, who?"

"Flaunting the wealth," Slennug said. "Waving it in our faces. And, frankly, the security measures are a joke. It's as if they *want* us to steal things, truly."

"Agreed," Semaj said heartily. "The only security forces worth anything are the people who came with you."

Wasim cleared his throat. "Am I correct in guessing that whatever it is that Mister Buchanan felt needed Naveed and Mister Gadhavi is, in fact, part of your plot?"

"He is *such* a bright boy!" Kram said with genuine delight. "It's a joy to work with intelligent people."

"We haven't agreed to work with you," I pointed out.

"You've met Lord Sominou?" Kram asked.

"Yes, we both have," I replied. "Why?"

"Do you like him?" Semaj asked.

I decided to be honest. "Not really, no."

"I don't, either," Wasim confirmed.

"We don't, as well," Slennug said.

"And why does this matter?" I asked.

"This entire display is his idea," Kram replied.

"Is it his idea to not have it guarded?" I tried to hide the derisive shock in my tone. The TCs all hooted laughs, showing I hadn't managed.

"I told you he was intuitive," Aeron said to Semaj.

"Is *he* planning to steal everything?" Wasim asked.

"Oh, no," Slennug said with a sly grin. "He's not a Gibb, after all." The other TCs all snickered.

"No, he's a supercilious racist." I looked at the trays. "What did we carry in here?"

"It's not a delicacy, is it?" Wasim added. The TCs shrugged and grinned at us.

I lifted the dome from my tray. There was a large, greenish, rather blah-looking ovoid sitting there. It looked pretty much like the alien caper Aeron had described. The others removed their domes as well. Six trays, six alien capers. But I doubted these were actually edible. "These aren't the items Aeron described to us on the way, are they?"

The TCs grinned and each karate chopped their caper. The outer shells broke apart, revealing large neon green, glowing, gelatinous blobs that reminded me of radioactive nuclear waste or badly made lime Jell-O. Aeron chopped my caper, but they moved Wasim's to the side.

"What happens when someone comes in here to get their things and they're gone?" I made sure the blobs didn't touch me or Wasim.

"We have a plan for that, of course," Kram said.

"Besides," Aeron added, "they're occupied right now."

Kram chuckled and went to the only door I'd seen since we entered, which was at the far side of the room, and gestured for us to follow him. He opened the door and we all looked out, though I was quite aware that Semaj was standing close behind me and Wasim. Maybe he just wanted a good look. Maybe he was ready to grab us if we tried to run or shout a warning. I decided to do neither, just in case.

Of course, if Wasim or I or all the TCs together had been shouting, no one would have heard us. I hadn't realized the rooms we were in were soundproofed, but I certainly hadn't heard the ruckus that was going on before us.

People were running around like madmen, screaming their heads off, waving their arms about as if they were trying to escape from something, only that something was all around them, so no one was actually leaving the area. I didn't see any of our people and had no idea if that was good or bad. What I did see were small, green, glowing things. If we'd been home, I'd have thought we'd discovered a new color of lightning bug—the same neon green as the gelatinous blobs that were sitting on the table.

"Where are those from our delegation?" Wasim asked, right on cue.

"I'd assume wherever your Mister Buchanan had Mister Gadhavi and Naveed help him get them to," Kram said cheerfully.

"As I said," Semaj added, "the only good security is your security."

"What are those?" Wasim asked.

"Pests," Slennug replied, as Kram backed us up and closed and locked the door. "A particularly nasty infestation of angry burrflies. They hurt, but they aren't deadly."

"Just extremely distracting," Aeron said smugly.

"What's really going on and why have you included me and Wasim in this plot?" I asked, rather more weakly than I'd have liked.

"Because we like you," Kram said. "And we'd rather work with you than give you a drug to make you sleep and leave you alone in the kitchens. How would that be protecting the young prince?"

"Oh. Yes. Of course. This is so much better." I managed, with supreme effort, to keep the sarcasm out of my voice. "So, you plan to take, ah, redistribute everything here to yourselves?"

The TCs all hooted laughs. In a different situation it would have been cute. Right now, it was unnerving.

"No," Kram said with a sigh. "We plan to teach them a lesson. And, I believe, once we explain it to you, you'll see why what we're doing is right."

* * *

"So," I said hurriedly, "these aren't the actual crown jewels. They're fakes. The TCs have taken the real ones." We'd been joined by every other Gibb working this event. They'd all gone out in groups of twos and threes, bold as brass, carrying armfuls of priceless items, using the main walkways. No one paid them any attention, they were too busy flailing about at the burrflies. Proof, for me, that the security in this system redefined the term "appalling."

"That's supposed to make this better?" Buchanan asked.

"No," Wasim said, "this is. All the 'stolen' jewels and antiquities and such are in a secure location. The Gibbs are trying to prove the point that they're better at security than any of the others, and that they should be given those jobs and positions of trust. They've taken these things to prove that they can, but they're going to return them to prove that they're trustworthy."

Everyone stared at us. "And, somehow, the two of you think that's the real plan, or if somehow it is the real plan, that it'll work?" Buchanan looked like he really wanted to hit someone but was using all his self-control to avoid doing so.

"Yes." I could say this confidently, because the linchpin to the plan was under our control. It was why the TCs had included us.

"The flying pests, they were part of the plot?" Gadhavi asked, looking thoughtful.

I nodded. "They're something the Gibbs created. They can and do function as you saw when they 'attacked.' But they can also combine and change their shapes." I pointed to the table full of "crown jewels" we were standing by.

"Those are made of the same pests?" Gadhavi asked.

"Burrflies," Wasim confirmed. "They have a variety of uses. Good and bad."

"Prove it," Buchanan said tiredly. "And then go on to explain why you bought this malarkey."

Wasim pushed his finger into the "crown" nearest to him. It boiled up, separated, turned into far too many burrflies for comfort, and then settled back down into the crown shape. Everyone else looked very impressed. Wasim and I had seen a burrfly nest in action already, so it was less of a thrill for us.

"We bought the malarkey because they took everything back to the main kitchen," I shared. "The goods are stored in the big freezers."

This earned the most shocked and horrified looks yet.

"Why?" Buchanan asked, sounding like the most resigned and tired man in the universe. "Just tell me why you thought that was okay."

"Because they feel that the only good security here is ours. I'll point out that you got Naveed and Mister Gadhavi, handled whatever distraction the Gibbs had created, then got all of our people to safety. And I know this because we didn't see any of you while the heist was going down."

"You sound so gangsta," Buchanan said. "I point back to the word 'heist' and ask why you think you haven't been conned."

"Because we believe them," Wasim said.

I nodded. "They wanted to ensure that the wealth was put somewhere safe, where they could guard it and return it easily, but where no one from this system would think to check." I cleared my throat. "That's why Wasim and I are here—we were waiting for someone, anyone, to come check on their priceless artifacts after the pests suddenly and mysteriously disappeared." They'd all come here, to create more of the fake jewelry.

"You all were the first," Wasim said.

Buchanan, Naveed, and Gadhavi exchanged a look. "You did say that we should verify that the prized possessions we've heard so much about were still in place," Gadhavi said to Buchanan.

"And you had mentioned that the pests seemed to leave in only one direction," Naveed said to Gadhavi, "and you suggested we investigate. Finding Prince Wasim safely here was an added bonus, but was not the original goal."

I nodded. "The Gibbs would like us to help them explain why they need to be put in charge of security. After today's events, I really can't argue with them. Oh, and after this is settled, we'll want to have them talk to our people about these burrflies. I imagine we'll have uses for them, and I've ensured that the Gibbs are willing to share how to create, nurture, train, and contain them in return for our assistance."

Of course, this wasn't good enough for Buchanan. We went back to the kitchens as a group, through the back corridors. I still had no idea where we were, but Buchanan never made a wrong turn.

The TCs were waiting for us, smiling, the only real alien caper—the one Wasim had carted all over—cut up and on display. It looked a lot better than the burrfly nests did. "Can we interest you in something tasty," Kram asked, indicating the caper, "or priceless?"

"Or something borrowed?" Aeron said, as she handed me a piece of caper.

"Something pretty," Slennug chimed in, giving a piece to Wasim.

"Or something that needs better care?" Semaj asked, as he handed the tray around to the others, most of whom took some. The caper was as delicious as promised, and maybe it would be worth all the work it took to get a piece.

"We have it all," Kram finished. "And we want it all. But we'll give it back, as long as we get to add on one more job that no one else here seems capable of doing."

Buchanan and several others checked the freezers. "It's all there, at least it looks like it," he said as they rejoined us. "And we touched everything and it remained inanimate."

"Do we have a deal?" Kram asked. "You help us and we return the goods?"

"If we don't help you?" Buchanan asked.

Kram grinned. "We take the money and run."

Buchanan snorted. "Then I guess we help you."

Before anyone could say anything else, several gorillas came running in, Lord Sominou in the lead. "We've been robbed!" he shouted.

"We know," Wasim said, sounding extremely regal and clearly using the Royal We, as he drew himself up to his full height. "And We have worked with your most faithful citizens to ensure that the thefts were contained. We will assist in the return of your items of incalculable value, as long as you will listen to Us and Our counsel, as We see a great need your people have, along with a way to fill that need expeditiously."

The gorillas all nodded. "Yes, your Royal Highness, we would appreciate your assistance." Sominou bowed. "We will follow your lead."

"Excellent. It begins with this. Lord Kram, if you would join Us?" Wasim asked.

Kram bowed. "As you wish, my Prince."

The gorillas gaped. "Lord?" Sominou asked, sounding like this was far more shocking than the fact that all the crown jewels of every planet had disappeared.

"Lord," Wasim said firmly. He nodded to me. "You will handle things here, Dion?"

"Yes, my Prince."

He turned back to the gorillas. "Then, let us adjourn to a different location, so that the rest of these fine Gibbs can continue to save the day." With that, Wasim left the kitchens, walking next to Kram, Sominou, and the other gorillas. Naveed and most of our Earth delegation followed them. Gadhavi, however, stayed behind with me.

Aeron smiled at me. "Thank you." Slennug hugged me.

And Semaj shook my hand. Gently. "It's always better to work with smart people, which was why we worked with you and Wasim. You're smart enough to be Gibbs."

Slennug winked at Gadhavi. "Of course, they're not the only ones."

Gadhavi chuckled. "I sense the beginning of a beautiful friendship."

All I sensed was that this alien caper was over, and Wasim and I had somehow managed to survive it, acquire new technology, and even avoid Buchanan's wrath. Travel really does broaden your horizons.

MAGICK ON
THE HALF SHELL

D.B. Jackson

Boston, Province of Massachusetts Bay, 18 September 1761

Ethan Kaille watched the tavern door, the cool protection of a warding spell already draped over him like a mantle, the words to an attack conjuring on his lips. His forearm, held below the edge of the table at which he sat, bled from a knife wound, self-inflicted, the blood intended as source for his next spell.

A pistol hung from his belt, also out of sight. A last resort in case his magick failed him.

All this in preparation for an afternoon engagement with the dangerous and inscrutable Sephira Pryce. As far as he knew, she wielded no magick of her own. She hardly needed to do so. She was deadly with a blade and she employed ruthless toughs, most of them as huge as seventy-gun ships.

Ethan didn't know what she wanted with him, but he was here, in the Crow's Nest, a run-down, disreputable tavern in Boston's North End, at her instruction. He would have preferred to avoid the woman entirely. She had all but declared herself his mortal enemy the first time they met, back in the spring. She was Boston's foremost thieftaker, the self-proclaimed Empress of the South End. He was a half-lame ex-convict who cobbled together a living recovering stolen goods for a bit of coin. That, though, made them rivals, in her eyes at least.

He hadn't seen her since their initial encounter, but her men had harried him repeatedly, dogging him as he conducted his inquiries, threatening his life, occasionally attempting beatings that, if not for his magick, a bit of wit, and a healthy dose of luck, might have made good on those threats.

He had honored her summons because he had little choice. He could avoid Sephira, he could defy her wishes simply by plying his trade despite her warnings of retribution, but to refuse an explicit request that he join her? Even Ethan wasn't so foolish.

Until now, it hadn't occurred to him that she might not show up herself. Had she lured him here so that her men could finally kill him? Had she alerted Stephen Greenleaf, the Sheriff of Suffolk County, to his imminent presence in the tavern so that the man might arrest Ethan and hang him for a witch? The cut on Ethan's forearm itched. A trickle of sweat tickled his temple.

The tavern door opened and a large, homely man lumbered in. Spotting Ethan, he positioned himself beside the door, crossed his massive arms over his chest, and stared straight ahead. Two more men entered. One was small, dark-haired and dark-eyed, the other yellow-haired and as big as the first. He had a long, horsey face and small icy blue eyes. This man—Ethan knew him only as Nigel— approached the table.

Ethan raised his arm enough to let the tough see his blood.

Nigel faltered mid-stride.

"No need for that," he said, drawling the words. "She wants a word is all. We're to take you to her."

"A word," Ethan repeated. "I'm to believe that?"

Yellow-hair's expression turned stony. "You believe whatever the hell you want, Kaille, but I'm here for Miss Pryce and I'm no liar."

"And you have no interest in revenge? For me putting you and your friends to sleep the last time we met?"

"Oh, I want revenge for that, believe me. And I'll have it eventually. But I have my orders and they don't include bloodying you unless you give me no choice." He grinned, exposing crooked teeth. "So, on second thought, go ahead: refuse to come along. That's all the excuse I need."

Ethan stood, his knife still in hand, the blade poised over his forearm. He could cast, cut himself, and cast again in the time it took Yellow-hair to draw a weapon.

Sephira's tough eyed the knife and the blood already on Ethan's arm before indicating the door with an open hand and a mocking bow.

Ethan raised his chin in the direction of the entrance. "You first."

Nigel chuckled and motioned the other two men out the door. He paused on the threshold, still grinning, and glanced back at Ethan.

"Without that witchery of yours, you're nothin'. You know that, right?"

"Of course. Just as you're nothing without your brawn and your friends. I suppose we have that in common."

The man's smile slipped. "Just come along." He stalked off toward Cornhill and the South End. As they stepped into the open, Ethan whispered a summons in Latin. The blood vanished from his arm and power thrummed in the cobblestones beneath his feet.

A ghostly figure appeared at his side. Tall, lean, dour, dressed in mail and a tabard bearing the sigil of the Plantagenet kings: Ethan's spectral guide, visible only to him and others who wielded magick. Ethan called him Reg, after a similarly ill-tempered uncle on his mother's side of the family.

"Stay close to me." He kept his voice low. "I don't trust these three."

Reg nodded, his eyes glowing like russet stars. Ethan rolled down his sleeve as he limped behind the toughs, but he kept his knife handy. Within the Crow's Nest, he didn't worry much about others learning he was a speller; in a tavern that catered to thieves and smugglers, customers made a point of staying out of one another's affairs. Out in the streets of Boston, though, a bloodied arm might draw unwanted attention and accusations that he consorted with the devil.

Pryce's men led him past the Town Dock and Faneuil Hall to the South End waterfront. This they followed around Fort Hill to Griffin's Wharf. Wisps of cloud feathered an otherwise azure sky and the autumn air smelled of brine and mud and ship's tar.

Ethan slowed as they neared the pier, reluctant to enter the hulking warehouse. He had thought they would lead him to Sephira's home, which lay farther south and west. A warehouse like this one seemed an unlikely place to encounter a woman of her refined tastes and inflated sense of her own importance. On the other hand, it might be a fine place to kill a man and dispose of his corpse.

"Come on then, Kaille," Nigel called, waving him on. The other two toughs waited for them by the warehouse door.

"I think I won't actually."

"She's in here, waitin' for you."

Ethan said nothing.

"You have my word, no harm will come to you."

Ethan bit his tongue to keep himself from commenting on the worth of Nigel's word. This struck him as the wrong time to further antagonize the man.

"If she's in there," he said instead, "tell her to come out. I want to see her before I go in."

He thought Nigel would refuse. After a moment, however, the tough turned back to his companions and said to the smaller man, "Ask her if she'll come out. Tell her Ethan here has suddenly turned shy."

The other two laughed. The dark-haired man slipped into the building.

To Ethan's surprise, the door opened barely a minute later, revealing Sephira, her lips curved in an amused smile. She was every bit as striking as he remembered from their previous encounter. She wore street clothes—black breeches and boots, a white blouse open at the neck, an embroidered waistcoat that hugged her form with the ardor of a lover. Sunlight sparkled in sapphire blue eyes and dark curls flowed like a cascade over her shoulders. A faint scar traced her jawline. Other smaller ones marked her temple, cheek, and brow.

"Good day, Ethan." She didn't raise her voice, but her words carried over the shouts of wharfmen and sailors, the cries of gulls, and the slap of waves against the pier.

"Good day."

She said something he couldn't hear to Nigel. He frowned, glanced at Ethan, and gestured to the other tough. The two of them entered the warehouse, leaving Ethan and Sephira alone on the wharf.

"Better?" she asked.

He approached her, his bad leg aching, and scanned the wharf for other toughs. Reg walked with him, ghostly pale in the sunlight, unnoticed by Sephira.

"You were surprised by my invitation."

Invitation? He had taken it as a command. "To say the least."

"I told you the last time we met that I would have use for you on occasion."

"Yes. When jobs demanding magick came your way. Aside from that, you made quite clear I was to stay away from any potential clients. I believe you threatened my life."

She laughed. It was her best quality, that laugh. Throaty, unrestrained, almost musical. He didn't trust it.

"You make it sound so dramatic. I merely wished to impress upon you that I don't take kindly to anyone who robs me of coin that's rightfully mine." She didn't give him time to respond. "But that's not what you're doing here." She opened her hands. These bore scars as well: keepsakes from a life spent in the streets. "I asked you to come because I have a client who you are...let's say, better equipped to help than I could ever be."

"A client."

"That's right."

"And this person has a problem of a...a magickal nature?"

"So it seems to me. You're the expert."

He weighed this.

"He's inside," she said, another twist of her hand indicating the warehouse. "Shall we speak with him? If you feel you can't help, there's no harm done. But if you can help him, it means coin in your pocket."

"And a rescue of your reputation."

"Precisely. We both benefit, which is the sort of association between us that I've hoped for from the start."

Ethan wasn't sure he believed that, but he hadn't had work in some weeks now and he had rent to pay on his room above Henry Dall's cooperage. "All right. I'll speak with your client."

She dazzled him with another smile. "Excellent."

Sephira led him into the warehouse, which was cavernous and warm and smelled of sweat and dust and stale ale. Nigel and the other toughs stood near the far wall, a short distance from a plump, bald man who sat on a barrel, appearing nervous and impatient. His clothes—brown breeches, a stained linen shirt, muddied boots, and a worn tricorn hat that he held in one hand—did not inspire in Ethan much hope of a generous reward for whatever labors this job might entail. He'd already given his word, though.

The click of Sephira's boot heels on the wooden floor echoed through the building. The bald man marked their approach and stood as Sephira neared him.

"Ethan Kaille," she said, "may I present Mister Frederick Denny? Mister Denny, this is Ethan Kaille, the associate of mine whom I mentioned earlier today."

Hearing her call him an "associate," Ethan glanced her way. She sent a warning glare in his direction.

"Ah, yes." The man proffered a hand. "A pleasure to make your acquaintance, Mister Kaille."

"And yours, sir," Ethan said, grasping the man's hand. Denny's palm was damp and clammy, his grip in return barely discernible. Ethan resisted the urge to wipe his fingers on his waistcoat.

"Tell him the story you told me," Sephira said. "Please."

"Yes, of course." The man cleared his throat. "I make my living off harbor and sea, Mister Kaille. I'm a lobst'man, an oyst'man, a fish'rman. I lobster in the fall and winter and durin' the summer I fish for cod, haddock, bass, scup, and fluke, among others. But for much of the year, except the warm months, of course, I make most of my livelihood harvesting and selling oysters.

"Inns and taverns can't get enough of 'em, especially these days with everyone eatin' chowders." He leaned closer to Ethan, his breath rank with the smell of tobacco. "And I know where to find 'em. I have a place, a spot I've been usin' for a couple of years now. Best I've ever seen. It was like a gold mine."

"Was?" Ethan asked.

Denny's glance cut to Sephira again. She nodded encouragement.

"Well, that's just it. I can't get there anymore. Or rather, I can get there, but it's no use. I can't do nothin' with the spot once I'm there."

"It's been over-harvested."

"That's not it, either. There's one man—he has no trouble findin' oysters there. Collects them by the bucketful. But when I go...nothin'. It's like the reef appears when he arrives and vanishes again once he's gone."

Ethan straightened and regarded Sephira.

"I thought perhaps you could help Mister Denny," she said, "seeing as you have far more experience with this sort of thing than I do." To the oysterman, she added, "Ethan spends much of his time in the mud."

"You're an oyst'man, too?" Denny asked, a proprietary iciness seeping into his tone.

Ethan suppressed a laugh. "Merely as a hobby. Searching out pearls for local swine and all that."

Confusion creased Denny's brow. Sephira glowered.

"You know, the oysters we get here, they don't really give pearls the way people think."

"Never mind that, Mister Denny," Sephira said, still staring daggers at Ethan. "Finish your story."

"Well, there's not much left to tell, honestly. This one man seems to have done something to my oyster reef and I'm facing a lean winter if he don't stop whatever it is."

Ethan thought he knew most of the spellers here in Boston, but a conjurer who specialized in stealing seafood...? "Do you know his name?"

"Well, I asked around a bit and got a surname. Sort of. Folks call him Cochran. I don't know his given name."

"And can you describe him for me?"

"Not too well, no. I've only seen him from a distance. He's tall, lanky-like, young, with a mop of red hair."

"Nothing else?"

"No, I don't—well, wait. One fellow mentioned that he had a gap in his teeth." Denny pointed at his upper teeth, just off to one side of the front ones. "Right about here. Other than that, though..."

"That's all right," Ethan said. "Between knowing 'Cochran' and having that much by which to recognize him—that's helpful. Can you tell me where the oyster beds in question can be found?"

At this, Denny scowled, dropping his gaze to the floor and scratching the back of his head with vigor. "Well, as to that, I'm not sure I wish to say. Like I've told you, this is my livelihood—"

"Do you want my help or not, Mister Denny?"

"Well, sure I do, but—"

"Then you need to tell me where to go. I'm not interested in stealing your oysters. I make my living, such as it is, as a thieftaker, not an oysterman."

The man pressed his lips thin. Ethan looked to Sephira and raised his brows.

"Ethan will not poach your reef, Mister Denny," she said. "You have my word on that. But he does require this information. If you won't confide in us, we can't hope to thwart Cochran in his scheming."

"Yes, all right. It's...it's off the Neck, at the Roxbury end of the Causeway, on the eastern shore there."

"Thank you."

"You give me your word—"

"Yes, Mister Denny."

The man flinched at Ethan's tone.

Ethan took a breath and when he spoke again he managed to gentle his voice. "That should be enough for me to start an inquiry. Us, I mean. For us to start. Again, thank you."

"Wait here, Mister Denny," Sephira said, laying a slender hand on his arm. His cheeks colored at her touch. "I wish to speak with Ethan in private. Nigel will get you anything you need."

"All right." He stuck out a limp hand again. "It's good to meet you, Mister Kaille."

"And you, sir." Ethan took his hand briefly. "I'll do what I can for you."

Ethan caught Nigel's eye and tipped his head, drawing a smirk from the tough. Then he followed Sephira out of the warehouse.

"Local swine?" she said, rounding on him as he stepped into the autumn sunlight.

He grinned. "Much of my time in the mud?"

She actually laughed once more. "Yes, all right." She indicated the door with a lift of her tapered chin. "What do you think?"

"The same as you. This Cochran fellow is using magick to conceal the oysters from Mister Denny. And others, I would imagine."

"So that is possible."

"Aye. The required magick isn't terribly difficult, although maintaining the spell for days at a time might take some effort."

"Have you been aware of such spells?"

"I haven't. But if they were cast out that way—along the Neck—I might have assumed that any magick I sensed came from...from others I know who live there."

Sephira smirked. "The African witch. Windcatcher. You wear your secrets poorly, Ethan."

His turn to glower. Janna Windcatcher owned a beat-up tavern— the Fat Spider—along the Neck. She was a friend, despite her cantankerous manner, and Ethan would have done anything to protect her from Sephira.

"Don't look at me that way," she said. "The woman has nothing to fear from me. I just like to remind you that you can't hide anything from me."

"How much is he paying you?" Ethan asked, eager to change the subject.

"Do you trust me to tell you the truth?"

"No. I'll simply add three or four pounds to whatever amount you give and consider that the true sum."

She laughed again, tipping her head back. "Oh, Ethan. I regret that you're so stubborn. I believe you and I could have quite an amusing partnership."

He stared back at her.

"Seven pounds. That's the truth. I'll pay you three. One and ten now, and the balance once you've dealt with Cochran."

"I'll be doing the bulk of the work. Why not two now and two later?"

"Without me, you wouldn't even have the job."

He opened his hands in surrender. "All right." He pivoted and started away. "Best of luck finding Cochran and defeating his spells."

She let him walk perhaps ten paces before saying, "Three and ten each? Half now, half upon completion."

He halted and peered back at her, but didn't say a word.

After another few moments she chuffed a breath. "Fine. The shillings mean more to you than they do to me. Four and three."

He walked back to her. "Two right now."

She dug into her pocket, produced her purse, and poured out the coins, counting them with some care.

"I want word as soon as you've met the man. If you need help finding him—or securing his cooperation—you're welcome to borrow Nigel and Nap."

"Nap?"

"The smaller man."

"Thank you. But I believe I can do this alone." He pocketed the coins and strode away from her again. "You'll hear from me soon."

* * *

Finding Cochran proved difficult. Few had heard the name and several of those who did know a "Cochran" sent Ethan in pursuit of the wrong man, an elderly wheelwright in the South End. This Cochran knew nothing more of oysters than that he enjoyed eating them with his ales.

The day after his encounter with Sephira, however, as Ethan spoke to patrons in yet another bar, this one near the Cornhill waterfront, an older gentleman in the back of the establishment beckoned to him with a waggle of grimy fingers.

Ethan joined the man, who seemed well into his cups. A platter of empty oyster shells sat before him on the worn table.

"Did I hear you say you're lookin' for Cochran?" the man said, his words somewhat slurred.

"I'm looking for *a* Cochran, yes."

"The one who sells oysters."

"You know him?"

"'S possible I do. What's it to you?"

Ethan produced two shillings from his pocket and rubbed them together, the ring of silver on silver drawing the stranger's rheumy gaze.

The man wet his lips. "I seen him not so long ago. A day or two. He likes to sit out nights by a fire, enjoyin' a bit of his catch."

"Where?"

"This side of the causeway, between Gibbon's Yard and the city gate."

Ethan set the shillings on the table. "Thank you, friend."

He stood, his chair scraping on the wood floor, and stepped away from the table.

"Folks say he's odd," the man called after him, making Ethan halt. "Dangerous, even. They say he walks with the devil."

Ethan gave a grim smile, his back still to the man. "Some have said the same about me." He left the tavern and started toward the South End.

* * *

That evening, with the sun slipping behind a bank of gray clouds on the western horizon and the first pale stars emerging in the deep blue overhead, Ethan made his way to the oyster beds Denny had described for him. He had cloaked himself in a concealment spell and warded himself with a second casting before leaving his room above the cooperage. He walked with as much care as the old wound to his foot would allow. He sent Reg away before setting out, but he knew he would need the spectral guide again before the night was through.

The mud flats were empty when he arrived. He couldn't tell if Cochran, or anyone else, had been there earlier in the day. Reluctant as he was to cast any spell and draw Cochran's attention—if the man was, in fact, a speller—he also needed proof that Denny's suspicions had some basis in fact.

After a moment's hesitation, he squatted, pulled a handful of marsh grass from the sour mud, and whispered, "*Revela omnias magias ex gramine evocatas,*" a spell intended to reveal all magicks used on the shoreline before him.

His conjuring vibrated in the ground, announcing to any spellers within miles that he had cast. Reg winked into view across from him, the color of a blood moon, his gleaming eyes fixed avidly on the mud between them.

Slowly, a nimbus of light emerged from the ooze—pale blue, like a hazed summer sky. Evidence of a spell.

"Can you see through the magick?" Ethan asked. "Are there oysters here?"

Reg nodded, eyes still on the mud.

"Can you tell from the spell how powerful this Cochran is?"

At that, the ghost met Ethan's gaze and shook his head.

"All right. Thank you. I need to find him now, which means I need for you to leave me, lest he spot you before I see him. *Dimmito te.*"

With the release, Reg faded from view. Ethan stood, returned to the causeway, and headed back toward the Neck, where the old man in the tavern had said Cochran might be found.

Before he had covered half the distance, he caught sight of a pale orange glow in the low brush. Ethan made his way in that direction, hoping the warding spell he'd cast earlier would hold against this man's magick. He preferred to avoid a magickal battle, but he wasn't confident that he could.

While he was still some distance from the small fire, a man's voice rang out, "I hear ya. And I saw your ghost before. So come on then, let me see ya."

He hadn't expected to take the man completely by surprise, but he had hoped to have a look at him, appraise him from afar before being discovered. Cursing under his breath, he closed the distance between them. As he stepped into the shifting circle of light cast by the man's fire, he pulled leaves from a bush and whispered a spell to remove his concealment.

Reg appeared again and eyed the other man.

The stranger was much as Denny had described. Even sitting on a thick piece of driftwood, he appeared tall, his limbs angular and lean. He had a bony face, handsome but severe. His eyes, beneath a swoop of red hair, were deep set and might have been green. It was hard to tell in this light. He greeted Ethan with a grim smile, exposing that gap in his large teeth.

He regarded Reg for a second, but appeared far more interested in Ethan himself, whom he studied through narrowed eyes. After a few moments of this, he reached down into a bucket Ethan hadn't yet noticed, picked out an oyster, and wedged it open with a blunt, silver blade. He shucked with the skill of a surgeon, tossed the top piece of shell onto an already sizable pile, and tipped back his head to slurp down the oyster and its liquor.

Facing Ethan again, he gestured with his knife to a spot on the ground. "Join me?"

Ethan hesitated. The man shifted his bucket so that it would rest within Ethan's reach. He pulled a second knife from the pocket of his mud-stained breeches and tossed it over the fire. It bounced once and came to rest near the oysters.

"Come on then. Sit. Eat with me. I know ya didn't come for a meal or conversation, but that doesn't mean we can't enjoy both before we fight."

Ethan regarded him, still standing. "I don't wish to fight you."

The man leaned forward and took another oyster. "No, I don't imagine." He gestured again with his blade. "Please, sit."

Ethan lowered himself to the ground, helped himself to an oyster, and shucked it with the second knife. He hadn't the other man's skill, but he managed to open the oyster without a struggle.

"Not bad. Ya've some experience."

"Some, yes. Are you Cochran?"

A thin smile flickered in the man's features. "I am. Stuart Cochran." He extended a large hand just to the right of the fire. Ethan gripped it. The man's handshake was as firm as Denny's had been weak.

"Ethan Kaille."

Cochran dropped his hand and turned his attention to his oyster. Ethan tipped his into his mouth. Briny and sweet, firm and rich. He ate oysters often in the city—they were a staple in most taverns, along with ales and flips—yet even the few hours it might take to get oysters from the waterfront to Boston's kitchens was enough to sap them of some flavor. These were as fresh as a dawn wind off the harbor. He was no expert, but he could taste the difference.

"Good?" Cochran asked, reaching for yet another.

"Remarkable." Ethan leaned toward the bucket, then stopped himself. "May I?"

"Take as many as ya want, Mister Kaille."

"My thanks." As he shucked this second one, Ethan said, "I'm here at the behest of a man named Denny."

"I guessed as much. Are ya with the city watch?"

Ethan laughed, ate. "No." He took another oyster from the bucket. "Sheriff Greenleaf would sooner cut off his own arm than welcome a speller onto his watch."

"I didn't know that."

"I'm a thieftaker. Mister Denny hired an *associate* of mine." He nearly tripped on Sephira's word. "She, upon realizing that magick had been used, turned to me for help."

Cochran had been about to swallow another oyster, but now he lowered his hand, considering Ethan across the fire. "A thieftaker," he repeated. "How odd. I've stolen nothing and, as far as I know, Denny has lost nothing that was his."

"You've used your magick to conceal the harvest from him."

"Ah! Well, that's hardly the same thing."

"I disagree."

"Tell me, Mister Kaille: this other thieftaker—yar associate...I assume ya refer to Sephira Pryce. I've heard of her. Most in Boston have. She's better known than ya, better situated than ya, she has men in her employ. I'm goin' to hazard a guess that ya don't."

He didn't give Ethan a chance to confirm this.

"Do ya accuse her of stealing when, by dint of her reputation and resources, she secures clients that pass ya by?"

"I'm not sure that's—"

"If Mister Denny was fishing for cod, and another fisherman used a bigger, better net to take in fish that otherwise might have been his, would ya accuse him of stealin'?" He watched Ethan, expectant, an eyebrow cocked.

"No, I wouldn't."

"Of course not. Well, my magick is my net. Just as yar magick is the one advantage ya have over Pryce. Ya wouldn't give that up, would ya, even if she insisted?"

Ethan didn't answer. The truth was, Cochran's argument hewed closely to the first conversation Ethan and Sephira had, when she spoke of their relative advantages and disadvantages in similar terms. He found the man's reasoning hard to refute.

"If ya've come to force me to stop using my magick, I'm afraid ya're goin' to be disappointed."

Ethan took another oyster, shucked it, and ate it, watching Cochran the entire time. "Mister Denny feels," he said at last, choosing his words with care, "that he found this particular bed first and that, in denying him access to it, you've unfairly hindered his ability to pursue his livelihood."

"He thinks he found it first," Cochran said, his tone flattening. His gaze turned flinty. After a few seconds he reached for the bucket and moved it back to his side, beyond Ethan's reach. "How 'bout this: if I were to forswear use of my spells, would he forswear use of a bucket?"

Ethan laughed. "I don't believe he would, no."

Cochran spread his hands. "Well, then..."

"I believe he would pay me, though, to accompany him to the beds each morning and use my magick to remove your concealment. That, according to your reasoning, would be a perfectly fair solution. Don't you think?"

The young man glared. "Ya wouldn't go with him every morning," he said after a long silence. "Surely ya have better things to do with yar time."

"I've been hired to solve a problem, Mister Cochran. Denny paid me, and Miss Pryce as well. We're honor-bound to do what we must to keep our word."

Cochran's breathing deepened and the muscles in his jaw tightened. After a moment, Ethan realized his lips were moving, though he made not a sound. A pale blue figure materialized at Cochran's shoulder— the spirit of a young man with hair like Cochran's. Magic growled in the ground.

Ethan braced himself and so managed to remain upright when the spell hit him. Even so, he reeled and grunted at the impact. It felt like he'd been kicked in the chest by a mule. He couldn't have said what Cochran's spell had been intended to do, but it might well have proved fatal if not for Ethan's warding.

"My turn," Ethan said.

He assumed Cochran was shielded with magick, so he directed a shatter spell at the log beneath the man. And he sourced his conjuring in the fuel he knew would most bother the pup. "*Discuti ex ostribus evocatum.*" At least half the oysters in the bucket vanished. Ethan's spell roared in answer and Reg reappeared beside him, his teeth bared at the other ghost.

The log upon which Cochran sat exploded in a cloud of wood chips and sawdust. The pup gave a cry and flopped onto his back, landing hard, air leaving his chest with a loud *ooomph*.

Ethan was on his feet before the dust cleared. He strode around the fire, dropped to his knees, and pounded a fist into the man's jaw once, and then a second time.

The first blow snapped Cochran's head to the side and addled him. With the second, the man went still.

By the time he woke again, his spectral guide had faded from view. Reg remained.

Ethan sat by the fire, which he had stirred and built up against the gathering chill of night. And he chewed yet another oyster before tossing the empty shell onto his own not-inconsiderable pile. He had nearly emptied the bucket.

Cochran moaned and propped himself up on one elbow. His jaw was already swollen and discolored. He dabbed at it with his free hand and winced.

"That was a good punch."

"Thank you."

Cochran pushed himself up into a sitting position. Ethan put down the shucking knife and picked up his own, which he laid against the skin of his forearm.

Cochran shook his head. "I'm not going to fight ya, Kaille."

Ethan lowered his arm, but kept hold of his knife, refusing to abandon all to trust.

"There anythin' left in that bucket?"

"A few." Ethan handed the pail to Cochran.

The young man felt around for an oyster and levered it open. "Did I hear ya right before? Denny hired ya and Sephira Pryce both?"

"Aye, he did."

"So, if I don't do as ya say, *she'll* be after me."

"Likely so."

Cochran blew out a breath. "Well, that's... Damn."

"No one else has hired us," Ethan said.

The man frowned. "Well, no I wouldn't expect so."

"Think, Cochran. *No one else has hired us.*"

It took the pup a few moments, but when the import of what Ethan had said came to him, he actually smiled, only to wince again and raise a hand to his bruised jaw.

"So, if I were to let Denny see the beds—Denny only—he and I could share the harvest. Just the two of us."

"I wouldn't have a problem with that. I don't think Sephira would, either."

Cochran considered this, at last giving a single nod. "I can live with that."

"Good. I'll arrange a meeting between the two of you for tomorrow. Sephira and I will be there as well."

"All right."

"How do I reach you?"

"Denny knows where to find me."

Ethan chuckled. One was as reluctant to speak of the oyster bed's exact location as the other. He had a feeling theirs would be a successful—if fraught—partnership. He wondered if he and Sephira might have a similar association, but quickly banished the thought. He didn't trust her and he was almost certain that she wanted not a partner but rather another employee—a magickal one at that.

"Very well." He climbed to his feet. "I'll leave you to your fire and the remains of your supper."

Cochran said nothing and Ethan started away. Before he was beyond sight of the man's blaze, though, Cochran called his name. Ethan stopped and turned.

"Ya've never had oysters as good as mine, have ya?"

"No," Ethan said, meaning it. "I never have."

The pup nodded, appearing pleased. Ethan walked on, intent on finding a tavern in which to sit and complete his evening. He wouldn't order more oysters. There were none he'd find that could compare with those he'd already eaten. But nothing went with oysters like a fine Kent ale.

APOCALYPSE CHOW

Jason Palmatier

Jenna looked down at her feet, preparing herself for whatever inane thing was going to come her way when she pushed open the moldy door. The reusable grocery bag on her shoulder dug in like it had for the last ten miles, but she ignored it. Instead she focused on the good things about this place: the fresh water of the creek on the far side of the cabin, the hidden location nestled in a gully, the warmth of its woodstove against the coming northern winter. She took a deep breath to calm herself and got a lungful of sick pungency, courtesy of the composting toilet inside. *Ugh. If that resort hadn't been burned down I'd be in four star heaven right now. Whatever. Just a few months, then it'll be spring and safe to hike out of here.* She turned the knob and walked in.

"You get me some capers?" Randy asked in his back-hills lilt before she had set a single foot on the torn linoleum floor. Jenna pressed her lips together and let her heel hit before looking up at the paunchy, middle-aged man lying blissfully in a fully-reclined puke-orange and brown chair. He was clothed in muddy hunting boots, ratty cargo shorts, stained t-shirt, and, of course, the obligatory flannel over-shirt. The brace made of shim slats on his leg was the icing on the Walmart Select cake. "You got me hooked on those things with that last wild turkey pick hotta' you made. Nothin' tastes right without 'em. Missing something..." Randy finished with what was probably supposed to be an introspective look.

Jenna groaned. "It was turkey *piccata*, Randy. And no, I did not get any Mystical Mountain Capers. They were all out." She walked past the small living room into the tiny kitchen, bypassing the stairs that lead up to the loft where her stolen sleeping bag lay. Randy used to stay up there, as evidenced by the giant Confederate flag on the wall, but they'd made his bed up in the bunk room behind the bathroom because of his foot. The cabin was falling-down shit, but it looked like a mansion compared to the speck of an apartment she had shared with her three friends back in the city.

"Pretty well looted down there, then?" Randy asked as he chivalrously clicked his chair into only a semi-reclined position.

His voice brought Jenna back from the front door of her apartment, right before she had pulled it open for the last time and left it for good. Left *them*...

She cleared her throat. "Yeah, it's pretty much all gone."

A part of her mind noted the increase in yellowed foam filling made of God-knows-what that was bulging up through the hole in the arm of Randy's chair. He must have been picking at the threads around it again while she was gone. Jenna set down the grocery bag and started unloading the kitsch bounty she was able to snag at the Mystic Woods Magic Mart down on old Route 26.

"That that mustard with the onion bits in it?" Randy asked from his throne.

Jenna nodded. Blurred looks of horror and pain had risen up before her and the stink of the composting toilet had taken on the sweetness of decomposing bodies. She clicked her LED lantern on by the stove with a shaking hand, even though the day's light was still fading. "They're garlic chives, actually. But yeah, that's it."

"Hmm," Randy said as he sipped from a beer bottle filled with creek water. "I don't like that much."

"I know," Jenna said flatly. She pressed a palm, *hard*, onto the ridge melted into the laminate countertop by an errant pot and focused on the pain. The smells and the pleading eyes faded.

"All they had, though?" Randy asked.

His voice cut through the moans, the buzz of flies on bloated corpses, replacing them with her first memory of him: a wild eye, sighting down a barrel as she panted outside the front door, fist held mid-pound, the howl of the wolf pack close enough to make them both jump. She felt his hand on her wrist, remembered the tug, the awkward, one-legged lunge past her as he slammed the door, the yelp as something fierce hit the other side...

Jenna shook her head and placed the last of the specialty jams and countrified salsas on the bare shelves above the countertop. The dark brown cabin walls came into focus, the past receding. She blinked the last of the memories away and looked up at Randy, his words finally registering.

"That's all I got." *Ah, geez, I'm picking up some of his lingo.* "Except for..." she paused dramatically, working to focus on the present. "This!" She yanked a brown paper bag with a fancy scroll-worked label out and held it up in triumph.

"What is that?" Randy asked, excited enough to actually sit up.

"Premium pancake mix," Jenna said proudly. "Found it stuffed between the register and ice cream counter. Must have gotten knocked off in the first big break in."

"Hell, bring it over here! I want to smell it."

Jenna walked across the rumpled orange shag carpeting with the three-pound bag and held it under Randy's nose. The redneck inhaled deeply.

"Ooo. That smells divine. Let me taste it."

"No!" Jenna said.

"Oh, come on, just a little dip of the finger?" Randy said as he licked the end of his unwashed finger and held it up.

"Absolutely not! This is going onto the shelf and getting used in something fancy. I'm not going to waste any of it on your dirty finger."

"I washed this finger two days ago!"

"Ugh." Jenna stalked back to the kitchen, shaking her head. She looked around at their supplies and tapped her foot, thinking about what she could make. *Thinking, thinking, always thinking. Got to keep thinking...*

"We not doin' pancakes for dinner, then?"

"I said fancy!"

"Mmm, that's a shame. Too bad there isn't anything else..."

Jenna narrowed her eyes as he looked sideways away from her. "What? What do you have?"

Randy fixed her with that crazy, wide-eyed redneck look he got when he was being mischievous. He dropped his hand down by the old knitting sack that held his hunting magazines and slowly pulled it up to reveal three respectably-large rainbow trout dangling from a line.

"You cheeky bastard!" Jenna shouted as her eyes blew wide-open in joy.

"You going British on me now?" Randy asked.

Jenna ran over and grabbed the fish, marveling at the shimmer of their scales and the delicate plumpness of their flesh.

"I'll gut 'em for ya'," Randy said, pulling his psycho-killer fillet knife from the sack.

Jenna didn't even blink at the handiness of the blade. "Ok! I'll start the frying pan."

She handed the fish over and sprinted to the kitchen. She smeared a fingertip of the remaining bacon grease in the old cast iron pan and turned the knob on her pilfered camp stove.

"Don't forget the window!" Randy called.

"Oh!" Jenna opened the window in the tiny kitchen to vent out fumes and grabbed a cookbook from over the stove. "Looks like pan-fried trout takes about 5 minutes per side. Ah, we could have cooked them whole, stuffed with lemon—if we had a lemon."

"I'll check the north forty for a snow-hardy lemon next time I'm out," Randy joked as he slapped the fish down on his old plastic TV tray and sunk the blade behind one of the gills.

Saw, saw, saw, flip! Saw, saw, saw, flip!

"One down, two to go. That pan hot yet?" Randy called.

"Nope."

Saw, saw, saw, flip! Saw, saw, saw, flip!

"Two down."

Jenna dipped her finger in her half-full, leftover water glass and flicked it at the pan. The water drops barely sizzled. "Still heating."

Saw, saw, saw, flip! Saw, saw, saw, flip!

"Come get 'em!" Randy yelled.

Jenna hustled into the living room and grabbed the tray, noting the fish remains stacked neatly next to the fillets. She tested the pan a few more times while she read up on making fish stock. She had just finished filling a pot from the creek and dumping the fish parts in when the flicked water finally sizzled in the pan the way she wanted. She laid the succulent fish flesh onto the hot iron and listened.

Tzzzzsssss

The sound was magical. Jenna's heart soared. She looked around the kitchen, a smile splitting her face. Her eyes fell upon the liquor shelf.

"We have to drink something with this," she declared. Randy pursed his lips in consideration and nodded. Jenna ran her hands across the modest stash and pulled off an old bottle. "This!" she declared.

Randy's face suddenly fell. "Nope. Not that one."

Jenna looked at the label. A forty-year-old bottle of Rebel Yell Kentucky Straight Bourbon Whiskey. "It's just a half-full bottle of whiskey."

"Nope. That bottle was given to me by my granddad for my tenth birthday and I'm saving it."

"Your tenth birthday? Really?" Jenna asked with a smirk. "What are you possibly saving it for?"

"For when things get really bad," Randy responded.

Jenna just stared for a moment. "Randy, ninety-five percent of the people on the planet just shit their intestines out and died."

"Yeah?"

Jenna gave him her best WTF look.

"But we're still alive, so everything's fine," Randy said, completely serious again. "Though," he held up a conciliatory hand, "your eyebrow piercings make my balls shrivel when I look at them, but I guess that's normal for you all."

Jenna flared her eyes and pressed a palm onto the counter. "'You all,' lesbians, or 'you all,' black people?"

Randy shrugged liked he wasn't sure.

"Oh, my God, Randy, I swear—"

"I will say that lesbian part seems very suspicious..."

Jenna clamped her mouth and shook her head, heat prickling her skull. Her hand sought out something heavy and lethal. "If it wasn't the end of the Goddamn world Randy..."

"Just sayin'. How much longer? Shouldn't you flip 'em?"

Jenna took her hand off the meat tenderizer and grabbed the metal spatula with half the wooden handle missing. She wasn't going to let Randy's hick ass mess up the best meal they'd had in days. Instead, she let the golden beauty of the cooked side of the fillet morph her anger into anticipation.

Five minutes later Jenna sank onto the rough corded upholstery of the living room couch with three steaming fish fillets on her plate. She put her nose over the vapors and breathed deeply.

Chomp, chomp, chomp.

Jenna looked up to find Randy stuffing half a fillet in his mouth. "Randy!"

Randy raised his eyebrows at her mid-chew.

"Food is to be savored and enjoyed, not just shoved and swallowed!" *How many times had she told him that?*

Randy mouthed an "ah" punctuated by a fish chunk falling back onto his plate. He carefully selected a smaller portion for his next bite.

"Savored and enjoyed," Jenna said as she turned back to her own plate and lifted her first delicate forkful. When the perfectly-yielding morsel touched her tongue she closed her eyes in bliss. The taste was absolutely fresh and clean, with just a hint of saltiness from the bacon grease. Heaven. Four forkfuls later she opened her eyes and said, "You know what this would go great with? Rice."

Randy nodded while lifting a small fish bit into his mouth with exaggerated care. After he chewed it for all of two seconds—and before he swallowed it—he said, "I know where some rice is."

"What?" Jenna said. "Where?"

"Over at Jackson's pond."

"Does he have a hidden stash over there or something? I looted that place clean." Jackson's pond was only two miles up the mountain road.

"No, it's in the pond. Jackson got all hot about wild rice. Thought he was going to sell it for big bucks to the city folks at the Mart. So he planted a mess of wild rice from Minnesota or somethin' in his fish pond. He gave up when he realized what a pain in the ass it was to hull it, but it's still up there."

"Do you know how to harvest it?"

"Sure. You just sort of bend it over and whack it. Need a canoe, though."

"Doesn't Jackson have a canoe?"

"He did…"

"Well, then…let's go get some!" Jenna said.

Randy looked at her for a second then shrugged. "All right. Tomorrow."

* * *

Jenna pulled the smelly old hunting jacket Randy had lent her tighter over her fall puffer to ward off a blustery, cold wind. All of the heat she'd generated hauling Randy's somehow still fat ass up the mountain road in his old firewood cart had long since dissipated. Cutting the chain on the canoe and slipping it into the water had been relatively easy. Getting Randy into the boat without soaking them both had not. But now they floated amongst the cattails and lily pads, seeking out the swaths of wild rice that had really gone wild. Geese honked in great Vs overhead, heading south, and squirrels busily buried nuts.

"Smells like snow," Randy said as he worked the tie string loose from one of the burlap sacks they'd found in Jackson's pond shed.

Jenna gave him a wry eye while she paddled. "Really? Is that your official NOAA prediction?"

"Nose-AA. It never lies," he tapped his red-tipped nose with one finger, then pointed at a tuft of rice grass. "Right there. Bring us up alongside of those."

Jenna accidentally pushed the wrong way with the paddle and they started spinning away from the patch. She tried to correct by paddling on the other side, but got that wrong, too.

"Want some help there?" Randy said with one raised eyebrow. "Don't want to end up on the other side of the pond, don't you know."

Jenna pulled the paddle out of the water to switch sides again and made sure some drips hit Randy's bare legs, below his shorts.

"Hey! Watch the shorts! They're my only pair."

"I know," Jenna said with a grimace. "I know."

A couple of tries later the canoe slid close enough to the rice that Randy was able to grab some stalks and pull them gently alongside. He gathered a fistful and bent them over the open sack he'd spread between his legs.

"So, old Jackson asked me to help him harvest one time because, you know, he was a lazy shit, and what he said you were supposed to do is hold it over the sack like this and then tap it." Randy gave the tops of the rice stalks he held a little tap with the broken handle of an oar they'd found in the shed and to Jenna's delight a handful of little grains fell out. Randy tapped it again and got about half as many. Then Randy pulled the canoe forward using the spent stalks and gathered another bunch.

After a few more tapping sessions Jenna asked, "Can I try it?"

"Sure," Randy said.

Jenna set down the oar and took the offered broken paddle. Randy pulled them forward and watched, amused, as she tried to gather a decent bundle in her hands. Finally, she settled for half the size Randy managed and gave it a little tap. Only a few kernels fell out. She tapped it again, a little harder and got a few more. Randy just nodded his head in that way he did when someone wasn't doing something exactly right but he was holding back on telling them. Jenna clamped her teeth and gave the bundle a solid whack. "Ouch!" she sucked on the skin that had come off her knuckle.

"You city folks don't whack rice with broken oar handles much, do you?" Randy asked. Jenna could tell by the slight twitch at the corner of his eye that he was trying not to laugh at his own joke. She looked at her red knuckle and grabbed the bunch again without responding.

A little harder, but not too much...

Tap.

A decent amount of rice fell into the sack. Jenna smiled, a strange sense of satisfaction washing over her. She whacked again and then grabbed another bundle. For the rest of that day, with fingers burning from cold and noses running, they tapped and pulled, tapped and pulled. Randy handed her an old cattail stalk to bend bigger bunches of rice over with while he held the canoe steady and fished. By the time the sun was sinking they had filled three large sacks and caught four fish. Randy then proceeded to pull up a dozen cattails and clean their roots in the water.

"What are you doing?" Jenna asked on the third cattail.

"Getting dinner," Randy said. "You can boil these up and eat them like potatoes. You just have to spit out the stringy tough parts. Someone told me you can make flour out of them too."

Jenna perked up. "Flour! How do you do that?"

"Don't know."

"Well, grab a few more and we'll find out!" Jenna said.

"Okay then." Randy grabbed another dozen and trimmed the stalks from them with his knife. He lay the bulbs in the bottom of the canoe and said, "Let's paddle for home. Gettin' dark and I saw some cougar tracks on the way up here."

That night, after roasting, hulling, winnowing, and boiling rice on the woodstove, they enjoyed a plate of pond trout with wild rice and a side of mashed cattail roots. Every muscle in Jenna's body ached from the long day, and she still sniffed occasionally from the cold, but the smell of cooking and the taste of fresh food made her feel alive.

"This five stars?" Randy asked as he lifted a small portion of mashed cattail on his fork and slid it delicately off onto his tongue.

Jenna pursed her lips and considered. "Yeah. This would be a couple hundred dollars at a swank place uptown."

Randy whistled around the cattail mash in his mouth. "See, ain't I a good provider?"

Jenna rolled her eyes but ended up looking down at the fish on her plate. "I guess you have your uses."

Randy nodded in agreement. "Can't cook though," he said. "You a chef in the city?"

Jenna looked up, startled. Randy had hardly asked about her past in the month she'd been there. "No. I was an actuary."

"Act-u-wha—?" Randy said with a confused look.

"I worked with numbers," she said, not wanting to get into it. "I always wanted to cook, though. Just didn't have the time." She stared into the flames behind the woodstove's glass front and thought about all the subway rides and crowd fighting she'd done only to arrive home too exhausted to do anything but nuke a burrito and fall onto the couch in front of the TV.

"Wouldn't a' guessed it," Randy said as he chewed.

Jenna looked over at him and then back down at her plate. She definitely ate better now. After a moment she nodded, lifted a forkful of rice, and chewed.

* * *

A month later Jenna trudged through the deep snow in a pair of Hello Kitty moon boots she had found outside a cabin halfway down the mountain. They were fake-furry and pink and white and ridiculous and absolutely warm so she took them, even though they weren't technically hers. She had gotten better at that over the last few months. Like always, she tried not to think about what had happened to their previous owner. Instead, she thought about Randy and his foot. He said he'd hurt it kicking his POS truck when it wouldn't start, right after everything hit the fan, but that was months ago. She was no doctor, but if he'd had it bandaged up that whole time it should be healed by now. What if it never healed? He couldn't get around by himself with it hurt and there was no one else around to help him... could she really walk away and leave him when the weather turned nice?

Hell yes! He's got a Goddamn Confederate flag on the wall! And it stinks to high heaven from that damn toilet!

But his foot...

Crack!

A shot echoed in the cold air, the report bouncing off barren tree trunks and rolling through gullies carved by trickling mountain springs. Jenna's head popped up, her eyes suddenly wide with fear.

"Randy?" She started to run, dropping the bag of books she'd carried in the snow. Bright kitty eyes flashed as she shoved aside branches and ducked, cutting across the edge of the old meadow instead of following the normal trail. An image that would never leave rose up: her roommate slumped against the bathroom wall, her ashen face a mask of fever and dehydration, of loss and acceptance; then her roommate's last, trembling effort, lifting that short barrel, putting it in her open mouth as Jenna turned to run; but the shot rang out before she could get to the door and she heard the thud of the gun hitting the floor and the slow slide of a body and—

"Randy!?" she yelled, the sound tearing at her throat.

"What?"

From above.

She stumbled to a stop and looked up, chest heaving, eyes tearing, to find Randy halfway down a ladder that lead to a tree stand. His rifle lay next to the tree trunk, a rope tied around it.

Relief flooded through her and she sat down, knees robbed of their strength.

"Thought I'd shot myself, did ya'?" Randy said matter-of-factly.

"Yes!" Jenna yelled, pissed at his nonchalance.

"Nope. Got a deer." Randy gestured over across the field with his chin.

"Oh, my God, Randy. I fucking swear."

"Apparently."

Jenna took a couple deep breaths to slow her heart. "How'd you get up there?"

Randy swung his bad foot off a rung and said, "Climbed."

Jenna narrowed her eyes. "With your bad foot?"

"Yep," Randy said, then proceeded to very clumsily hop down.

Jenna moved back a bit, intent on letting him fall to his demise for the scare he had put into her, but he made it down with only a couple small slips. He kept his balance by holding onto the tree and said, "Let's go gut something."

"Ugh." Jenna rolled her eyes but stood to give Randy a hand limping over to his kill.

The deer was still breathing. A large chunk of flesh was missing from the top of its neck, exposing vertebrae.

"You missed its heart!" Jenna said. She'd seen enough deer targets standing in yards on her trek out here to know that was the spot to aim for.

Randy nodded. "Shot its spine. Sometimes they still run with a heart hit."

Jenna covered her mouth as a single frightened eye rolled to look at them. Nothing else on the deer moved. "You paralyzed it," she whispered in horror.

Randy slid his arm off Jenna's shoulder and knelt down, pulling his hunting knife from the cracked leather scabbard on his waist. He placed a hand on the deer's neck and patted it gently before lifting its head. The blade slid across its throat, cutting deeply. Blood welled and Jenna turned away, not wanting to see it stain the snow, not wanting to be reminded. Something whole and good and beautiful had been struck down and it had lived long enough to know it–*to know it*– before the final blow came. She walked away, wiping at the tears that sprung to her eyes. She watched the cold wind rattle branches, only a few leaves still clinging on. *Would all the leaves blow away?* She crossed her arms and hugged herself to squeeze away the pain. When it had subsided and the tears had dried, she turned to see Randy stroke the deer's head one last time before pulling out his rope.

"I gut it, you haul it," he said, as he tied knots around the deer's small antlers, then picked his knife back up.

Back at the cabin, sweaty and tired from dragging, she helped him throw the rope over a limb of a black cherry tree near his truck and haul the gutted deer into the air. Randy secured the rope around the trunk with a couple knots, scrubbed his blood-covered hands clean in the snow, and asked, "What's for dinner?"

Dinner...

"Oh, the books!" Jenna ran up the trail and came back a second later, breathless, but beaming. "Check. This. Out." She held up a book with a brown cover.

"*A Guide to Canning, Freezing, Curing and Smoking Meat, Fish and Game*," Randy read.

Jenna gestured to the gutted and hanging deer behind Randy with a flourish and an eyebrow raise.

"And this!" Jenna said proudly.

"*Edible Wild Plants and How to Prepare Them*," Randy read again with his funny reading squint.

"Got 'em at the state park's living heritage museum gift shop. We're going to eat like kings" Jenna nodded with confidence.

"Okay then," Randy said. But she could see that twitch at the corner of his eye. He was trying not to smile.

Jenna beamed.

* * *

Jenna stamped thick snow off her boots and closed the door. The smell of the smoker they'd rigged up outside wafted in with her and, in her hands, she held four strips of its bounty. It was from the deer she'd shot last week and gutted herself. Randy had leaned on a tree near the cabin and watched her work without a word. When she dragged it past him on the skid he'd built, he just nodded and puffed on the pipe he'd started smoking to "keep out the cold."

Jenna took a bite and held a strip out to Randy as he hastily finished poking something into the fire and closed the door on the old wood stove.

"What'cha doin'?" she asked in her best backwoods twang. Four cold months trapped in a cabin with a racist yokel had driven her mildly insane. She found the silly things took the edge off.

"Nothin' much," Randy said as he took the meat strip and sat back. Two actual potatoes they'd pilfered from Widow Hansen's overgrown garden sat steaming in tinfoil atop the woodstove. Jenna nodded in approval at the forethought and smell. They'd moved Randy's chair closer to the fire so he could tend it easier, which had triggered a latent, bored-as-hell cooking gene in him. Unfortunately, it hadn't done much for the smell of the place. Now the composting toilet had competition with Randy's overly warm hick B.O. Jenna flopped onto the couch and lifted her hands to the fire. The silence lengthened but wasn't awkward. Watching the flames gingerly dance against the glass front always mesmerized her and the muffled crackles and sharp smells were fast becoming harbingers of home.

Home.

Jenna twitched her head and swallowed, faces rearing up before her. The soft hiss of a wet log turned into a sob overheard through a hallway door as she stole out, the Mystic Woods Resort and Spa flier clutched tightly in her hand, her bag tugging on her shoulder. She had been planning to get away before and she needed to get away then and where else was she going to go? She swallowed and blinked but the memories stayed.

Randy's voice, oddly pitched, broke through it all. "You see a lot, gettin' here?" he asked, eyes looking away from her back to the fire as his fingers worked the hole in the arm of his chair.

Jenna started and stared at him. He had never asked her about that before. She didn't know how to answer. How do you describe watching the world die right in front of you? Watching your roommates get it and wave you away when you want to take them for help because they know—*they know*—there is nothing anyone can do, nowhere to go, and they hang onto that one tiny shred of hope that what they have isn't it and that they'll survive, but they're wrong and they know they're wrong twelve hours later because you can see it their eyes. The horror. The pain. And the end. She had to leave. She couldn't take being there anymore, a rag held over her face from the smells, a hoodie cinched tight against the sounds from the bathroom, from the apartments next door, from across the street. Death and dying everywhere. Except for her.

She started to shake. *Why me? Why not others? Why Randy?*

Everything crashed in.

"My wife died a while ago."

Jenna ripped her eyes from the flames in the stove, looked at the side of Randy's face as he kept staring at them.

"Got the cancer," he said, fingers working the threads. "Couldn't do nothin' about it." His hand flattened and ran across the exposed yellow foam. "She wanted to stay home. So, we did. Dialed the I.V. up when we had too, to cut the pain, but..." Randy's flat palm patted the yellow foam. "She died."

Jenna watched as Randy nodded, his wet eyes staring at those dancing flames.

"It's hard watching someone die," he said finally.

Jenna pressed her lips together and looked to the floor. She nodded and ran a hand across her nose. The fire crackled, its reddish light dancing off the half-full bottle of whiskey on the shelf. Jenna pulled the brown and white polyester afghan from the couch back and wrapped it around herself, sinking into the beaten down cushions. The moon rose and the clouds cleared. When she finally went up to bed with a silent nod to Randy, she felt more tired than she ever had. And as she pulled her sleeping bag tight against the chill, her mind dimly registered the moonlight glinting off the fake wood paneling where Randy's Confederate flag should have been. But then the sweet embrace of rest touched her and she let it carry her away.

* * *

The garbled chirping of robins and dripping of snowmelt woke Jenna one morning; she had stopped counting the days. She rolled onto her back and stared up at the smoke-stained ceiling. *Spring. I can finally leave...*

She pushed herself up and slid out of the sleeping bag.

Randy sat in his chair, looking at the fire he'd just stoked in the woodstove. His fingers worked over the last remaining threads on the chair arm and she frowned. After a pick-free period during the coldest months he'd started up his old habit with a vengeance.

"You want some cattail hash cakes?" she asked as she tied her braided hair on top of her head. "I got some leftover mashed root on the porch. Sounds like it might be thawed out now."

Randy patted the foam on the arm of his chair and nodded, but Jenna got the impression he wasn't nodding at the hash cakes. He turned to her and said, "I got something to tell you."

Jenna stopped piling her hair. Her frown deepened. *Oh, no. I don't want no "I'm in love with you" bullshit from this yokel. He knows I don't like men...*

Randy stood up.

Jenna cocked her head to the side, thinking of where the knives were in case Randy had finally cracked and came after her.

Randy took a step. And then another. Without a hint of a limp.

She looked down at this bad leg. The braces were gone.

"Randy, what's going on?"

"My leg's fine."

"I can see that. How long has it been fine?"

"Since about a week after you showed up."

Jenna stood there, head slowly canting to the side.

"A week?" she asked.

Randy nodded, pressing his lips together in an oddly guilty grimace.

"So you've been faking it this entire time?" Jenna asked, heat building at the base of her neck, a heat that rapidly expanded to envelope her entire head.

Randy nodded, face turning red enough to match his neck.

"What the fuck, Randy? Why didn't you tell me?"

"Well, you know..."

"What, you wanted me to be your servant? Cook for you? Clean for you? Haul your fat ass all over this mountain like some sort of pack mule? Is that it?" Jenna's muscles bunched in outrage at all the work she had done because Randy was "injured."

"No, I just..."

"Just what? Just exactly what possessed you to lie to me for six months, huh? Six months! Stuck in this cabin with you and your hick body odor, sleeping next to a Confederate flag—"

"I burned that flag!"

"Don't interrupt me! You used me for half a year and the entire time I believed you. I *believed* you, Randy! And I was actually worried about what I was going to do when spring came because you couldn't take care of yourself. Well, guess what? I'm not worried anymore, 'cause I'm leaving right now!"

Jenna grabbed her pilfered hunting backpack from the hook by the door and started shoving stuff into it. She'd been thinking all winter about what she'd need to take and she ticked off the items easily, despite her rage: rifle from the wrecked truck at Spruce Creek, hunting knife from the Mart, collapsible fishing rod from the canoe rental place, hatchet from Jackson's shed, her lantern...

Randy stood in the living room and pleaded with his dirty palms held at his side.

"I'm sorry, I just didn't want you to go."

"Oh, really? I seem to recall a gun pointed at my face when I showed up."

"I didn't know who you were!"

"Well, now you do, Randy. I'm a pissed-off lesbian who's about to hike off this mountain for the last time."

"I just didn't want to be alone!" Randy shouted.

"Even if it meant living with a black person?" Jenna said viciously.

Randy held up a hand. "I have been rethinking my previous stance on race relations—"

"You hate black people, Randy! Your flag said so!"

"I admit, I have said that in the past. But..." Randy held a finger up to elucidate his next point. "I had never actually met a black person before."

Jenna stopped shoving venison jerky and pemmican cakes into a thrice-reused gallon freezer bag and looked up at him. "What?" She could only imagine what her face must have looked like at that moment. "You spent fifty years of your life hating black people and you had never met one?"

"They're not very common around here. I mean, before."

"Oh my fucking God, Randy. I can't...I...I just can't." Jenna shook her head in absolute disbelief. After a few mind-blown seconds she returned to shoving cattail flour, salted trout, acorn cakes, and shelled hazelnuts into her bag. She paused only briefly when she lifted the small sack of wild rice from the bin. She shoved it in, zipped it, and pounded up the stairs for her sleeping bag.

"Don't go!" Randy said from down below. "It's dangerous out there! Bears will be waking up hungry, and there's the wolves and cougars!"

"Don't care, Randy! You taught me to shoot. I got a hammock." She shoved the hammock home in the front pocket and started tying her sleeping bag on the bottom of the backpack.

"Ah, come on! I only lied to you for half a year!" Randy said, in a voice that clearly displayed his lack of perspective on honesty.

Jenna did not feel a reply was necessary. She pounded down the stairs, flung open the door, and stomped into slushy snow.

"Jenna, don't do it!" Randy yelled after her. "Just come back, I promise to do more stuff and not be an asshole!"

Jenna marched down the trail, muttering, her mind on fire. She hitched her backpack up, tightened the straps around her waist, then snugged the straps over her shoulders. She'd make it fifteen miles today on pure rage and that would be fine with her. The more distance between her and Randy the Racist Con Artist, the better.

Randy's pleas cut off with a final, "You were a really good cook!" Then she turned out of sight onto the lower fork trail. Five steps later she set her jaw against the odd twinge she felt at not hearing his voice anymore. She resolutely soldiered on. The morning flew by at a brutal pace that brought her to the looted Magic Mart, which she bypassed with a bitter shake of her head. A hastily-chewed pemmican cake, eaten without stopping, staved off her hunger as she marched farther than she'd ever been down Route 26.

As night fell, she worked her way warily up an overgrown road past a broken sign that read "Country Gardens Bed and Breakfast." There were no signs of tracks, save the obligatory deer trail through the overgrown lawn out front, so she opened the unlocked back door to find herself in a fully stocked, professional kitchen. For a moment, she just stood, taking in the stainless-steel appliances, the high-end pots and pans hanging above the massive island cooktop and the pantry—*the pantry!*—stuffed with boxes upon boxes of shelf-stable vittles. She swooned and put one hand out to catch herself on the edge of the granite countertop.

She turned a knob on the stove. Gas hissed. She lit a match from a box on the pantry shelf.

Fwoosh!

Blue flames tipped with yellow sprang to life, perfectly formed by the immaculate burner.

Suddenly renewed, she began to cook. Canned crab, dried onions, an unopened bag of vacuum-packed bread crumbs, an absolutely not natural block of shelf stable cheese from a holiday gift basket, and a little olive oil later she sat down and inhaled.

"Oh, my goodness. That smells so good."

She cut a delicate bite with the side of her flower-embossed fork. She lifted it to her mouth. She slid it off onto her tongue. She chewed.

"Mmmm..."

No one grunted a reply.

She took another bite.

"It's good, but it's missing something..."

She looked around for an agreeing nod. The darkness outside her lantern light met her eyes. She frowned and swallowed. The next bite went in. She chewed it without noticing, listening to her own jaw work in the silence. Twelve unnoticed bites later she sat back, realizing she was full. An entire crab cake remained. She had automatically made enough for two.

"Damn it, Randy!"

She unrolled her sleeping bag under the kitchen table with a rough throw and crawled in, glaring. Eventually, she fell asleep.

* * *

Her foot kicked the empty bottle of Rebel Yell as she stepped onto the back porch of the cabin and peered into the failing light at the snoring form in front of her.

"Randy?"

A snort. A moan.

"Randy!"

"Wha—" Randy jerked awake, dropping the rifle whose barrel lay just under his chin. He fell from the recliner he had hauled onto the porch with his two perfectly-good legs.

"Jenna!" His bloodshot eyes registered equal parts confusion and disbelief. "I thought you hated my ass."

"I did. I do," Jenna said, picking up the bottle and looking at the faded label. "But it turns out food doesn't taste as good without some company."

Randy rubbed at the hangover on his face and raised both eyebrows.

Jenna glanced at the rifle, held out the bottle. "I thought you were saving this for when things got really bad?"

Randy looked right into Jenna's eyes. "I was."

Jenna nodded, pressing her lips together. "Here." She tossed him a tinfoil packet. Randy bobbled it, picked it up off the deck, and opened it.

"Is this crab?" he asked, incredulous.

"Yep. It's a little old, but it probably won't kill you. Much. You like crab?" Jenna asked.

"Never had it," Randy said.

Jenna shook her head. "I swear, Randy, you are the hick-est hick I have ever—"

Randy took a nibble. He gave a considering nod. "Hmm, looks like I do."

Jenna tried not to smile, but she couldn't help it. She at least made it grudging. Randy took another bite.

"Wait," Randy said, with a mouth full of crab cake, "it's missing something…"

Jenna threw a small glass jar at him, which he caught one handed. Randy looked down at the label.

"Capers!"

SIX SANDWICHES TO PLACE INSIDE A PENTAGRAM TO SUMMON ME TO YOUR PRESENCE

Gabriela Santiago

Dear Kam,

1. Bread and butter

The bread should be cheap wheat bread, too soft but also too crumbly, so dry that it sticks in the mouth without the addition of the butter. It doesn't have to be butter; margarine is fine, or better. If you get your butter or margarine in a plastic tub where it curls to form a belly-button, then swirl your knife around the belly-button, saving that beautiful center for last. Use just one piece of bread and fold it in half. Dunk it in milk before eating.

I survived most of my first seven years on bread and butter, dipped in milk. Everyone always chopped off the belly-button of the butter first thing. So do this for me, okay, Kam?

There's something like genetic memory in the taste of bread and butter. Something where you can feel your ancestors stretching out behind you like a wool blanket around your shoulders, sitting in their peasant huts and eating what was probably better bread and better butter, since it was local and fresh, only less of it. Always less of everything. But still that brief moment of comfort, the sweet trace of honey in the dense give of the bread, the fat of the butter sticking to your bones and shutting out the cold. Their milk would have been warm, too.

It'll be awhile before we have real bread here—we're still doing tests on the kinds of wheat that grow best in the dome, and we're still fiddling with the bug numbers. The other day the gravity went off, only for five seconds, but it messed the spiders up like hell for the rest of the day and we think some of them died of shock. My team's arguing about what bees to unfreeze first; it's probably going to be classic honeybees because we have the biggest supply of them, but there's a faction arguing for some of the smaller wild bees to help diversify the pollen-spreading, which I personally think is a mistake since we're not certain how the bees will adjust to navigating. We think they navigate primarily by local landmarks, but if they've been using the stars or the sun or the moon this whole time we're going to be pretty screwed unless they've got the best learning curve ever.

No butter, of course; GenEd's dairy line is still at least a decade in the future, no matter how fast they fuss with the embryos. Maybe we'll have oat milk in a year, but did you know it has seventeen grams of sugar? That's more than a candy bar. I feel like I'm just eating candy bars, sometimes; no matter what the ingredients are they always seem to load the rations with beet sugar; I don't know if it's to cover up the taste or keep up the energy or keep up the morale. Everything's sweet and chalky—they load it up with calcium supplements too.

I guess this all sounds like I am complaining, but it's not all bad. The work keeps me busy and the air is purified here; no bad days like when the breeze off the Mississippi makes you reach for your inhaler. Remember that time you were just wheezing and wheezing and I had to prop you on my handlebars and pedal all the way to Children's? The wait in the ER was so long we just went home when you stopped.

Dad said you're keeping busy with the apartment algae farm for your work credits to graduate. I'm so proud of you. Tell me all about it.

Love, Elle

Galactic Stew

* * *

Dear Kam,

2. Peanut butter and cheese

The bread doesn't really matter here, cheap or fancy, as long as it's wheat. The peanut butter matters even less; have you ever met a bad peanut butter? No such thing. I prefer crunchy but I know you might be starved for choice with most of the grocery stores selling out of all the brands except the top-line mixes; you could try checking the farmers' markets for the raw peanuts and crush them in my old mocajete. Look for the Hmong stalls. Lots of kinds of cheese work, but the absolute best will be a bright orange cheddar, sharp or mild.

The important thing is how you eat it: squash it flat, then peel off the crusts and eat them first, dipping in milk as necessary to soften. Then, using your fingers to measure out straight lines, nibble away to create a perfect rectangle. Peel away—or if the texture of your bread or peanut butter does not cooperate, nibble away—one side of bread and then the other. Roll the remaining peanut butter and cheese into a ball of sweet, comforting fat that can be devoured in three bites.

This is how I have always eaten peanut butter and cheese sandwiches.

This is how I eat them even now—well, I guess how I ate them before I left. There is such security in doing something the way you have always done it. A small handhold that you do not have to let go of. I have let go of so many things that I would have been terrified to abandon in childhood—you know, because we were the same child in so many ways. Or do you? I was a teen—the same age you are now—when you were born. I remember how you cried at foods touching on your plate, at specks of brown in your white rice, at plans that changed after you had been told how your day would go. I heard you cry and I wanted to tell Dad to stop yelling at you, that you couldn't help that you felt the cruelty of the world so keenly in the way I always had. It was never the touch, the specks, the yellow bus to the park instead of the blue train—it was always the change, and the fear that it might spread to everything, that all this solid world might be a lie. That if things could not go exactly as we planned, they might completely fall apart.

Was that what got you into all this pentagram stuff? That there might be some greater plan? Don't worry, I'm not going to make fun of you this time. I don't think I ever told you, but I wanted to be a goth in high school, would've been if I could have afforded it—the black pants with silver chains, the lace corsets, the thigh boots with an infinity of snapping buckles like ultimatums. If I'd had the money, I would have eaten up everything in Hot Topic with a spoon.

Once after a protest I fixed myself this sandwich. I had not been hungry on the way to the protest—I'd had chicken and waffles for lunch—or during—I was filled with adrenaline—but as soon as I got home, I came down from the high of chants and whistles and stomped feet and music, and I was ravenous. I had been heckled by counter-protestors on the way home—they called me a fat lesbian who hadn't been able to get laid in high school—and I remember mostly feeling confused, that our country had gotten to this point where our languages had so divided that they could perceive these things as insults. I turned around and said that just because they had never stood up for anyone in their lives, didn't mean everyone else was the same. One of them said, "I stand up for my own. Who do you stand up for?" And I said, "Whoever needs it." And I took the cold train home to the apartment and my hunger erupted in the cold apartment and I tried not to wake you and Dad as I opened the cupboards for bread and peanut butter and cheddar and a paper plate and a flimsy knife. I ate the sandwich with chamomile tea and I listened to you and Dad sleep and I was tired, but I felt alive with the comfort of the familiar as I took it into myself and I thought of all the counter-protesters screaming hate in the name of a god I had not been able to believe in since I was younger than you and it seemed to me like they felt the comfort of that hate like a blanket and I chose the comfort of peanut butter instead. I said to myself, in that way of sleepy thoughts that makes them seem profound even if they are absurd, that if their god was hate then my god was peanut butter.

Anyway, I guess that was pretty ridiculous and probably more ridiculous than your goth thing, so I guess I'm saying sorry for laughing at you that second-to-last time I saw you, and I'm saying I'd like to hear more about how you got into it and what you like about it and what else you're into these days. I know it's probably been a busy couple months with the work credit thing and also the ACT and SAT coming up. Are you still pretty dead-set against the community college? That's fine; it's a good program but you should go somewhere you want to go and I know Dad has the carbon credits for it if he gives up his motorcycle for a couple years.

Love, Elle

Dear Kam,

3. Mrs. Bunny sandwich

You can get nice bread for this one if you want, but it has to be toasted. Spread one side with mayo and bacon (try Cecil's or Holy Land for beef bacon if you don't have a local hookup for pork yet; I just read about another case of trichinosis in Wisconsin), the other with peanut butter and a crunchy lettuce—butter lettuce, or a nice red romaine. Good lettuce now—none of that Iceberg crap. Cut it into triangles and serve.

I know it sounds strange, but if you give it a chance you'll love it. It's a wonderful play of taste and texture—the crunch of the lettuce and bacon and toasted bread, the smoothness of the peanut butter and mayonnaise. The umami and salt playing against toasted grains playing against the refreshing sweet light tang of the greens.

It was named after Mrs. Bunny, its creator. You remember my first girlfriend, Dianne? Her mother and aunts and uncles worked for a woman called Mrs. Bunny throughout all their college years. I never met her, she was long dead, but I imagined her house like a page out of *The Secret Garden*: peeling paint, waterfalls of ivy over steep gables, mysterious nooks with crumbling concrete statues whose originals were marble in some faraway museum, weeping willows through whose branches you could pass like a veil between worlds— maybe fall down a hole into Wonderland between the roots, maybe find a fairy door nestled at the base of the trunk. I guess a part of me has always wanted to escape to another world.

You won't remember this, but Dianne used to invite us sometimes to celebrate Mrs. Bunny Day, a holiday that fell one to seven times a year, whenever the whole family wanted to get together and eat this sandwich and listen to stories of the koi in the old fountain, the Persian rugs in the study, the strange things Mrs. Bunny would say like an old wizard in a fantasy novel that always made sense later.

We have new holidays here. I'll have to time these letters so that you don't summon me before Blossoming. That's another holiday irregularly scheduled. We can mostly predict it, but plants are stubborn—I think sometimes more stubborn than us, more eager to survive and at the same time more determined to die if they don't get their way. Look at me, talking about plants like they're people. But they become people to us up here. There are so few people up here, you get tired of people, you want them to be quiet like plants and at the same time you're so lonely you wish the plants would speak to you. You wish they'd say what they want, unfurl their leaves and whisper across the room how you've angered them, what it was you said or did, what you have to say or do for them to forgive you. How you can help them grow. You wish you could explain that it's not all a selfish wish for sustenance and continued life, but that you love them—that you've held them when they were so small and it terrifies you to see them grow, and wilt, and maybe pass back into the soil from where you both came.

Do you remember last Christmas, how the warm weather had fooled the trees into putting out buds and then the rain came down cold and fast until all the trees around the park looked like a forest of glass? They made a sound like wind chimes in the morning and bass drums in the afternoon when the weight became too much and the branches crashed to the ground.

What do the trees in the park look like now?

Please write when you can.

Love, Elle

Dear Kam,

4. Tomato sunflower seed sandwich

Cheap wheat bread. This sandwich works best when the other ingredients can seep into the bread and hold it together, so it needs to be softer than a pillow, the kind of bread you can smush into a ball, but don't do that. Spread with mayonnaise. Slice tomatoes. Any kind of tomato will do; the tastiest heirlooms for the sandwich are Green Zebras or Pineapple or Pink Brandywine or Black Beauty. But the very best tomato for this sandwich is a sweet tasty little cherry called Sun Gold—like pure drops of sugar, so irrepressible it splits on the vine. Once you've covered one piece of bread with little yellow half-moons, pour sunflower seeds (roasted salted is best, though all other varieties will suffice in a pinch) on top. Pour a lot on top. You're not done until you have a little hill of sunflower seeds shedding strays to each side of your sandwich on the plate. Put the top bread piece on, mash it down to hold together, and cut into quarters, squares this time.

This is the taste of summer, available only late August through early October, sometimes not even then. Remember how last summer we paid for the heat of the coasts with cool rains in the Midwest until the bottom of my shoes rotted away and I had to wear your big black boots for a week? It was even harder to tell us apart then. You taller, your face a little more square. But both of us bespectacled, curly-haired, dark and quiet. I never did tell you how much I loved how alike we looked. It seemed like something that Dad could never—oh, you know how he is. He always wants you to achieve so much. He always had such high hopes for you, even before you were born, even before we knew you were going to be born.

You've made this sandwich before; maybe I didn't need to leave the instructions. Maybe I could have just said "tomato sunflower seed sandwich" and you'd have known. Do you remember how I would make these for you after school in early fall? You'd tell me all about your day. I'd tell you a story and make you tell me one back. I'd hold you upside down and swing you in a circle ten times and tell you to do your homework. You were so smart even then; you'd finish it all in ten minutes.

How did the tests go? I hope they went well. I saw an article about the algae tank project in the *Star Trib*; they mentioned your name in a big list but they didn't quote you and I couldn't find you in any of the pictures.

I think memory is a kind of spell. You know I don't believe in spells but I hope you know that I don't think you're stupid for believing in them. I would never think you're stupid. Do you remember how worried you got about global warming when you were seven? You came home and cried. I remember being so proud of you for understanding when so many adults couldn't. Do you remember how I hugged you? I told you it made sense to cry.

Love, Elle

* * *

Dear Kam,

5. The Hellbeast I made when I was nine

This is not a good sandwich.

All the others were good sandwiches—yes even, yes especially, the Mrs. Bunny one—but this one is not. It is supposed to summon me after all, and I'm human, and all humans are messed up and flawed and we do things that make no sense and we hurt each other with so little thought. Yesterday I was talking to Dad on the eight minute phone and he was so angry that I wasn't going to be home for the big march and I said what good did the marches really do anyway and what I meant was that there were a lot of ways we could all fight and they could all help but how it came out was like I thought he was wasting his life and it wasn't true, I wish I could be at the march, Kam, I do. But I only seem able to fall short of things and lash out; when you were very little I whispered into your ear that I was sorry that he was all you had and that it was okay to hate him, and even though you didn't speak English yet you looked at me in such shock and I have never forgotten it: how the words I wanted to be a balm are always a weapon and here I am writing to you anyway but I never wanted to hurt you, Kam; I only wanted to find a way to not leave you entirely.

Why haven't you written me, Kam?

This sandwich can only be made when you are so hungry and bored that it is the only thing about you anymore. If you didn't make this sandwich you would do something else bad, because the house is empty and you have read all the books and the heat advisory has auto-locked the doors to prevent children from going outside. It is peanut butter, and then cheddar, and then parmesan shaken out of the green container in the fridge door because that's a cheese too, and then maple syrup because you know peanut butter goes well with honey and maple syrup is the closest thing you have to honey in the cupboard, and then anise seeds because of the Norwegian cookies you made last Christmas for a class project that were so delicious as long as you remembered to keep them locked up tight in their Tupperware and if you didn't they became as hard as rocks, teeth-shattering, stomach-rending boulders.

The first bite you think will be fine; the second is a little cloying, the third is too much, you overstepped, you took too much of what was good too greedily, as if not tasting everything meant you would starve; you cannot bear to bite down the fourth and fifth and sixth bites because you know it will only get worse but you know that you have to because you have already used up precious resources and you cannot waste them because that will be a sin and that will be admitting your mistake and that will be change, a change that is all your fault, that you could have prevented if you only stopped and thought.

This sandwich doesn't have a name because I only made it once, but let's call it the Hellbeast because that is what it is: an orgy of excess and poor decisions and regret.

We can see the forest fires from up here.

A whole quarter of the world is a cloud of ash.

Can you even go outside now?

Maybe you were right. Maybe I could have helped stop this if I stayed. And you were right that this was cowardly, to run away. I wasn't thinking; I was so tired, Kam. I could not bear it any longer, the long grind of hopelessness and the pressure of one billion hateful eyes and Twitter comments telling me I was less than, that I should die. I think sometimes, we all should—humanity, what a failed experiment. Who told us we could conquer the stars? Who told us conquering was the point of anything?

I entered the calculations wrong and we lost half our genetic data for einkorn wheat. Something is wrong with the tomatoes; we've adjusted and adjusted for heat and moisture and soil composition but they won't sprout. Stupid dreams borne of Butler's *Earthseed* and the kind of escapism she could never write. Somehow I read all her *Parables* and I didn't get that things change. I thought I could control how things change, I thought I would never have to give anything up, and especially not you. I don't want to limp away while watching Earth die, but I have signed papers and committed to this course and will not be allowed to waste the precious resource of rocket fuel even if I admitted that I am afraid. Do you remember when you used to have such vivid nightmares? Was that real? Kam, if you don't write

This is your big sister then. Four letters of fluff and passive-aggressive begging and then this, the truth, failure. There is no sixth sandwich. You have enough to see me clearly.

This is all I am.

I'm sorry.

Love, Elle

* * *

Dear Kam,

6. Banh mi!

I forgot banh mi, Kam! How could I forget banh mi?

Do you remember the last time you let me hold you without embarrassment? You were thirteen. We had banh mi in the fridge from iPho: fresh cilantro and jalapeño and tender slices of spicy pork meatloaf. We slouched on the big bean bag chair with crumbs of French bread collecting on our laps and globs of spicy mayo falling on our chins. It's not an authentic food. Neither of us is authentic. Authenticity is something we chase like stars, and we fill our belly with delicious compromise.

When we were done, you read me your story while you leaned into my side, my arm around your thin shoulders, the softness of your hair something I have never forgotten.

I don't have any instructions for this. I don't have time for instructions if I did. You'll need to use your Xfinity minutes to Google something, or make a new friend, I don't know. You love learning. You'll do great.

My friend Cat figured out the tomatoes. They needed the sun. How do you forget the sun? But we did, we filtered too much. Maybe we'll get skin cancer now, but that's the risk we take for a taste of home. There are white and yellow flowers peering up at the dome now. The engines are warming up. The eight-minute phone is tied up and anyway, I know you are at the march. I hope you have brought your extra inhaler. I hope you read this letter, even after the last one. I am sorry about the last one. I hope you will not remember me that way. It is true, but so is this.

Kam, I think maybe there is no such thing as good and evil in this whole universe, only moments and decisions. Only love like air and mistakes like thorns pricking our skin and catching us. I think there is only people, only us—our sharp spiky edges, our five hours of sleep, the last book we read, a lyric repeating in our brains, the taste of peanut butter on our tongues, our hands swinging uselessly at our sides when we have forgotten how to hold on. I think there is only this, over and over, only life and death and the seconds that stand out like fires in between, where we felt love and that love made it all worth it, all the mistakes we can never take back but only try not to make again, even if everyone else will.

Find some banh mi. It's so good. I won't taste any here for years, but I will hold the memory of it ahead of me like a star. Do you remember when I woke you up to look at the satellites falling like stars?

I love you.

I will miss you every day.

I will be awaiting your summons.

Love, always,

Elle

ABOUT THE AUTHORS

R.S. BELCHER is an award-winning journalist and author of the Golgotha series (The Six-Gun Tarot, The Shotgun Arcana, The Queen of Swords, and The Ghost Dance Judgement coming in June 2020), the Nightwise series (Nightwise, The Night Dahlia), and The Brotherhood of the Wheel series (Brotherhood of the Wheel, King of the Road),currently in development for television.

DERRICK BODEN's fiction has appeared in numerous venues including *Escape Pod*, *Daily Science Fiction*, and *Flash Fiction Online*. He is a writer, a software developer, an adventurer, and a graduate of the Clarion West class of 2019. He currently calls Boston his home, although he's lived in fourteen cities spanning four continents. He is owned by two cats and one iron-willed daughter. Find him at derrickboden.com and on Twitter as @derrickboden.

CHAZ BRENCHLEY has been making a living as a writer since the age of eighteen. He is the author of nine thrillers, two fantasy series, two novels about a haunting house and two collections, most recently the Lambda Award-winning *Bitter Waters*. He has also published fantasy as Daniel Fox, and urban fantasy as Ben Macallan. He lost count of his short stories long ago; a "best of" collection will be published in 2021. In his fifties he married and moved from Newcastle to California, with two squabbling cats and a famous teddy bear. He can be found on Facebook, Twitter and Patreon, and at www.chazbrenchley.co.uk.

PAIGE L. CHRISTIE is originally from Maine and now lives in the NC mountains. She is best known for *The Legacies of Arnan* fantasy series (#1 *Draigon Weather*). She strives to tell stories that are both entertaining and thoughtful, and that open a space where adventure and fantasy are not all about happy endings. When she isn't writing, Paige is director of a non-profit, runs a wine shop, and teaches belly dancing. She is a proud, founding member of the Blazing Lioness Writers, a small group of badass women writing badass books.

ANDY DUNCAN's fiction has won a Nebula Award, a Theodore Sturgeon Memorial Award and three World Fantasy Awards. His third collection, *An Agent of Utopia: New and Selected Stories* (Small Beer Press, 2018), was a Locus Award finalist, and its title story was a Locus Award and Nebula Award finalist. A Clarion West graduate, he has taught at Clarion and Clarion West multiple times and was final judge for the 2020 Kurt Vonnegut Prize. A South Carolina native, he is a professor of writing at Frostburg State University in the Maryland mountains. He haunts Facebook at andy.duncan.39794 and Twitter @BELUTHAHATCHIE.

Nebula Award winning author **ESTHER FRIESNER** has seen the publication of forty-one novels, over two hundred short stories, nine anthologies, and three collections of her work. She created the popular Chicks in Chainmail series (Baen Books), and the Princesses of Myth series of YA novels (Random House). She keeps busy.

DIANA A. HART lives in Washington State, speaks fluent dog, and escapes whenever somebody leaves the gate open—if lost, she can be found rolling dice at her friendly local game store. Her passion for storytelling stems from a well-used library card and years immersed in the oral traditions of the Navajo. Her work has also appeared in *Writers of the Future, Vol. 34* and *Zooscape*. Diana tweets about wine, writing, and nerd life @DianaAHart. Her website lurks at https://www.diana-hart.com/.

D.B. JACKSON is the author of the Islevale Cycle (TIME'S CHILDREN, TIME'S DEMON, and TIME'S ASSASSIN), as well as the novels and short stories of the Thieftaker Chronicles, a historical fantasy set in pre-Revolutionary Boston. As David B. Coe he has written epic fantasy, urban fantasy, and media tie-ins. He is best known for the Crawford Award-winning LonTobyn Chronicle. David has a Ph.D. in U.S. history from Stanford University. His books have been translated into more than a dozen languages. http://www.DavidBCoe.com; http://www.dbjackson-author.com; http://twitter.com/davidbcoe; http://twitter.com/dbjacksonauthor

HOWARD ANDREW JONES is the author of the Ring-Sworn heroic fantasy trilogy from St. Martin's, starting with *For the Killing of Kings*, the critically acclaimed Arabian fantasy series starring Dabir and Asim, and four Pathfinder novels. He's the editor of the print magazine *Tales From the Magician's Skull*, among other things, and can be found lurking at www.howardandrewjones.com, where he blogs about writing craft, gaming, fantasy and adventure fiction, and assorted nerdery.

GINI KOCH writes the fast, fresh, and funny Alien/Katherine "Kitty" Katt series for DAW Books, the Necropolis Enforcement Files, and the Martian Alliance Chronicles. She also has a humor collection, Random Musings from the Funny Girl. As G.J. Koch she writes the Alexander Outland series and she's made the most of multiple personality disorder by writing novels, novellas, novelettes, and short stories in all the genres out there and under a variety of other pen names as well, including Anita Ensal, Jemma Chase, A.E. Stanton, and J.C. Koch, all with stories featured in excellent anthologies, available now and upcoming. www.ginikoch.com

MIA MOSS is a science fiction and fantasy author living in a Bay Area warehouse guarded by feral cats. Her writing explores the ways often trivialized, feminine-coded activities and interests can subvert power. She also writes a lot about food. You can find more of her work at her website, magicrobotcarnival.com, or subscribe to her weekly sci-fi recipe newsletter, the Breakfast Serial at thebreakfastserial.substack.com. You can also follow her on Twitter @ladyglitterpunk.

JASON PALMATIER is co-creator/co-writer of the fantasy graphic novel *Plague* published by Markosia Ltd. and a contributor to the indie comic series *Lords of the Cosmos* by Ugli Studios. His short stories have appeared in the Zombies Need Brains anthologies *Clockwork Universe: Steampunk vs Aliens*, *All Hail Our Robot Conquerors*, *Guilds and Glaives*, and *Portals*. He has completed two novels, *War Mind*, a near future military thriller about a dystopia controlled by music; and *Xenoslammer*, a parody/rage piece that is best described as "Cards Against Humanity meets Aliens".

GABRIELA SANTIAGO's work has previously been published in Clarkesworld, Strange Horizons, The Dark, and Lady Churchill's Rosebud Wristlet; she is also one of the people of color destroying science fiction and horror in the anthologies *People of Colo(u)r Destroy Science Fiction!* and *People of Colo(u)r Destroy Horror!* She is the founder and curator of Revolutionary Jetpacks, a science fiction cabaret centering the futures imagined by BIPOC, queer and trans, and disabled artists. You can follow her @LifeOnEarth89 or writing-relatedactivities.tumblr.com.

MIKE JACK STOUMBOS is an emerging fiction author, disguised as a believably normal high school teacher. Recently, his work has appeared in *Dragon Writers: An Anthology* and *The Cursed Collectibles Anthology*. His previous writing work has included online academic and marketing content, stageplays, and a self-published novel, *The Baron Would Be Proud*. Mike Jack lives in western Washington with his wife and their parrot, and he has been routinely spotted at the best karaoke spots in the Seattle area. He can be found online @MJStoumbos on Twitter and as Mike Jack Stoumbos (Author) on Facebook.

A.L. TOMPKINS is a writer from Ontario, Canada. She holds an honours Bsc. in Biology, and is usually found working surrounded by animals, the bigger and more likely to eat her, the better. When not writing, A.L is usually reading anything she can get her hands on, or getting overly invested in the lives of video game characters.

ABOUT THE EDITORS

DAVID B. COE is the author of more than twenty novels and as many short stories. He has written epic fantasy – including the Crawford Award-winning LonTobyn Chronicle – contemporary urban fantasy, and media tie-ins, and he co-edited *Temporarily Deactivated*.

As D.B. Jackson, he writes the time travel/epic fantasy series The Islevale Cycle (*Time's Children*, *Time's Demon*, *Time's Assassin*) and the Thieftaker Chronicles, a historical urban fantasy set in pre-Revolutionary Boston.

David has a Ph.D. in U.S. history from Stanford University. His books have been translated into more than a dozen languages.

http://www.DavidBCoe.com
http://www.dbjackson-author.com
http://twitter.com/davidbcoe
http://twitter.com/dbjacksonauthor

* * *

JOSHUA PALMATIER is a fantasy author with a PhD in mathematics. He currently teaches at SUNY Oneonta in upstate New York, while writing in his "spare" time, editing anthologies, and running the anthology-producing small press Zombies Need Brains LLC. His most recent fantasy novel, *Reaping the Aurora,* concludes the fantasy series begun in *Shattering the Ley* and *Threading the Needle,* although you can also find his "Throne of Amenkor" series and the "Well of Sorrows" series still on the shelves. He is currently hard at work writing his next novel and designing the Kickstarter for the next Zombies Need Brains anthology project. You can find out more at www.joshuapalmatier.com or at the small press' site www.zombiesneedbrains.com. Or follow him on Twitter as @bentateauthor or @ZNBLLC.

ACKNOWLEDGMENTS

This anthology would not have been possible without the tremendous support of those who pledged during the Kickstarter. Everyone who contributed not only helped create this anthology, they also helped solidify the foundation of the small press Zombies Need Brains LLC, which I hope will be bringing SF&F themed anthologies to the reading public for years to come...as well as perhaps some select novels by leading authors, eventually. I want to thank each and every one of them for helping to bring this small dream into reality. Thank you, my zombie horde.

The Zombie Horde: Karen Dubois, Michael Kahan, J.P. Goodwin, Dawn Vogel, Jan Hendriks de Geweldenaar, Joe Hauser, Heidi Cykana, Jeanette Glass, Stephanie Cranford, J.T. Arralle, David Zurek, Céline Malgen, Jörg Tremmel, Mitch Eatough, Duncan Shields, Paul Bulmer, C R Lofters, Mark Zaricor, Kat D'Andrea, Christine Hanolsy, Herbert Eder, Jeremy Audet, Benjamin C. Kinney, Sarah Liberman, DeAnne Stefanic, Treefrogie, Ruth Olson, John T. Sapienza, Jr., Nicole Wooden, Reese Hogan, Michele Fry, Cade Cameron, Anne Schoonover, Matthew, Kiya Nicoll, Wendy Dye, J W Anderson, Mike Sloup, Sabina Perrino, Sam Ludzki, Jonathan Leggo, Merrie Haskell, Brian Dysart, Max Kaehn, Jakub Narębski, David Eggerschwiler, Duncan & Andrea Rittschof, Eric Hendrickson, Cindy Cripps-Prawak, eric priehs, Kat Haines, Linda Scott, Megan Beauchemin, That Blair Guy, Maria Haskins, Ginger Lee Thomason,

Evan Ladouceur, Richard Ohnemus, Pam B, Pat Knuth, Michael A. Burstein, Bruce Shipman, Paul D. Smith, Nancy Pimentel, Bruce Glassford, Jon Woodall, Patrick Thomas, Adrienne Wise, James H. Murphy Jr., LetoTheTooth, Brooks Moses, Mark Chick, J. M. Coster, Michael Hanscom, Dirk, Steve Salem, Clare Deming, Stephanie Lucas, cassie and adam, Alli Martin, Jason Febery, Keith West, Future Potentate of the Solar System, Margaret St. John, Shawn Marier, Joe Abboreno, Christopher Wheeling, C Preyer, JustiN, – Andy Funk–, Jamieson Cobleigh, Chris Gerrib, Brendan Lonehawk, Cait Mongrain, Wes Rist, Natalie Reinelt, Del W, Sharon Sayegh, Chris Kaiser, Joe Gherlone, John Winkelman, Ken Huie, Deborah A. Flores, Cynthia Harper, Elise Power, Holly Elliott, Juli, Gareth Jones, Carol B, Susan O'Fearna, Jeff Scifert, Leah Webber, Regis M. Donovan, RJ Blain, Tommy Acuff, Margaret Bumby, Kate Malloy, Colette Reap, Raymond Rigo Jr, Susan Carlson, Chris Abela, Elektra, Konstanze Tants, Neil Clarke, Jeff Nylander, Christine Ethier, eerian sadow, John Paul Ashenfelter, Raven Oak, Marty Poling Tool, Morva & Alan, Stephen Ballentine, David Rowe, Anna Rudholm, Dave Hermann, Douglas Park, Joanne Burrows, RM Ambrose, Aysha Rehm, Michael Halverson, Robert Claney, Scott Raboy, Iva Ferris, Megan Riker, Risa Scranton, Robbin Webb, Sheryl Ehrlich, Matt Downer, Rebekah Lange, Alex Swanson, Ashley McConnell, Tasha Richards, Kris Dikeman, Ron Oakes, Sharon Altmann, Marsha Baker, Lorraine J. Anderson, Scott Raun, M Taylor, James Conason, Christopher J. Burke, Vicki Greer, Ronald H. Miller, Steven Peiper, Sheelagh Semper, Dina S Willner, PDXRobin, T. England, Lavinia Ceccarelli, Christine Hale, Gretchen Persbacker, Ian Glover, Jarrod Coad, Noah Bast, Robert Tienken, Erin Penn, Kerry aka Trouble, Deanna Harrison, Niall Gordon, Aurora Nelson, Jenn Whitworth, Lark Cunningham, Jaymie Larkey Maham, Rebecca M, Mark Newman, Patricia Bray, Penny Ramirez, Daryl Putman, Todd Stephens, Anne Hamilton, Jesse N. Klein, Dev Singer, Mark Lukens, Larisa LaBrant, Rachel Sasseen, Dan Tappan, Justin Pinner, Nancy BlueSpider Tice, Tibicina, John Appel, Rich Riddle, Bárbara y Víctor, Kenneth Skaldebø, Michael Abbott, Jean Marie Ward, Cyn Armistead, David Futterrer, Erin G, Cory Williams, Nate Givens, Mark Kiraly, Amy Matosky, Jerrie the filkferengi, Bruce Arthurs, Chris Lynch, Adam Rajski, Accelerator Ray, Doc Holland, Ian Chung, Howard J. Bampton, Mark Carter, Shel Kennon, pjk, Jenelle Clark, Ane-Marte Mortensen, Katrina Coll, Patti Short, Brad L. Kicklighter, Brynn,

L.C., Mark Slauter, Sheryl R. Hayes, Deanna Lukens, John Markley, Mint, Eugenio Monasterio, Rhiannon Raphael, Su Minamide, V Hartman DiSanto, Stephen, Lisa Kruse, Walt Bryan, Connor Bliss, Charibdys, Cliff Winnig, Jake Harrison, Miranda Floyd, Katherine S, Ed Ellis, Carl Wiseman, Khinasi, jjmcgaffey, Yaron Davidson, Mary Alice Wuerz, Jonathan A. Gillett, Elisabeth Fillmore, Elyse M Grasso, Chris B, Simon Boynton, Amanda Cook, Chad Bowden, Uncle Batman, Jo Miles, Paul Zuckes, Arej Howlett, Alan Smale, E.M. Blade McMicking, D.I., Michael Ball, Michael Cieslak, Ryan Marriott, Erik T Johnson, Deborah Hartigan, Dino Hicks, Louisa Swann, The Palmatiers, Megan Miller, PaulG, Nirven, J. M. Britten, Tina M Noe Good, Cracknot, Jason Palmatier, L. E. Doggett, Carl Dershem, Kathy Blain, Deborah Kwan, Kristi Chadwick, Matt Hope, Brenda Moon, maileguy, Heidi Lambert, Michael Niosi, Anne M. Rindfliesch, Michele Howe (neverwhere), Linda Pierce, Tim Jordan, K Kisner, D. Stephen Raymond, Todd V. Ehrenfels, Mandy Stein, Cat Girczyc, Heidegger & Mocha, James Reston, Julia Haynie, J.R. Murdock, Len Berry, Lace, Jessica Enfante, Tory Shade, Craig Hackl, Tami Hawes, Sharon Wood, Ross Hathaway, Crazy Lady Used Books, Deirdre M. Murphy, GMarkC, Kevin J. "Womzilla" Maroney, Rick McKnight, Liza Furr, Carol J. Guess, Gary Phillips, John H. Bookwalter Jr., Jessi Harding, Phoebe Barton, Joshua Bernard, Larry Strome, Fred W Johnson, Jim Gotaas, Paul McErlean, Andrey, Cathy Green, Marzie Kaifer, Jaq Greenspon, RJ Hopkinson, Sarah Cornell, Tsutako, Bobbi Boyd, CK Lai, Karinargh, Robert Gilson, Deeply Dippy, Simon Dick, Amy Brennan, Jenny Barber, Michelle Johnson, Piet Wenings, Ivan Donati, Alison McCormick, Sasha, Hoose Family, Ergo Ojasoo, Craig "Stevo" Stephenson, Brandon Butler, Jenni Peper, Mervi Hamalainen, Regenia Alcock, Judith Mortimore, Jennifer Crow, Revek, Brendan Burke, Bill and Laura Pearson, Sam Stilwell, Rolf Laun, Kristin Evenson Hirst, rissatoo, Vikki Ciaffone, Mustela, Cheryl Losinger, Patrik Andersson, Ian Harvey, Russell Ventimeglia, Tanya K., F. Meilleur, Caitlin Jane Hughes, Brian Colin, Cherie Livingston, Mitchell A Johnson, Helen Ellison, Susan Oke, SwordFire, Bill McGeachin, Joe and Gay Haldeman, Meyari McFarland, Jaime Bolton, Christian Bestmann, Beth Byrne Lobdell, Lorri-Lynne Brown, SusanB, Andy Miller, Dr. Kai Herbertz, H. Rasmussen, Deborah Blake, Patrick Osbaldeston, Jared and Tasha, Misty Massey, Megan Hungerford, Fred and Mimi Bailey, Jeanne, Tracy 'Rayhne' Fretwell, Sue Martin, Dave, Ash Marten, Michael M. Jones, Shana

Jean Hausman, Udy Kumra, Patrick P., Rhel ná DecVandé, Becca Harper, RKBookman, Nathan Turner, Andy Clayman, Sally Novak Janin, Gavran, Leila Qışın, William Leisner, Annalise Lightner, Paul Alex Gray, Dana Scopatz, Catherine Gross-Colten, Gina Freed, Liz Tuckwell, Tobias Z. Salem, Melanie McCoy, Brittany Hill, Darrell Z. Grizzle, Brian Gilmore, Justin Lowe, Theresa Derwin, Michael Kohne, Jeff Eppenbach, Mary Kay Kare, Rebecca Crane, Bill Harting, Chris McLaren, In Memory of Ruth Duggan, Jonathan Adams, CG Julian, Samuel Lubell, M. Stephens, Louise Lowenspets, Shane Alonso, Yosen Lin, manicmarauder, Kayliealien, Ilene Tsuruoka, Alexandra Garcia, Alexandru Orbescu, Mr Armstrong, Jennifer Della'Zanna, Phillip Spencer, NewGuyDave, The Steiners, Yankton Robins, Tiffany Newhill-Leahy, Meg Anderson, Sabraizu, Sharan Volin, Steve Feldon, Havok Publishing, Lily Connors, Jason Tongier, Chantelle Wilson, David Holden, Frances Rowat, Steven Halter, Eagle Archambeault, R.J.H., Colleen R, Elaine Tindill-Rohr, Michelle Palmer, Randall Brent Martin II, Shayne Easson, Frank Nissen, Michele Hall, Evergreen Lee, Elizabeth Kite, Emily Collins, Jennifer Berk, BELKIS Marcillo, Sharon M, Michelle "ChessyPig" Taylor, Jennifer Flora Black, Nick Martell, Cheyenne Bramwell, Julie Pitzel, Heather Fleming, G. Fitzsimmons, Angie Hogencamp, Karen Franks, Shane Ede, Lee Dalzell, Alex Shvartsman, K. Nelson, Dale Cozort, Lish McBride, R. Hunter, Risa Wolf, Sharon Kae Reamer, Rob Riddell, C. C. S. Ryan, S. Worthen, Keith E. Hartman, Deb Atwood, Dagmar Baumann, Rebecca Wagoner, Michelle Botwinick, J. L Brewer, Jerry Wayne Howard, Kimberly M. Lowe, Peter Okeafor, John & Susan Husisian, Carol Snyder Foltz, Morgan, David Boop, Gabe Krabbe, Nickolas Schnell, Tasha Turner, Axisor and Mike, Crystal Sarakas, Catherine Sharp, ron taylor, Cyhiraeth "Rae" Ybarra, Missy Katano, Edi und Luibär, Bernie & Di Brown, Jennifer Dunne, Michael Fedrowitz, Meredith Jeanne Gillies, Chris Brant, Moshe Feder, P. Christie, Kitty Likes, Josie Ryan